CHARMING MISS STANDISH

Willful Winterbournes
Book Six

Sandra Sookoo

ARE YOU SIGNED UP FOR DRAGONBLADE'S BLOG?

You'll get the latest news and information on exclusive giveaways, exclusive excerpts, coming releases, sales, free books, cover reveals and more.

Check out our complete list of authors, too!

No spam, no junk. That's a promise!

Sign Up Here

www.dragonbladepublishing.com

Dearest Reader;

Thank you for your support of a small press. At Dragonblade Publishing, we strive to bring you the highest quality Historical Romance from some of the best authors in the business. Without your support, there is no 'us', so we sincerely hope you adore these stories and find some new favorite authors along the way.

Happy Reading!

CEO, Dragonblade Publishing

Additional Dragonblade books by Author Sandra Sookoo

Willful Winterbournes Series
Romancing Miss Quill (Book 1)
Pursuing Mr. Mattingly (Book 2)
Courting Lady Yeardly (Book 3)
Guarding the Widow Pellingham (Book 4)
Bedeviling Major Kenton (Book 5)
Charming Miss Standish (Book 6)
Teasing Miss Atherby (Novella)

The Storme Brother Series
The Soul of a Storme (Book 1)
The Heart of a Storme (Book 2)
The Look of a Storme (Book 3)
A Storme's Christmas Legacy
A Storme's First Noelle
The Sting of a Storme (Book 4)
The Touch of a Storme (Book 5)
The Fury of a Storme (Book 6)
Much Ado About a Storme (in the *A Duke in Winter* anthology)

The Lyon's Den Series
The Lyon's Puzzle
The Lyon's Redemption

Dedication

To Claire G. Phillips. Thanks for being you and letting your unique light shine into the world. Enjoy the book!

CHAPTER ONE

December 5, 1820
Ashdowne House
St. James Place, London

"WHAT THE H-H-HELL is wrong with y-y-you?"
Edmund Ashdowne—Viscount Evermore—shook his head while continuing to sit in a negligent manner. He slouched in a brocade chair with an ankle resting on one knee. There was something about needling his older brother that appealed to him, and today was no different. "Sorry, but I'm quite sought after around Town, so you will need to narrow down the *one* event which set off your ire."

"Do not think to antagonize me f-f-further, Edmund. I am not of a g-g-good temperament." Graham Ashdowne, the Marquess of Grantley—or rather, Edmund's older brother and the head of the family—crossed his arms at his chest and glared. "Things just now are r-r-rather stressful."

Well, Edmund would give him that, for his brother had been recently married within the last year, and now was expecting his first child at the end of next month. To say nothing of the fact that the whole Ashdowne family had been rocked by scandal last February, when it became known their father hadn't, in fact, sired any of them. Instead, that paternity lay with the former Earl of

Ettesmere. Which meant they were illegitimate Winterbournes, though for all intents and purposes they were the legal children of their marquess father.

While he didn't mind creating scandal for himself, he was rather annoyed when someone else did it for him. Living in London with the gossip flying had been difficult, and quite frankly, he wanted a change but didn't know how to bring that about.

Perhaps the holier-than-thou Graham would have a suggestion.

"I am not trying to be difficult; I truly don't know to what you refer." In the last month, he'd done any number of things that might have come down on the side of scandal. He glanced at his sister Beatrice, who'd come by because Graham had summoned her as well. Apparently, this was a family crisis. "Help me out. It's not as if I haven't been acting this way most of my adult life."

"I'm sorry, darling, but I have been quite distracted since the summer. There has been much going on, you see." She shrugged and offered him a wry smile. "It cannot be so bad, can it?"

In August, his sister had become engaged to a former military man who'd attained the title of major. He had two children from a previous marriage while Bea had a daughter. During the remainder of the summer and part of the autumn, she'd been scarce around the house, for she'd been preparing for her nuptials later this month as well as preparing to launch her daughter into society, which had occurred last month.

Knowing she waited for an answer, he said, "That largely depends on which on-dit reached Graham's ears."

They both looked at their brother, who fairly seethed as he paced in front of the windows. Tall, blond, with blue eyes that were the apparent traits of the Winterbournes, Graham had recently come into his own even though he struggled with a stutter and a title that was land-heavy but coffer-poor.

"I suppose the incident with the opera s-s-singer has escaped your m-m-memory?" he finally asked. Annoyance flashed in his eyes. "How you were f-f-found on stage after the performances e-e-ended, letting her pleasure you orally?" His voice broke on the last word.

"Oh, her." Heat crept up the back of Edmund's neck, but he couldn't help his grin. "Damn, but she distracted me for most of October." What her lips and tongue could do! That bird had the most luscious body he'd been fortunate to make use of. And she'd been his last liaison, for no one else had managed to catch his eye. He'd moved on to other vices, but there was only so much drinking and gambling and wagering a man could do before that also grew dull. When his siblings just stared at him, he sighed. "But that affair has been over for a while."

More's the pity. He was feeling quite restless and the next step after that meant he'd be randy without a ready woman.

Graham chopped the air with a hand as he paused by one of the windows. "You have no r-r-respect for yourself, your f-f-family, or for society in g-g-general." Heavy censure hung on his words.

"And why should I?" No longer able to keep still, Edmund launched himself from his chair. "Ever since the scandal broke about our family, there have been nothing but innuendos and whispers. Gossip that has nothing to do with me precedes me into a room; I'm already tainted by the time I arrive at a *ton* event." That irritated him, for he wanted the attention on him to be of his own making, not that of his skewed bloodlines. "The two of you might have accepted all of this, but I haven't." Hot anger still coursed through his veins. "And I don't know if I ever can."

His sister made a soft sound of displeasure. "You truly should. I thought the same as you, but then I came to the realization that family was more important than holding a grudge against people long dead. Their sins were their own."

"Perhaps, yet those effects are lingering." Then he glared at his brother. "And don't think to come at me with lectures on your lips when your own history isn't sterling nor without scandal." Hell, the man had coupled with a widow during his first foray into society at a masquerade. Yes, he eventually wed the lady—an heiress to boot—but that didn't prevent the gossips from dining out on that morsel for weeks.

Graham didn't buckle, which served as a testament to the confidence he'd found with his wife, Mary. "The difference being that I am m-m-married, and you are not. Something m-m-must be done."

A discreet scratching at the door interrupted the charged argument. The butler, Harrod, stood there, with a rather large willow basket in his arms. While he was a man of perhaps sixty, he was neat and tidy, and there must have been some military service in his background, for he kept his back ramrod straight and his bearing dignified.

Except his expression was one of shock as he bounced his gaze between the basket and Graham. "Ah, Your Lordship, there has been a delivery for Lord Evermore."

"What?" Edmund frowned. "What is it?" That basket looked far too ominous.

"Uh, it appears to be a baby, my lord."

All three Ashdowne siblings stared at the butler, then Beatrice and Graham transferred their shock to him.

"What have you done this time, Edmund?" Bea asked as all the color leeched from her face. "It is hard enough to launch my daughter into society with the scandal surrounding our name, but if you've heaped more upon our heads…."

"Let us not panic just yet." How any of this rested at his feet, he had no idea, but he slowly made his way across the room and reluctantly took the basket from the butler. "Did you recognize the messenger who deposited… this here?"

Harrod's frown was as fierce as Graham's. "I did not, but I was given instructions to bring the basket directly to you."

After Edmund brought the basket over to a chair, he set it onto that piece of furniture then gently peeled back a delicate white muslin blanket trimmed with lace. A babe's face stared back at him, all strawberries and cream complexion with large blue eyes—Winterbourne eyes—with blonde hair beneath a muslin bonnet with strings tied beneath the chin.

The babe stared back at him—he couldn't be sure of its sex just by looking at a face—but the mouth held a sweet Cupid's bow, and the lashes were long. An envelope rested on one side of the basket, and that was what Edmund snatched up.

"Good heavens," Bea breathed from behind him. He hadn't heard her approach. "What a gorgeous infant. Those eyes!"

Graham crowded the space behind him while the butler departed. "Well? Is it y-y-yours?"

"I don't know." A pit of worry opened up in the pit of his stomach as he broke a green wax seal and yanked a single piece of stationery from the envelope. The cloying perfume that wafted to his nose indicated it had undoubtedly come from a courtesan, and it was a scent he'd certainly smelled before.

"Read it aloud," his sister said, as she drew a trembling finger along the baby's cheek.

It wasn't a long note.

"Evermore,

"Nine months ago, you withdrew your protection, which forced me to seek out another. Six months ago, I was delivered of a daughter, who I have named Poppy. One only needs to look at her to know she is yours. She looks exactly like you.

"However, I cannot keep her. Being a mother is at cross-purposes with being a courtesan, and my current protector isn't best pleased with having my attentions split. After being raised in an orphanage myself as well as various homes as domestic help, I don't want the same for our daughter. At least with you, she has a chance to survive and thrive. It is better than a life of workhouses and such.

"Forgive me, but I never wished to be a mother, and

sometimes protection against pregnancy fails. I hope you can give Poppy a good life, and I hope you can make peace with her as well. Please don't call on me. I will refuse to see you, for you are part of my past.

"Yours,

"Nancy."

With raised eyebrows, Edmund looked at his sister and then silently handed the missive to her. "I barely remember this woman." She had been a string of many, and he didn't keep mistresses around for long. "What the hell do I know about raising a child?" Panic rose in his chest, for seeing the infant in the basket meant the situation was entirely too real. "She'll need food and constant care. I suppose that means hiring someone—people." He shoved a hand through his hair. "My pockets are already much to let, unless you wish to—"

Bea shook her head and held up a hand. "Oh, no. I have already raised my child. And I'm going to add two more to my personal family later this month. I have no intentions of having a baby in that mix."

"This is o-o-outside of enough!" Annoyance rose heavy in Graham's voice. He bounced his gaze between Edmund and the babe. "I have no other choice." When he advanced on Edmund, he drilled a forefinger into his chest. "You m-m-must reform. No more vices. Otherwise, I'm completely cutting you off. F-f-from your family as well as the purse s-s-strings."

"How the hell would you like me to do that? I have literally had no purpose in life." Anger exploded out of his chest and through his voice. "Father didn't give two farthings about me. Of course, now I know why, but I was cast adrift while you were trained to be the damned marquess." He verbally pushed back against Graham while Beatrice gasped. "So don't blame me when I have done nothing more than what society has expected from a second son from a family with too many damned scandals to their name."

When the infant in the basket began to fuss, another wave of panic rolled over him. For whatever reason, he'd been thrust into this situation, and no one would do anything about it. Oddly enough, the thought of having a child—even an illegitimate child—with his blood and looks appealed. Perhaps it was the only human on this earth who might love him unconditionally, who wouldn't think of him as a disappointment, wouldn't assume he'd cocked up his life beyond repair. Moving to the basket while Bea tried to calm Graham, he gently scooped the child into his arms, brought her out of the nest of blankets, and then awkwardly held her against his shoulder.

Never before had he held a baby. He'd not wanted children, and he'd reached the age of seven and thirty without falling into parson's mousetrap, had made certain he did his part to not father children. To say nothing of the fact there weren't many children in the Ashdowne connection with the exception of Bea's daughter, yet Graham had forged a new path in that area with his first child coming by the end of next month. As gently as he could, Edmund patted the child's back, and he continued on that vein of thought. There *were* children in the Winterbourne family, of which he was now a part of, for the earl as well as the earl's sister had nearly grown children. Hell, beyond that, Ettesmere's wife had just had a boy infant in late September, so it seemed that fate wasn't nearly done with the Winterbournes yet.

But none of that meant Edmund wanted this one.

As the babe fussed against his shoulder, he glanced at his siblings. "I cannot keep her." The soft muslin gown she'd been dressed in was as delicate as she, and there was a certain lovely scent of the baby's skin he hadn't smelled before.

Graham snorted. "Perhaps you s-s-should. It is time you actually reaped the c-c-consequences of a scandal. It might change your l-l-life."

"I think Graham is correct." Bea drifted close. She clucked and fussed at how he held the child. "Be careful of her head and neck. Make sure she feels safe and secure."

"It's humiliation personified." To say nothing of the expenses a baby would incur on his already strained purse-strings. "What the devil should I do? The babe's mother doesn't want her. Hell, *I* don't want her, but I don't want her to have a horrible life."

"Then adopt her out or send her a-a-away to a couple that will raise her." The exasperation in his brother's voice indicated he was completely done with the conversation.

"Oh, no!" Beatrice shook her head. Compassion shadowed her eyes as she stroked the baby's head. "You can keep her, raise her yourself. It might give you some self-worth and a purpose. For the immediate time being, you could probably ask the countess to share her wet nurse until you are settled."

Edmund snorted. "How the devil can I do that? My own life is a wreck." When his voice raised, the baby fussed harder, so he modulated his tones in the hopes she would calm. "And it would be frowned upon for a bachelor to raise a child, let alone a girl." God, how had life become so distorted?

She showed him how to hold the babe so that it was more secure, how to tenderly bounce her so she might settle. "You could marry."

"First off, I don't have any prospects. And secondly, why should I merely to give this child a mother when her own didn't want her?" Experimentally, he bounced the girl. "And third, there is not much in my coffers, so I rather doubt I'll get by on my charm alone. Women want to have their futures settled." Never had he been so ashamed of his current circumstances as he was right now.

What would Poppy think of him as she grew?

Graham released a huff of apparent frustration. "I don't see that y-y-you have much choice." He shook his head. "Put yourself out there f-f-for more than vices, do the p-p-pretty, and charm someone q-q-quickly." Consternation lined his face. "I have run out of patience with you, and by the t-t-time the year is out, you will be tossed out of t-t-this house, too."

"Oh, Graham." Bea sucked in a breath of surprise. "I realize you have a child on the way, but what will Edmund do?"

His brother shrugged. "Go to Kent." His tone brooked no argument. "It is t-t-the only other property available." Then he rested his hard gaze on him. "I swear, I'll wash my hands of you, Edmund, and you'll have to f-f-fend for yourself. I will not start my l-l-life as a father with your mess on my doorstep."

"Or my taint of scandal to touch your precious heir, if the babe turns out to be a boy?" Annoyance and anger once more welled within his chest. The baby continued to fuss, and since he didn't know what to do or how to soothe her, he put her back into the basket and tucked her in. "I'm trying my best," he whispered to the infant, even though in his heart of hearts he knew it was a lie. Quickly, he swallowed around the lump of emotion in his throat. Fate was apparently determined to crush him, but he wouldn't let that happen.

Bea gave him a sad smile. "Until you can procure a wet nurse and a nursery maid—"

"Which means I'll need an actual nursery," he muttered beneath his breath.

"And that means you n-n-need your own townhouse," Graham said with his usual matter-of-factness that drove Edmund to the brink of madness.

"Yes, yes, I am well aware of the gauntlet that stretches before me." But he wasn't a Winterbourne—illegitimate though that may be—for nothing, and there was a stubborn, willful streak in him that refused to be quieted. He rested his gaze on Graham and then transferred it to Beatrice, then he stood at his full height. "The two of you might want me to fail in some misguided thought that I need to learn from my mistakes. However, this is my notice to you that I don't intend to fail. Whatever you may think of me and my life choices, that's fine, but I don't need your judgment or your censure." He paused to think over his next words, cast a worried glance to the fussing baby, and then nodded. "I *will* succeed, and I don't particularly care if that estranges us."

"Oh, Edmund, you've taken our words and distorted them." When Bea went to reach for his hand, he waved her away.

"No. The two of you had scandals in your own lives, but you seem to forget that now you're married or soon will be." It wasn't fair, but then he'd always been out of pleasure with the family. "I will forge my own path, just like I always have. Without the support of the family."

Graham nodded. "Perhaps that is b-b-best."

"I believe it is." He picked up the basket. "Now, if you will excuse me, I have much to do. Least of which is finding someone who can help me get this child fed until I can make other arrangements."

Though he left the drawing room with a ramrod straight spine and an uplifted chin, inside he was quaking with fear. What the devil was he going to do with an infant, and how the hell would he ever attract any sort of decent woman to wed with his life a mess?

He didn't know but he would rather die than let his brother see him fall. Above everything, he wasn't his father.

CHAPTER TWO

December 7, 1820
Mattersfield House
London, England

MISS ANNA STANDISH, only daughter to Sir Mattersfield—a wealthy baronet—rocked slightly forward as she sat on a cushioned bench in front of her much-loved piano. Moderate rain fell outside. It drummed steadily against the window glass while she went through each new passage of the piece of music she played. As life went, this was a lovely day.

Her father came into the room, but there was a rushed energy about him, so she didn't think he would stay long. "Hello, dove. You are quite fetching in that color."

"Thank you." She'd chosen a silk-wool blend dress of a rich wine hue today, for it reminded her of the berries she used to pick in the country before tragedy had changed her life. "I'd like to think it's cheerful."

"It is, quite." He chuckled. "I have several business meetings this afternoon, my love. Will you be all right here by yourself?"

By willpower alone, she stifled the urge to snort in derision as her fingers stilled on the ivory keys. When was she not alone? "Of course I will, Papa."

Her father had acquired the title through services for the

Crown during the war. What, exactly, those services were, she'd never thought to ask. He wasn't a particularly brave man, nor was he one to rush into danger upon a battlefield. Papa had one thing in his life that he was excessively proud of, and that was the fact he was allegedly related to Myles Standish from the Plymouth Colony as well as the Mayflower, but that blood connection had never been substantiated, since the lineage sprang from a child of a tryst. Yet, he still clung to it as if it made him better, somehow, in the eyes of the *ton*.

But then, it was something that made him unique, and she loved him all the more for it.

"Ah, that is good to hear. And remember, if you should need to go out and run errands, please take one of the footmen and a maid with you. The streets of Mayfair are difficult to navigate even if one has the full use of their sight."

As if she were a child of eleven instead of a woman grown at two and thirty. "Don't I always?" In his own way, he looked after her the best he could, but fate had beat him down with the same hand that had touched her, and his idea of living with the aftermath was to keep busy so he wouldn't need to think about it.

Anna had lost most of her sight following a horrible fever she'd contracted at the age of ten. Though she'd survived, suffering with a fever that high had done severe damage to her body. She could only see if something was very close to her nose. Otherwise, everything was lost to splotchy shifting patches of darkness and dull white light. That fever had also left her weakened and delicate, which she never really grew out of no matter how many specialists her father had taken her to see. For the longest time, they'd remained at their home in the Derbyshire countryside, for that was the easiest way of letting Anna live on her own terms. But eventually, his work with coal had brought him the notice of men who wished to take that knowledge and change the world, which made being in London more convenient.

So she'd accompanied him to Town, and that was where

they'd been for the past few years. Yes, she missed the peaceful tranquility of the countryside, but London was so vital and exciting that she rarely complained. There was a pulse, an energy here that she felt throughout her body, and she didn't need sight to enjoy that.

The one thing that made her sad and would always leave a hole in her heart was the fact that that same fever had taken the lives of her mother and older brother. Many in their small village had been affected, and if one didn't make strides to purposefully move forward, they would be lost to grief and the past.

That was much what would happen to her papa if he ever paused in his business dealings.

"I am only thinking to your safety, pet." He came close and rested a gentle hand on her shoulder. "You are all I have left, and if something were to happen to you...." His voice broke on the last word.

"I know," she said in a quiet voice. "But I am here, and I don't foresee anything changing in my routine soon."

More's the pity.

"Good. Good." He patted her shoulder. "You will always be my girl."

Anna stifled the urge to huff in frustration. "Of course, Papa. Have a good afternoon. Will you be home for dinner?"

"I am not sure just yet, but if I am not, I'll send word." Then he bussed her cheek and fled the room, for no matter how much he claimed to adore her, knowing his only daughter was blind made him remember that horrible time years ago when he'd lost everything.

It was something she couldn't help him come to terms with unless he wished that for himself, so she once more returned to music, and as her fingers flew over the keys, a sense of peace stole over her that she was beginning to need more and more often as she grew older.

Music was her balm, and though she'd learned the basics before the fever, all the music she played now she'd memorized by ear—sometimes after hearing a piece only once—and though she often made mistakes with the notes, she had natural talent that she'd always wanted to do something with. Hours of practicing each day had perfected a handful of pieces, and whenever her father did entertain, which was rarely, she was often called upon to entertain those parties with her fantastical skill.

She was happiest at her piano or playing for people who had never heard such pieces performed in front of them before. Bringing the gift of music to others was quite fulfilling, and if she had her way, she would travel all over the world in an effort to learn all that she could of different forms and styles of music, learn how to play them merely as a way to take those notes and movements unto herself and appreciate them all the more.

Of course, there was always the tiny little dream in her heart to perform on stages in front of the world's elite and titled, but she rather thought that would never happen.

With a sigh, Anna gave herself over to the notes flowing through her that prompted her fingers to dance over the keys with starting precision. In the twenty-two years since she'd lived with her blindness, she had come to terms with her lot in life, and though she had greater latitude than many who'd been ravaged by the fever, it was still a lonely existence. Above all, she wanted to be loved by a man and to give that in return, yet the blindness made anyone wishing to take her to wife leery and usually kept them away.

The trouble was, she was already a wealthy heiress, for her mother had left her a rather large inheritance—she was the great-granddaughter of a duke on her mother's side—but additionally, Anna was the sole heiress to her father's fortune that he'd made with coal and whatever he'd done to warrant the title of baronet. Many young men had come sniffing around, but the interest in her was only for the coin and not for her as a woman. Either she'd asked them to leave, or her father had, but regardless, much of that contributed to her lonely, unfilled life.

For several minutes, she gave herself over to the music so the thoughts circling around her head like ponies on a loop would quiet.

The rub was that in order to find a man who might look past her affliction, she needed to circulate within society, but doing so made her nervous, so she has avoided it for far too many years. Now, her age was a detriment along with the blindness, so why should she even try? Not even once in her life had she experienced marriage or had she ever been wanted, and as a result, Anna feared all of those things together had made her far too awkward or rather desperate. Which made her take refuge with her piano even more.

Why cannot life, for once, just be easy?

When a loud crashing noise outside of the townhouse reached her ears, she flinched on the bench and her fingers came together on the keys to make a discordant sound. What in the world was happening outside? The frantic shouting of men and the whinnying of horses indicated an accident had possibly occurred, but since the Hanover Square neighborhood wasn't in a prominent section of Mayfair, it was odd that anything like that might have happened here.

All the same, Anna rose to her feet. "Jacob! Please come here." He was the latest footman assigned to watch over her in the afternoon hours, and though she had protested long ago that her father coddled her, it had been easier to give up that particular fight.

Feet pounded against the hardwood, and then he skittered to a stop just inside the drawing room. "Yes, Miss Standish?"

She turned her head, but all she saw was a grayish blob throughout much of her field of vision. "Is something amiss outside? There was the sound of a large crash and there are shouts on the street."

"I am not certain, but I can find out." Not long after he left, Jacob returned. Clearly winded, that didn't stop him from relating what he saw. "There has been a carriage that collided with a larger vehicle, nearly in front of this building." He paused to suck in a breath. "Many men are on the street because traffic is jammed."

Well, that didn't happen every day, and it was rather interesting. "Was anyone hurt?"

"I wouldn't know, miss."

Of course not. "If they are, please bring them inside so they can be taken care of while I inform the butler of possible injured guests."

"Very well, miss." When the sound of his feet retreating faded, Anna made her way across the room.

Inside her own townhouse, where she knew down to the inch where everything was placed, hung, or located, she possessed loads of confidence. It was when she found herself in unfamiliar environs that she tended to panic. With her fingers gliding along the wall, she reached the staircase, and then using the rail, she navigated the treads with the ease of someone sighted. Though her world was constantly in fuzzy colors of black, white, and gray, that didn't stop her from imagining what the rooms and their furnishings—and even the servants—must look like, and oftentimes she amused herself doing just that.

"Barton?" As soon as she reached the ground floor, she called for the butler. "Where are you?" One thing she especially appreciated about him was that he rarely left his station and always seemed to be there when she needed him.

"I am here, Miss Standish." Perhaps the same age as her father, he was always soft-spoken and solicitous. He touched her elbow. "It has become quite busy here of late."

"Oh? Jacob told me about the accident on the street."

"Indeed. There is a man in the parlor who suffered a few scrapes and has a tender ankle because of the accident. He is being given tea as we speak."

"Then I shall go there and see if he needs medical assistance." Not that she could do much in that regard, but surely there must be a physician or surgeon close by they could summon if need be.

"Very good, miss. If you have need of anything else, please ring and one of us will be there in a thrice."

With excitement buzzing at the base of her spine, Anna glided the fingertips of one hand along the wall as she walked the corridor toward the parlor. As soon as she entered, the change in the air was immediate. The man who occupied the room filled the space with his presence even though he sat on a low sofa, but it was the scents of sandalwood, orange, and leather that wafted through the air and teased her nose that made her pay attention.

"Good afternoon. It seems you've come to this house because of an accident." Oh, what she wouldn't give to see what their guest looked like! A man who smelled that delicious had to be at least a little handsome.

"Yes, it was rather unfortunate, and the rain didn't help." Not an overly deep voice, but the rich tenor of it brought awareness tingling over her skin. When he made a move to stand, she tsked her tongue and held up a hand.

"Please, remain sitting. My butler told me you were injured."

"I am, slightly, I suppose." A hint of annoyance went through the tones.

"Ah." Anna approached his sofa and then seated herself in a chair near his location. It was odd being so close to a man without her father crying alarm or one of the servants rushing in to make certain she wasn't taken advantage of, but she refused to waste this opportunity. Sadly, it was the most excitement she'd had in months. "Well, I am glad that you were able to be brought inside on your own cognizance." She allowed herself a short chuckle. "I am Miss Standish, but you may refer to me as Anna. I don't hold to the strict rules of society, for I hardly ever find myself in that muck anyway. Welcome to Mattersfield House."

"Thank you. The name is vaguely familiar."

"My father is a baronet."

"Ah yes, the chap that's got piles of coin, or so the rumors at the clubs go, and has set an enormous dowry on his daughter's head." Then he gasped, and though she couldn't see his face, his embarrassment was acute. "Of course. *You* are his daughter."

"I am." She offered a small smile, for the whole conversation thus far had been amusing.

"I apologize. I should have phrased that better, and there was no disrupt intended." The clink of china against china indicated he'd fit a teacup into a saucer. "I am Viscount Evermore, but if we aren't standing on ceremony, you may call me Edmund or Evermore if you prefer."

"What a lovely title!" Reminding herself to rein in her enthusiasm lest she come across as a ninny far too enamored by the aristocracy, Anna blew out a breath. "How are you feeling? Do you wish for an apothecary or even a doctor to be summoned?"

"I am well enough." He snorted as if it were all a joke. "However, I have had better days. A few cuts and scrapes. Mild pain in my bloody ankle, but I don't think it's broken."

"If you don't mind me asking, what happened? I was upstairs in the drawing room playing the piano when I heard the commotion on the street."

"Well, it doesn't reflect well on me." A self-depreciating laugh followed, that tickled through her chest. "I was apparently woolgathering, not paying attention to the road. Ah, some concerning things in my personal life have me at sixes and sevens." When he paused for breath, she continued to smile at him, for she adored the sound of his voice. "Someone with a large wagon hit me while I tried to make a turn. One of the wheels on my carriage broke. The vehicle turned onto its side with a rather large dent in the door. As I attempted to extricate myself, I twisted my ankle. The blasted rain didn't help matters either." He huffed. "My brother will no doubt ring a peal over my head. Again."

Since she had no idea who his brother was, she shrugged. "It sounds as if you are no stranger to scandal or drama."

"Ha!" His chuckle once more sent skitters over her skin. "If you only knew, Miss Standish—Anna." Then he leaned forward and touched her hand. Flutters went through her belly. "Thank you for the hospitality."

"Well, I am not very current about what goes on within the *beau monde*, and since my father was awarded his title, we aren't truly of the *ton* to begin with." Unless one counted that thin, thin connection left over from her mother or *her* mother's side. It was probably best she make that known from the start. "But it all sounds very exciting." She was all too interested in him, but it was probably just her silly self. Just because he'd touched her hand didn't mean there was a future between them. What a ninny she was.

"Perhaps that is just as well. Since my reputation doesn't precede me here, you cannot pass judgment on me." Relief threaded through his words. "I thank you for your kindness, but I should probably return home."

And put an end to their lovely visit? "Or perhaps you can send 'round a note to your family assuring them that you remain uninjured and you will arrive later." She offered him another smile, and even though she couldn't see him, she felt rather than saw his answering grin. "Do you want to stay to dinner? My father won't be home until late, and even then, he'll no doubt linger at his club, but I wouldn't mind the company. I get it so rarely." *Oh, do stop talking, Anna, lest he think you're desperate!*

"Let us see." After he set his cup and saucer on the low table in front of him, the viscount stood, put weight on his ankle. A soft cry of pain echoed in the room, and he swiftly sat back down. "I would enjoy taking dinner with you, and it will allow me a chance to rest my ankle further... if you don't mind me not dressing correctly for the occasion."

A genuine laugh escaped her. "In the event you haven't noticed, Lord Evermore, I am blind, so it wouldn't matter to me what you wore, but we should have a splendid time anyway." She stood and went so far as to hold out a hand to him. When he took it and brought her fingers to his lips, another round of flutters went through her lower belly. "I will find you some stationery so that you might write a note explaining your absence and your location."

"Thank you. I appreciate that."

Anna nodded. "I'll inform Barton that you are staying to dinner." It was odd that life hadn't changed in so many years, but then a rainy afternoon blew this entertaining stranger right onto her doorstep. *Well, I'm certainly not going to waste the opportunity.* If nothing else, he was someone to talk with who wasn't on her father's payroll.

CHAPTER THREE

THIS TRULY WAS a new experience for Edmund, and one in which he didn't know exactly how to act. For the bulk of his life, he'd gotten by on his looks and charm as well as his reputation, but the woman sitting across from him at the dinner table was blind, so most of that was lost on her.

Not that such a thing didn't come with good tidings. From all the talking they'd done over tea and then as dinner and dessert wound to a close, it was fairly easy to discern that Miss Anna Standish didn't have a blessed clue who he was, and better yet, she didn't know who his family was, which meant she hadn't heard the gossip surrounding the Ashdowne and Winterbourne names. And she certainly hadn't heard of the gigantic scandal that was the baby who'd been dropped off at his home two days ago.

It was odd and left him with a blank page and possibilities he could explore without having his hand forced or excuses made, and that made him more reckless than he might usually be. Her cook put out a decent dinner, and the plum cake they were in the process of finishing was superb, but the real reason he'd stayed this long at the table was the conversation, and for a man who preferred beguiling a woman into bed and avoiding talk as much as possible, it boggled his mind.

Of course, knowing exactly who Miss Standish was made everything that much more appealing. Oh, she was an heiress all right, of first one fortune and quite another once her father died. Did it matter to him that she was blind? It was difficult to tell currently, but she was a wonderful conversationalist and seemed to be intelligent on the most popular topics of the day. Though she couldn't read, apparently there was a companion that read to her from many different books and subjects, and from all he'd gleaned, she filled the rest of her time by playing the piano.

It was quite refreshing in some ways to meet a woman who wasn't vapid or filled her head with fripperies and frocks every chance she got. Could he charm his way into her good graces? And what was more, could he manage to romance her enough that she might agree to a marriage? He reeled from that shock, for never had he willingly wanted to put himself into parson's mousetrap. Yet the woman was past the first and second blooms of youth and perhaps more his age than a debutante would be, which meant she hadn't many offers, and that meant she might be sitting on this side of desperation. It sounded harsh, but there wasn't much opportunity for women in their world, and even less if said woman was blind. It would certainly solve a couple of his more immediate problems and perhaps even some of hers, but he would need to come to know her better.

"You are far too quiet, Lord Evermore… Edmund."

Damn, but the sound of his name in her dulcet tones had gooseflesh racing over his skin. "I suppose it has been an overwhelming day."

"And here I am being a terrible hostess by keeping you at the table." When she shot to her feet, he touched her hand.

"Hold. I didn't mean that we needed to relocate." But having her standing so close gave him leave to study her.

On the petite side, she probably stood no more than a couple inches over five feet, and her build was slight, almost delicate, which brought out protective instincts he didn't know that he had. Clouds of black hair, as dark as a raven's wing, was caught at the back of her head in a messy bun, as if she didn't give much thought to fashion or style, but it was her emerald eyes that drew his attention time and again. Even though she was blind, her eyes weren't milky or clouded. They were clear and fathomless. She'd dressed in a cream-colored gown shot with brown shimmering thread, which only added to the assumption that she might have escaped from a woodland fairy camp somewhere if one were to look quickly enough.

"Oh." Clearly, she was conflicted, for she kept darting glances to the open door. "Perhaps we should adjourn to the drawing room, though. You will be more comfortable there and able to prop up your ankle on a footstool."

"All right." He was definitely curious about her as well as her life to this point. "Though the pain in the ankle has gone down considerably since I first arrived." After she'd brought him a piece of stationery as well as pen and ink, he'd dashed off a missive to Graham explaining his absence and beseeched either him or Bea to care for Poppy until he could return home. Being away from the infant this long discomfited him, for the past two days, he'd been constantly in her company, and that, too, made his mind reel.

"Even more reason to move away from the table." When she took his arm, he immediately crooked his elbow. "Not that I'll ask you to dance or anything like that. Between your ankle and my sight, that might prove a disaster." The giggle that followed was so enchanting that already he thought of new ways to make her do it again.

"There is that, though I've been told I'm an excellent dance partner, especially during waltzes." That was how he usually charmed women into his bed. There was nothing so intimate as a dance when one used their whole body, their words, and their eyes to charm their partner.

"How lucky you are, for I have never danced a set in my life." A hint of longing went through her voice as they quit the room. With each footfall, the initial pain in his ankle ebbed. "Since I went blind at the age of ten, my parents hadn't yet engaged a dancing master for me. Now, it's anyone's guess if I could even do such a thing."

"I rather think you can do anything you set your mind to." As they traversed the corridor toward the room next door, he breathed in the delicate scent of apple blossoms. Perhaps a tad too faint for a woman of her age and personality, but somehow it worked and blended well with her woodland fairy appearance.

"Oh!" A blush went through her cheeks as she guided him into the drawing room. "What a lovely thing to say. I don't know how true it is since I haven't much confidence, but I'd like to think it is."

The second he stepped foot into the room, he realized this was probably where she spent the bulk of her time, for the room fairly resonated with her personality. Done in varying colors of green, the furniture was arranged in such a way that it would be easy to navigate. A piano occupied a space in the corner by the windows on both sides, and it must look wonderful in the sunshine. On one of the tables, a wooden chessboard had been set with marble pieces.

"Do you play chess?" How intriguing, for he'd never met a woman with such mental prowess. Or rather, he'd either not paid attention or they hadn't told him.

"On occasion I match wits with my father. He taught me at an early age, and I've found the game is something I can continue that doesn't require sight. I can simply feel where the pieces are in conjunction to mine." She guided him over the Aubusson carpeting to a sofa that she apparently favored. "I have tried to play opposite Meredith, but between you and me, the woman has not the head for it."

Edmund frowned. "I beg your pardon, but who is Meredith?"

"Oh, she is the companion my father hired, so I would never be alone. She helps me navigate through life, I suppose, though she leans toward being a sourpuss warden."

Unexpectedly, the mental image she conjured of a woman he'd yet to meet had him chuckling. "I wonder if you find any chance to slip the noose if you can."

She turned her head toward him, and when she smiled, a stab of pure lust went through him. The woman was made for bed sport. There was nothing that indicated she wouldn't enjoy that sort of activity, for one didn't need sight for a good tryst. What would those full lips feel like pressed against his, or better yet, wrapped around his rampant length? "I do try, but somehow Meredith always manages to find me."

"Then you're not doing it right." Once she settled onto the sofa, he did the same but made certain there was a cushion of space between them. Already, being alone in her company was flirting with scandal and disaster, but a glimmer of an idea was trying to form in his mind, and he wasn't worried too much about what might happen. "You need someone more skilled in evasion to teach you the tricks."

"Why do I suspect you are well-versed in such things?" They shared a laugh, then she sighed. "Ordinarily, the only person I take dinner with is Meredith, but since I rather think she would break apart before she'd make a joke, it has been great fun having you around today. When we have company over, she has to dine with the servants."

Pleasure warmed his chest from her praise. It was a simple thing, really, but it had been difficult to come by as of late. What would she say if he told her that he had an infant to care for and said child had been dropped off two days before? Instead, he pushed such thoughts from his mind. "Tell me about your dreams, Anna. What do you wish for above everything else?" It would help him to better understand her.

"Oh, that's simple. I would like to play my piano on stage in front of crowds. Can you imagine making people get caught up in music that I make?" The animation in her face was a thing of beauty, and he couldn't imagine an ounce of the talent she must have. "However, if that were never to happen, I would hope my second dream might come true."

"Such as?" Why the devil was such anticipation filling his belly?

Anna loosed a sigh that sounded as if it came from her toes. "Quite simply, to be loved. To find a man who wants me merely for me and not access to my fortune. To have a family of my own, but I fear time is running out due to my age."

It would seem she had completely different goals than he, but perhaps they could manage to work together after all. With a tight chest, he asked, "How old are you?"

"Two and thirty."

"That's hardly ancient." He snorted. "Why, many women are just coming into their own at that age. It is when they learn what they want and won't stop until they've achieved it." Was it a bit of flattery? Of course, but then he rather suspected she'd had little of that in her life.

"Thank you for infusing me with renewed hope." She threaded her fingers together from where her hands rested in her lap. "My father is too overprotective since I became blind. And since his business ventures have taken off, he doesn't allow me to leave the house due to worries of me being kidnapped or taken advantage of by fortune hunters." She briefly worried her bottom lip with her teeth, and once more his attention fell to her luscious mouth. "That's why he hired Meredith, so I would never be alone."

That sounded like a ghastly life. Edmund hadn't considered how personally dangerous it would be to have a fortune at play but not be able to discern if men were after that money. By willpower alone, he prevented himself from shuddering. "Is that what you wanted?"

"Of course not." She huffed out her annoyance. "I'm never alone!" Though she turned her head toward him and her eyes roved over his person, he doubted she could truly see him. It must happen by impulse. "There are times in my life I don't want to be with people. I just want to hear myself think without inane chatter or censure."

"That is quite understandable, and perhaps I out of all the people you could have plucked from the street today do sympathize and even empathize with your situation." He rather liked that sudden show of spirit. It meant she wouldn't be so quickly cowed by the *ton*.

Or anyone else for that matter.

"You are an interesting man, Edmund."

He scoffed. "I don't know about that." Perhaps it was time to turn on the charm to see how it would work on her. Women were women, right? "I have never met anyone so inspiring as you, though. I would imagine many men would do a fair number of illicit or stupid things merely for a glimpse of your smile or your regard."

"Oh, my." Another mad rush of dark pink color infused her cheeks. Of course he would have expected it in a much younger woman, but since Anna had been coddled and sheltered and essentially kept away from nearly everything life offered, perhaps she hadn't experienced anything that a woman in society should have by this age. She cast her eyes downward to her lap, and the black fringe of her lashes against the paleness of her cheeks suddenly stoked his ardor. "I think, perhaps, you had better return home. If Papa comes home and finds you here with me, he'll fly into the boughs."

Dear God, the thought of teaching her everything she didn't know had the capacity to turn his brain into mush. "We wouldn't want that so soon after our first meeting, hmm?"

"Not if we wish to repeat this visit." Slowly, she stood, and Edmund scrambled to his feet. "This was all too lovely."

"Indeed, it was." Unexpectedly, he wasn't ready to return home, but obviously he couldn't linger. It was poor form. "However, I am much grateful for your hospitality and your willingness to tend to any injuries that might have been severe."

"I am only trying to help." Another blush suffused her cheeks. "I'm glad the accident put you here, for I enjoyed this visit quite a lot."

"As did I." Oddly enough, he felt a certain protectiveness toward her. Her father was correct in thinking she shouldn't be on her own, but he didn't know if having a handful of servants about her was the wisest choice. She was intelligent, but there was a certain restlessness about her, a longing in her eyes that indicated she was ready to spread her wings and fly. "Perhaps I'll see you again while in society."

"Oh." Her expression fell from lively enjoyment to sadness. "I don't accept invitations very much. Society makes me uncomfortable."

"Ah." It appeared she was the direct opposite of him, for he thrived on attention and the mad crush in ballrooms and drawing rooms. "That is too bad; I'd hoped to encounter you again." Once more, the glimmers of a plan danced about in his mind. It would solve most of his problems and perhaps some of hers. If she would agree to it. He needed more time to plan because on paper it would be complete madness, let alone trying to have his family agree to it.

"Perhaps I shall encounter you at the shops, then. Or if you're involved in another carriage accident in the vicinity." A giggle followed as she led him across the room, and it was as enchanting as the first time he'd heard it. "Do you want me to tell the butler to bring out Papa's carriage?"

"No. I'll walk. It's not that far." And the cool air would clear his head so he could think. This wouldn't be the end of their association, though. He racked his brain for an excuse. "I'm scheduled to attend a musicale evening and dinner tomorrow at my sister's home, and my presence is demanded at her behest, for her soon-to-be stepdaughter will be performing." It was as good an excuse as any. Additionally, she was also musically inclined so she might enjoy herself. "If you should wish to mingle within society, this would be a good opportunity."

"What an intriguing offer." Her expression had brightened. Once more amusement danced in her all too-arresting green eyes. "Perhaps I shall see you there."

It had been all too easy to lead her on a merry chase. Not that it was overly dishonest, for once his plan coalesced, it would benefit them both. Additionally, it would needle Graham, and that was more than enough motivation for him. "If you *do* come, tell the butler you are my guest."

"All right, but I don't have the address."

"An easy remedy." He cast about the room, and spying a small secretary in a corner, Edmund dashed over, took a piece of paper from a stack, and wrote out Bea's address in Mayfair. Then he scribbled a quick note on the paper that would work to further encourage her to meet him there. Once he'd returned to her side, he took one of her hands in his, brought it to his lips, kissed the back, and then pressed the now folded paper into her palm. "I wrote the address on this paper, but then I also wrote something personal just for you."

"Oh?" She curled her fingers about the paper. "What did you write?"

Daring much, he leaned close and put his lips to the delicate shell of her ear. "It says, 'Thank you for the dinner and charming conversation, but meeting you and having you all to myself for a few hours was, by far, the best thing about my day.'"

"How lovely!" Her expression was more than a little star-struck, but he tamped down a grin. "Thank you for bringing a bright moment to an otherwise boring monotony of a week."

"Truly, it has been a pleasure, Miss Standish." Then, with a grin that felt rather too cheeky for the occasion, Edmund made his way to the staircase. As he descended, he waved to her even though he knew she couldn't see the gesture. Though there was every possibility someone within the house would inform Anna what sort of a man he was, he didn't care. She would need to make her own decisions, but he would keep on with the charm for as long as needed, for neither of them could keep on in the same vein as they had been.

Nothing different was ever obtained if one remained in the same spot they had always stood in, but God he needed to get away, perhaps even leave London for a time until he felt like himself again.

If that were even possible.

CHAPTER FOUR

December 8, 1820
Delacourte House
London, England

ANNA'S NERVES WOULD get the better of her if she didn't find a way to calm, but it wasn't every evening that she went out into society.

As her father's closed carriage waited in a line to let other passengers ahead of them disembark, she smoothed a gloved hand down the front of her navy satin gown. It had been an age since she'd gone to an event, and since this was a musicale evening, it held special meaning for her. Perhaps she could make friends with some of the performers. How lovely would it be to talk about music and the playing of such with like-minded people?

The gown itself was plain, but there was a silver net panel that overlaid the front which sparkled each time she moved, or so her maid had told her. A simple navy velvet ribbon had been tied about her throat as a choker and pinned to the ribbon was a cameo pin of a lady wearing a towering, powdered wig that had once belonged to her mother. It was the best she could do, for she didn't own any jewels of value; there had never been a need since she couldn't see them. Or so she'd been told by various people who'd come in and out of her life. Yet if it had been her choice, she might have enjoyed wearing a bejeweled necklace so she could feel the coolness of the gemstones against her skin, but frankly, no one ever asked her what she wanted. Everyone assumed that in being blind, she had no opinions… on anything.

It was quite aggravating.

Additionally, her dear maid had been beside herself with delight as she'd piled Anna's hair on her head and secured the curls with pins and combs. Occasionally, she wove navy ribbons through the mass and finally declared her good enough to hobnob with the *ton*. Then Meredith came to claim her.

"I wish my stomach would settle. It feels as if I swallowed a flock of butterflies." She pressed a hand to the window glass, and even through the kid glove the chill reached her. Then she pulled the matching pelisse tighter about her person.

Her companion sniffed, as if the trip itself was an affront to her. "I don't know why you took it into your head to go out into society. In the past few years, you have done nothing of the sort, yet you seemed perfectly content."

"Oh, yes, content to remain in the ivory tower my father put me in, so I won't be hurt." Sarcasm dripped from her words. One couldn't be hurt when wasn't allowed to do anything. "Now I have a chance to experience other things."

"All because of *that man's* visit yesterday." Annoyance wove through Meredith's tones.

"If you refer to Lord Evermore, then yes." Anna couldn't help the smile that curved her lips. "Having the viscount visit was a remarkable distraction from what has become a rather dull, a rather *predictable* life."

"Do you think to see him tonight?"

"Well, considering this is the home of his sister, and he did invite me, it would be the height of rude not to at least acknowledge him." The carriage lurched forward, and she hoped they would be allowed to exit the vehicle soon. "Stop being such a spoilsport, Meredith. This should be an evening of fun. And music is always a good idea." She breathed out a huff of frustration. "Besides, it's well past time that I left the house and started enjoying life before I'm a dried-up old maid."

And that probably wasn't far off, since being two and thirty without having been wanted by a man or even kissed by one was tantamount to falling into that state.

Meredith grunted. "What of your safety?"

"What of it?" Why did the woman need to be so impossible? "Nothing has happened recently. I shall be fine, and this might be good for me. I can connect with other musicians." And that might give her avenues she hadn't thought of before. Dreams couldn't come true unless one wished to work for them.

"Your father won't be pleased." From the sound of Meredith's voice, neither was she, but then she had always been much of a cold fish and didn't enjoy trying anything new.

"As much as I love him, Papa can go hang. I have spent far too many years in a prison of sorts. I want to find my freedom." Or at least the chance to spread her wings and see what she could do away from the cloying and repressive protection.

"Ha." Meredith's laugh sounded like a rusty gate. "You intend to find freedom at a musicale evening?"

Anna frowned. "Or perhaps with a certain viscount." Where had that thought come from? She'd only met him yesterday, but was she one of those women so desperate for change that they glommed to the first man who paid them attention? As much as she hoped not, she feared he might be her only hope to break out of the bind she'd been put into.

"He is far too scandalous." Censure threaded heavily through Meredith's voice as the carriage rocked. Seconds later, the driver pulled open the door and greeted them as he put down the steps.

"Perhaps everyone could do with having some scandal in their lives," Anna murmured while scooting along the bench toward the open door and the chilly air that poured into the vehicle. When the driver grasped her hand, she stifled a sigh, for this silly conversation with Meredith was finally over. "Thank you, Sam."

"My pleasure, Miss Standish." His voice was as rough as the man himself, but each time he assisted her into or out of the carriage, his touch was as light and gentle as a nurse to a babe. "Enjoy yourself tonight. I'll return in a couple of hours."

"I'd appreciate that." She waited while the driver helped Meredith out of the vehicle. The companion didn't say anything in the way of thanks or gratitude, and that provoked another frown from Anna. Why must the woman be the sourpuss in everything? She acted as if she had a vile dislike of life in general and nothing would make her grateful for the life she did lead. When the woman finally linked their arms, Anna stifled a sigh. "I hope you will enjoy yourself tonight, dear."

Meredith snorted. "I am not one for music."

Of course not, because anything that might bring Anna a modicum of joy was off limits. Without comment, she let the companion lead her up a short walkway. The soft advisement that there were a few steps warned her to watch her own, and then they were admitted into the blessed warmth of an entry hall.

Already, the buzz of excited chatter punctuated with bursts of laughter and giggles met her ears. As she was instructed to hand off her pelisse and bonnet to Meredith, more knots of uncertainty pulled in her belly. Pungent scents of pine and candle wax met her nose, and she smiled. Had they already begun decorating for the Christmas holiday? It made sense if they were entertaining.

What a lovely prospect!

Then Meredith once more gripped her arm and propelled her along a corridor that echoed with gay conversation and revelry. "The staircase is to your right. We will reach it in about ten feet."

Whatever else Meredith was not, she gave direction well.

Before they reached the area, though, someone hailed her. Gooseflesh raced over her skin and prickled the hairs on her nape, for she recognized that voice. She lifted her head, but since she had no idea the layout of the house or where the call had come from, she swam in a sea of confusion, which further added to her feelings of unease.

Then *he* was there. The comforting scents of sandalwood, orange, and leather preceded him, and seconds later, she felt the presence of the viscount as he stood at her other side. "How lovely to see you here tonight, Miss Standish," he said in a bright voice that indicated there were other people he knew in the vicinity.

"Hullo, Lord Evermore." It was far too natural to smile at him. Then she turned her head in Meredith's direction as butterflies once more danced in her lower belly. "Why don't you go ahead up and find a seat? I would like to talk with the viscount for a bit."

Edmund cleared his throat. "I shall escort her up once I've introduced her to my sister."

A slight huff came from Meredith, but she released her hold on Anna's arm. "Very well."

Leaning closer to her, the viscount put his lips near the shell of her ear. "She's quite the scare, isn't she?"

"Oh, stop." But she giggled, nonetheless. "Meredith means well. She is just prickly around the edges."

"Prickles neither of us need to brave just now. Come." He took her hand and threaded it through his crooked elbow. "I wasn't lying when I said I wished to introduce you to my sister. The last I saw of her, she lingered just outside the drawing room door. Will you be all right navigating the stairs?"

"I haven't reached this age without being carried up and down them to this point, if that's what you're asking." She couldn't help but joke with him, yet the idea of being securely fitted in his arms as he did just that had excitement buzzing at the base of her spine. "I shall be fine. Merely instruct me on when they begin and end."

"Of course." With murmured instructions from him, they navigated the stairs without incident, and she rather enjoyed having him so close. "We are turning left now. The drawing room will be on your right in about ten feet."

"Ah, Edmund!" Interest propelled the cry into the air. "I'm so glad you actually came upstairs. I had originally thought you'd duck into one of the card rooms for the evening."

Before Anna had a chance to comment, slight pressure on her arm had her moving ahead. "Good evening, Beatrice. I'd like to introduce you to Miss Standish. She was the one who offered her home to me yesterday afternoon following the accident." For whatever reason, there was a forced cheerfulness that rang in his voice she didn't understand.

"Oh, yes. Of course." Then Anna's free hand was scooped up by the woman who was apparently Edmund's sister. "I am Lady Beatrice Ashdowne-Delacourte, soon to be Kenton, and the hostess of tonight's event."

The tones were welcoming enough, but there was a note of confusion, even speculation there. What was the dynamic between the two siblings, and why did it feel as if there was unresolved tension there? Not wishing to appear rude, Anna nodded. "It is good to meet you, my lady. Lord Evermore was the model guest yesterday at dinner, and I hope he is none the worse following the accident." Perhaps she should have inquired, but there hadn't been time.

"I am well, thank you," he said in a low voice that sent shivers twisting down her spine. "My sister will marry later this month."

"Yes, and to me." The new male voice was a tad deeper than Edmund's, but his gloved hand replaced the lady's as he brought that appendage to his lips and kissed the back of it. "I am Major Kenton, and my daughter will be performing during the recital."

"It is lovely to meet you, Major." She barely had time to disengage from him before her hand was taken up by a girl who pumped it with enthusiasm. "You must be the daughter."

"Yes! I am Miss Kenton, but you can call me Mary. I'm playing a piece on the piano tonight, for Papa said I should at least give it a go before I decide the direction of my future." Her voice was bright and bubbly, and Anna rather doubted she was much older than eighteen. "I'm so glad you're here."

"You are?" Did anyone even know who she was?

"Oh, yes. Uncle Edmund said you played the piano as well."

"He did." It wasn't a question. "I barely talked about it yesterday, and I certainly didn't have an opportunity to play for him."

"I've never met another lady who has wished to play professionally. Most of my friends only dabble because it's something to fill the time until they catch a man."

Laughter went around their group after the bold statement.

Why couldn't a lady play professionally and also wish to catch a man? Was that not done within the *ton*? "Well, I hope I live up to your expectations, and I'm looking forward to hearing your piece." Finally, the girl released Anna's hand. "Perhaps we will talk later." She'd met more people in the last five minutes than she'd met in all of last year combined.

"I would enjoy that very much, Miss Standish."

From her side, Edmund chuckled, and the sound reverberated through her chest with a tickling sensation. "If there is someone missing on the roster tonight, perhaps Miss Standish can fill in."

"What a lovely suggestion." This from his sister. If the company was curious about her eyesight, they were too well bred not to mention it. "You should find seats. It won't be long before the recital is underway." She touched Anna's shoulder. "I'm happy to meet you, for you seem to have made an impression on my brother."

"I have?" In such a short time? How fascinating. It was something she wished to explore.

"Don't mind my sister. She is forever trying to match couples now that she is so happy in her own relationship."

"Ah." That made sense, but did that mean he didn't think she was good enough to be his match if that were to happen?

Eventually, Edmund showed her into a chair and then sat beside her. He kept up a whispered monologue of what the people directly around them looked like, how they acted, what they might be thinking, and it was enough to banish her anxiety, even cajole her into a better mood.

During the first half of the musicale evening, she was treated to some lovely performers and some not-so-wonderful musicians. Before and after each performance, she and Edmund held short, whispered conversations, whether pertaining to the music or not. However, when Mary was onstage and played a piece from Beethoven, Anna was impressed with the girl's talent.

"Your sister's soon-to-be stepdaughter is quite amazing. To have such a grasp on the finer nuances of the piano and music at that young age is awe inspiring."

"I shall be certain and tell Beatrice that. She rather dotes on the major's two children."

"Of course she should." When there was an announcement by the lady herself that this was an intermission and there would be a half hour break before the second half began, the room erupted into low conversation as many people left their seats.

"Would you care for some punch or even a glass of champagne?" he asked her while they both stood and his hand was at her elbow, guiding her through the crush of the room toward the corridor beyond.

"That would be lovely. I *am* rather parched." The fact remained that she'd talked more tonight than she had in the whole of last week, and having the viscount next to her, treating her as if she were a regular person instead of a pariah or a china doll, made such a difference. Society would prove not so bad if she could always have him with her.

But that was naught but a foolish imagining from a soon-to-be spinster.

Eventually, they reached the refreshment table that had been set up just outside the drawing room's double doors. The noise from the multiple conversations was almost deafening, and there was quite the crush in the corridor, which frequently jostled them together. Anna thrilled each time a part of her brushed a part of him. And if that wasn't enough, she adored how he gentlemanly put a hand to the small of her back and guided her away from the high-traffic areas when the crowd swelled too much.

"Let us stand to the side of the table," he whispered into her ear as he put a glass of punch into her hand. "And might I say, you are lovely tonight in navy. I particularly like your necklace."

"Thank you." Heat seeped into her cheeks from his praise. "The pin belonged to my mother." Though she couldn't see him beyond a darker blob moving against a lighter blob, the solidness of his body beside her and the warmth that emanated from him was the height of comforting. "Oh, goodness. This is a rum punch," she whispered with some excitement in her voice. The slight burn of the alcohol caught her by surprise.

Edmund chuckled. "Bea probably wished to treat everyone to a taste of the upcoming holiday season." He made a sound in his throat. "But yes, it's quite strong, isn't it?"

She didn't mind, for it was a treat indeed, and she finished the contents of her glass in short order.

Then the atmosphere shifted slightly, and didn't seem as gay as before. As she gave her cut crystal glass to the viscount, she frowned, for something didn't feel right. Anna cocked her head to further listen to the subtle clues. A brief kerfuffle erupted at the side of the table near their location. Apparently, a couple of men weren't pleased to see each other. A few glasses tumbled onto the floor as if the table had been strongly bumped. Then the smell of burning fabric reached her nose, and she wrinkled that append-age.

"Oh, my dear!" A lady close by yanked on her arm. "The back of your gown is aflame!"

"What?" Panic welled in her chest, for she didn't know what to do. Obviously, without being able to see the potential danger, she couldn't do the needful and help herself, but before she could call out for assistance, the viscount was there, stamping on her hem, patting the gown down.

"Stay still, Miss Standish. I've got this under control." Inevitably, part of her gown in the back tore. "A candle has tipped over and fallen off the table during the melee."

The heat of embarrassment went through her cheeks as murmurs erupted through the crowds around them. Oh, this night was ending in a disaster! Not knowing the state of the fire, she stood there with a pounding heartbeat while Edmund worked. Finally, one of the footmen brought out a pitcher of water, which was poured upon her backside until the fire was well and truly doused. She put her gloved hands to her burning cheeks. Not only had her gown caught fire, but everyone was no doubt staring at her, the fabric was ripped, torn, and now soaking wet, and there was still the second half of the recital to go.

"Oh, Edmund, please remove me from here. I cannot abide the scrutiny." Perhaps it had been a mistake after all to leave her house.

"All will be well." He was there with a hand to the small of her back and another holding onto her hand. "We are making our way to the staircase and will go down to the lower level. The parlor will be just the place to shield you from prying eyes until other arrangements can be made."

The sound of his voice and the confidence therein soothed her as she let him lead her away from the refreshment table and the drawing room. She clung to his arm as they made their way down the stairs, and once they reached what she assumed was the parlor, she nearly cried with relief, for here it was quiet and without the mad crush of people.

"You are safe now." Gently, he brought her deeper into the room. "How are you feeling?"

"A little worse for wear and quite embarrassed." A shuddering sigh escaped her. "Or perhaps overwhelmed is a good way to describe how I feel. That, and happy."

"What?" Confusion hung on that one word. "How so? Some of those pieces were eardrum shattering."

"True." Anna couldn't help her smile. Now that she'd been removed from the crowd and the embarrassment, she was beginning to relax. "However, this is the most excitement I've had in years. Though the ruined gown is saddening."

"True, but then, what is life without the unexpected." His chuckle tickled through her chest. Once more, his hand was at the small of her back, and she was shuttled all too close to him. "Perhaps this will make up for that." Before she knew what he was about, he'd pressed his lips gently to hers.

Oh, dear! If possible, her heartbeat accelerated even faster than it already was. So stunned was she that Anna froze and stared at him. With him being so close, she could finally see what his features looked like, and good heavens, he was perfection itself! Blond hair arranged into what she assumed was a popular style, eyes of a deep cornflower blue that were intensely looking back at her. Autocratic lines which swept the planes of his face, from his eyebrows to his nose to his lips, indicated he was indeed descended from nobility. The tiny hint of evening stubble on his cheeks and chin made him nearly irresistible.

And still he waited as if wishing for her permission to continue.

Butterflies danced through her belly as she gawked at him. "That was my first kiss," she admitted in a barely audible whisper. To think that this man had given it to her set her mind to reeling. So much had already happened since she'd met him, it was stunning.

"Truly?" The viscount cupped her cheek, drew the pad of his gloved thumb along her bottom lip and grinned when she trembled.

"Yes." The heat had returned to her cheeks. "I told you my father sheltered me regardless of what I have wished for my own life. There are so many things I've not experienced in this world that I'm breathless with ignorance."

"We cannot have that." With another grin, Edmund reeled her into his arms, settled her more comfortably there. "Perhaps we should begin your education." Then he once more pressed his lips to hers, but the difference between kisses was like day was to night.

As he moved over her mouth with confidence, Anna curled

her fingers into his lapels, for it was heady stuff indeed to be kissed twice by the same man. His lips were both firm and soft, and they cradled hers as if born to do it. With tiny nibbles and licks, he introduced himself to her through that medium, and after the shock of it wore away, she followed his lead, tried to mimic what he did to her. Oh, good heavens, but she could soon find herself lost in such a kiss, and slowly, she slipped her palms up his chest to loop about his shoulders. He pulled her ever closer while continuing to kiss her without pressure, didn't attempt to deepen the embrace or do anything that might frighten her, and for that she appreciated his discretion.

A sharp gasp from the doorway had them springing apart. "Lord Evermore, for shame, taking advantage of Miss Standish." The censure in Meredith's voice was unmistakable. "I heard what happened and came to check on you." She rushed to Anna's side and took up one of her hands. "Are you all right?"

Well, that largely depended on which event the woman referred to, for her senses and head was still spinning from that kiss.

"Yes, of course, but my gown is ruined. I can't return to the drawing room." Not that she minded if Edmund would stay with her here.

"We should go home immediately." Meredith tsked her tongue. "Finding you like this at the mercy of such a man means scandal is surely in the offing."

"He has been nothing but lovely."

The viscount cleared his throat. "Be careful lest you overstep, Miss Grafton." There was no mistaking the veiled warning in his voice.

Anna pouted. "Perhaps going home is the logical choice since my gown is wrecked." Yet she hadn't had nearly enough time with Lord Evermore.

Again, as if sensing the direction of her thoughts, Edmund came close and took up her other hand. "Would you be agreeable to me calling on you tomorrow?"

"Yes." Oh, dear, her voice was far too breathless. She

squeezed his fingers. "Please do come for tea. We had such fun last time."

"We did indeed." He lifted her hand to his lips and pressed a kiss to the back of her gloved hand. "Then I will see you tomorrow, but thank you for spending part of the evening with me. I know my sister appreciated your support."

She and Meredith didn't meet many guests on the way out, for the second part of the musicale evening must have already begun. Once in their carriage, her companion's heavy sigh threatened to take away some of the magic from the night.

"I don't trust Lord Evermore by half. He is trailing scandal with pockets near to let, but his family has money." Meredith huffed. "If one can overlook the fact that family is also surrounded by scandal."

"I don't mind." He was the first man to ever see for herself. In this, she would gladly antagonize her companion. "I think he is lovely and interesting, and he's the first man to pay me attention in years."

"All the more reason to steer clear. He wants your inheritance."

"Ha." Anna scoffed as she clasped her hands in her lap. "I only just met him." Surely a man who was a bounder wouldn't kiss her so sweetly. "You are just grasping at the worst of what could happen."

"Time will tell." Fabric rustled as Meredith settled on the opposite bench from hers. "Let us hope his attention will stray and he soon leaves you alone."

A rebellious streak wrapped up Anna's spine. *You can wish for that, but I am going to hope for the opposite.* It was definitely time to test her wings and see where she could go from there.

CHAPTER FIVE

December 9, 1820
Ashdowne House
St. James Place, London

EDMUND YAWNED. DAMNATION, but he'd never been so tired in his life. Dawn had barely broken, but Poppy was fussy, and he didn't want her to wake the rest of the household so as he laid in bed, he had her next to him, tucked securely next to him and surrounded by pillows on the other side.

The women he'd hired to care for her wouldn't start with him until the day after tomorrow. In the meantime, he played the role of a nursery maid while he'd temporarily paid the wet nurse the Countess of Ettesmere used to help him out as she could. In the interim, Graham's cook had shown him a different option in feeding the baby with a bottle and some goat's milk she added a couple of things to. That helped him, and though he was doing the best he could, he feared it wasn't enough. Was she getting enough nutrition? Enough interaction? Enough attention? Would she even like having him as a father once she grew and learned things about him?

When the baby cooed and kicked her feet, he gave her a tired grin.

"Regardless of how your life started, you are a pretty little cherub, and I am glad you are here." That admission shocked him, for a handful of days ago, he was a confirmed bachelor who'd wanted nothing to do with anything that smacked of domesticity. Now? Well, now he was a reluctant father to a baby girl who had enough of his features that anyone could see she was his. As she looked at him with those Winterbourne blue eyes and grabbed at his fingers as he teased her, his resolve to prove his family wrong still burned strong. "You and I are going to take on the world, Poppy." He stroked her little downy head. Already, little ringlets were trying to form in her golden hair. "Come hell or high water, we are going to show them all that we are both meant to be here, and we have purpose."

Perhaps it was a good thing he'd been too busy to attend his clubs, for he'd managed to avoid gossip that way, but he hoped since the baby's existence had been kept behind the walls of the house, tattlemongers and scandal wouldn't soon visit.

God, I need a break from that.

Another yawn threatened to split his jaws. Yes, being a father without help was an exhausting endeavor, but he had a plan, and it all hinged on the enchanting piano player he'd unexpectedly kissed last night. She was interesting enough in her own right, had a face and figure that weren't unsavory, and she was intriguing enough to hold his interest for a bit. Would she be able to look past his indiscretions once she heard of them? For her self-righteous companion would make certain she would, but she'd seemed so overwhelmed and embarrassed after her gown caught fire in a freak accident that he'd wanted to set her mind at ease. Oddly, he wanted to protect her in the usual sense of the word, which wasn't in his style at all. And him, being him, had kissed her, for it was the only way he could think of.

Had he enjoyed that embrace? Yes, yes he had, probably more than he should, since he knew very little about the woman. Would it have grown out of hand had they not been interrupted by the Friday-faced companion? It was difficult to say, for the pianist was woefully inexperienced in all things carnal, but he wouldn't have minded teaching her a thing or two. The remembrance of those lush lips pressed against his brought shuddering awareness to his shaft.

But he wasn't in the market for a wife… or not a real wife, that was. A wife in name only? It was definitely the best for everyone concerned. Anna would provide funding, stability, and more importantly be a mother to the baby. In return, he would give her the freedom she desired, a way to meet her goals, and a husband as well as the family she wanted. Above all, he would demand a marriage of convenience, for he didn't wish to give up his mistresses or courtesans. To say nothing of the fact his heart had been broken years ago and though it had healed with time, he was leery of going down that path again.

Especially now, when he needed to think of Poppy's future.

"What do you think I should do?" he asked in a whisper of the babe.

She merely smiled and cooed and kicked her little feet as if she found the whole prospect too much of a joke.

First and foremost was taking care of the infant. Her mother might have given her up, but he would not. In the whole scope of scandal that had rocked his family's name, this was a mere hiccup and could be weathered accordingly, but he needed help.

"Did you know that your mother named you Poppy?" Edmund didn't know if he liked the moniker but there was nothing he could do about it. "I don't know why, for you haven't red hair, but perhaps it was a name she liked." When she tossed her head about and stared at him with those big blue eyes, his chest tightened. Though she heavily resembled him, she also looked like her mother. He barely remembered the woman; she was just one of many he'd had in his bed over the years, but this was the first time he'd been aware he had offspring. "The only thing I remember about your mother was her affinity for jewelry." Damn, but he'd often spent all the allowance Graham had given him each quarter on baubles to keep the woman happy and beneath his protection.

In the end, she'd grown bored of him and he with her. They'd gone their separate ways, and he'd had nothing to show for the jewelry he'd given her during the months they'd had together.

Except for the baby.

In many ways, he was fortunate. Again, he dangled his fingers over her head. Poppy reached up a hand and then wrapped her little fingers around one of his. "God, but you are determined to charm your way into my heart, aren't you?" That organ squeezed. She was of his own flesh, a part of him. Now she was his responsibility. His family might be under scrutiny from scandal, but her life didn't need to be affected by that. "I am going to protect you to the best of my ability. No words or people will be able to hurt you, and you will grow up strong, determined to change the world. Just like me."

She smiled once more and put her tongue out. When he chuckled, she kicked her feet and flailed her hands as if she were pleased with his reaction.

"Your mother was wrong, Poppy. Despite the odds, despite everything, *I* want you." And that shocked him to his core. "If all goes well, I'll take the first steps in making everything right, in giving you a future you can be proud of. A future I will be proud of. We only need Miss Standish to agree to the plan."

His family be damned.

Mattersfield House
London, England

ONCE MORE, EDMUND was shown into the parlor where he'd come after the carriage accident. Knots of worry pulled in his gut, for this was either the greatest plan he'd ever had or the stupidest, but he had to try.

Last night, Graham had given him a lecture that included him destroying a carriage and having no respect for others by bringing his bastard daughter into Graham's home without a plan for her care or future. When Edmund had tried to argue the point saying things were expected to clear up soon, his brother had none of it and reiterated his intentions of withdrawing support by the first of the year.

He had finally quit the room, telling his brother he would have an answer for him in a few days, then he'd gone up to his room, dressed his baby for nighttime sleeping, did the same for himself, and slept as fitfully as the infant's schedule would allow.

As he waited for Anna to make an appearance, he paced in front of the fireplace where a cheerful fire danced behind a metal grate and tried to stifle a yawn. Again, it was raining, which wasn't uncommon for December in London, but it put a damper on his uplifted spirits. Above it all, his nerves felt strung too tight, for he'd never once considered asking for a woman's hand before.

Especially within these circumstances, and as a matter of survival.

The butler came into the room with a tea tray. Edmund nodded his thanks, and before he could seat himself, the sound of voices in the corridor beyond alerted himself to the imminent arrival of Anna and her companion. With excitement and dread twisting together down his spine, he clasped his hands behind his back and waited until the woman came into the room.

Anna had her hand wrapped about Meredith's upper arm, but she turned her head, seemingly already knowing where he stood in the room, and a glad smile curved her raspberry-hued lips. "Lord Evermore. I am so glad you came."

"As am I." He bounced his gaze to the companion, who stared at him with narrowed eyes. Her brown hair had been scraped back into a tight bun and was about as uninteresting as the brown crepe dress she wore. "If you don't mind, Miss Grafton, I would like a word alone with Miss Standish."

"So you can perhaps encourage her into a compromising position?" It was a waspish comment and they both knew it.

Edmund stifled the urge to huff with frustration. "No. I have the utmost respect for Miss Standish, but there are things I would like to discuss without an audience." He shifted his stance, crossed his arms at chest level. "You may rush in after an hour has passed and make certain she remains unharmed."

Anna patted the other woman's arm. "It is all right, Meredith. I trust the viscount."

"You shouldn't. Mark my words, he'll be your downfall and you'll have nothing but regret and tears." But she left in high dudgeon.

"What a pill that woman is." If Anna agreed to wed him, the first order of business would be to dismiss the companion.

"Please don't mind her. We have been together a long time and she is rather overprotective in a different way than my father is." As she crossed the room toward the sound of his voice, Edmund met her in the middle and led her to a low sofa. "But let us not talk about my companion. I have thought about you all day." Today, her gown of moss green silk brought out the color of her eyes and once more put him in mind of a woodland garden where she'd surely escaped from.

"You have?" He sat after she settled, and when he would have poured out tea, Anna did the task herself. Not a drop spilled. Impressive. "Why is that?" Yes, he wanted to hear her say she'd enjoyed his kiss, but then, he was a vain rogue most of the time.

"Of course." When she offered him a delicate porcelain cup, he took it and made certain their fingers brushed. "When a man kisses a woman as you did me last night, she will always hope he'll come calling the next day." A giggle followed as she poured out her own cup. "Besides, it was enough to send Meredith into the boughs, which meant she gave me a lecture this morning, but I don't care. I am old enough to make my own decisions in life."

There was the opening he needed. "I am glad to hear that." For long moments, he sipped his tea and hoped his stomach would settle so he could get through this next bit without casting up his accounts from nerves. "Uh, since meeting you, I have been impressed with your determination as well as the dreams you have for your life. Also, I have been horrified that you have lived much as if you have been imprisoned."

She nodded. "It has been something of an ordeal, but since I met you—only two days ago—I feel as if I'm hovering on a precipice of change."

"You aren't far off." Quickly, he downed the remainder of his tea, regardless that it was still quite hot, and then set the cup and saucer on the low table in front of him. "Since meeting you, I think we can be good for each other, help each other through life's foibles as it were."

"What does that mean?" A frown tugged at the corners of her highly kissable lips.

Why the devil couldn't he stop staring at her mouth? It wasn't as if he hadn't had countless liaisons with women in the past and had never kissed any of them. Pushing such thoughts from his mind, Edmund turned toward her on the sofa. When their knees bumped, heat streaked up into his groin. He took her hands in his. "It means I can give you the freedom you want, and you can give me the stability I need." When she frowned again, he sighed. "In short, I wish to know if you have any interest of entering into a marriage of convenience with me as soon as it is convenient."

"What?" She tugged her hands from his hold as shock rounded her eyes. "You cannot possibly mean that. Are you asking me that in jest?"

"No, of course not! I have carefully thought of nothing else for two days." Perhaps he needed to go carefully so as not to spook her again. "It is an easy thing, really. You want out from under your father's thumb in order to explore everything that life might offer you. I need a wife to show my brother I am not the layabout cockup that he and the gossips think I am." And lest she get the wrong impression, he added in a rush, "This would be a marriage of convenience. We would both have the legitimacy of marriage but with the added freedoms it would entail."

And he would be financially solvent with a mother for his

child.

"Why?"

"Why not?" He shrugged. "We obviously rub along well enough together."

"True, but then that is difficult to ascertain after two days, for you are far too charming for your own good, I'll wager." Anna narrowed her eyes. "Are you a rogue or a bounder? Meredith has had some choice things to say about you and your family."

Of course she did. Edmund stifled a groan. There was no point in lying, for she would find out in any event. Regardless, he chuckled. "Some might say yes. In the past, my name has been linked to more than a few courtesans and scandals." Heat crept up the back of his neck, for he'd never given thought to his lifestyle before now, and in some ways, he regretted those days, for he probably appeared problematic in her estimation. "In fact, just this last week, one of those affairs resulted in a baby. My former mistress has decided she didn't want the babe any longer, so she sent the infant to me." Uncertainty filled his chest as he looked at her. "I desperately need help with the babe, and Poppy needs a mother."

"Oh, you poor things. Both adrift, essentially." She squeezed his fingers. "And I did say one of my dreams was being a mother." Indecision warred with need on her face. "How old is your daughter?"

"Six months, and she is quite the taking little thing." His voice broke of its own volition. "I'll admit, I have no idea what I'm doing; I never thought I would be a father. What if my bumbling attempts are already harming her development?" Quickly, he told her that he'd hired the appropriate people to help with her care lest she think he was a complete nodcock.

"At least you are making the effort." With a sigh, Anna scooted closer to him and then leaned into him in an apparent attempt to look into his face. He would need to ask her why later. "I can see the conflict in your eyes, the struggle, but there is also anger there too. You aren't happy with your life or yourself."

Oh, God.

"In the past year, life has been… trying. I'll leave it at that."

"Fair enough." Though she nodded, she continued to examine his face, and he hoped to any deity that was available she found something redeeming in him. "What of love in the future? Is there no chance?" This time it was her voice that broke. "Is that something I should warn myself not to hope for?"

That tiny tell of longing nearly sent him to his knees, and he didn't know why. In an ordinary situation, he didn't give two farthings about a woman's thoughts or feelings. "I don't know. We will need to see how things go, but this will give us both what we want and change our immediate circumstances."

For the space of a few heartbeats, she held his gaze. "Would we take a wedding trip?"

"If you wish it." Surely, he could manage that… or encourage Graham to send them on one. In that way, he would be out of Graham's hair, and they could both cool down. Of course, the very nature of this union would see that his brother remained annoyed for a long time to come. "I'm certain I can find some place to go. My brother has a property in Kent. Would that be acceptable?"

"I have never been anywhere except London and my father's estate in Derbyshire."

Edmund cleared his throat. "Is that an agreement? Will you marry me in name only?"

"Yes." As if the clouds cleared away from the sun, she smiled, and his world righted once more. "I agree to marry you and enter into the convenience of it for the good of us both. At least now I won't die a spinster. Perhaps an old maid since it won't be a true marriage, but that is better than the alternative." When she giggled, his shaft tightened. "The sooner the better. It will be lovely spending the Christmastide season with my own little family."

Damnation, he'd forgotten about the impending holidays. Remarkably, he relaxed by increments, for it would be good to be away from Town… and all that he would be missing. "Thank you." Cupping her cheek, he brushed his lips over hers in a chaste kiss. "I will speak with your father if he's in residence."

"I believe he is in his study." She leaned forward and bussed his cheek. The scent of apple blossoms lingered in his nose. "I am not naïve enough to think this isn't a huge sacrifice on your part, but I do appreciate what you're doing for me, for you, for the baby. Perhaps it is what we all need, and we will discover that in time."

"Perhaps." He nodded, and suddenly tears misted his eyes. Since the advent of Poppy, he'd been beset by foreign emotions he didn't quite know what to do with. "Thank you. I should probably speak to your father now. If you wish to wed quickly, there is much to do before then."

And God help them both.

CHAPTER SIX

December 12, 1820
Ashdowne House
St. James Place, London

ANNA REPEATEDLY TOLD herself there was no reason to suffer through nerves, but they persisted in feeling strung too tight as Meredith escorted her into the drawing room at Ashdowne House. Her husband-to-be had told her next to nothing about his family, and even less about himself, so she would go into her nuptial ceremony as blind as she truly was.

Perhaps that was just as well, for she hadn't put too much stock in the gossip Meredith delighted in repeating. She would have the truth or nothing, and she would make her own judgments about Edmund. As of yet, there was no one else in the drawing room except them. The butler had said to expect the family imminently.

Still, everything had happened so quickly after the viscount had asked her to marry him. Though it would be a marriage in name only, it would change both of their lives forever, and the knowledge that he had an infant in his care from a prior mistress managed to send knots of worry into her belly.

Would he remain faithful to her? That remained to be seen, but she had to maintain some sort of hope. Otherwise, the alternative couldn't be contemplated.

"Drat, but I'm so nervous," she whispered to her father as he switched places with Meredith and placed her hand on his arm. "Perhaps this is a mistake."

"Nonsense, poppet. This marriage is quite strategic and a good match for you." He patted her hand. "I always wanted at least that for you."

That might be the truth, but the truth of the matter was he no doubt looked forward to not having the care and protection of her any longer. It would certainly free up his time.

"You know I don't care about positioning within the *ton*. I merely wish to be taken care of and have someone that I can love." Would Edmund be exactly that? Again, it was too soon to contemplate, and she would merely need to be patient, but his kisses made her feel like flying, so at least they were slightly compatible.

"Every union is much like a gamble, but I wish you the best of luck." He pressed a kiss to her forehead. "I'm told that Lord Evermore's family is interesting and with quite a blue-blooded pedigree. You will be someone of power."

She couldn't bring herself to ask about the gossip that apparently swirled about the family collectively and Edmund specifically. "I suppose the dowry you offered him was generous."

"Of course it was. I won't let the Ashdownes intimate me with their position and wealth."

At the last second, she stopped herself from rolling her eyes. "I see." If Edmund was truly a fortune-hunter, at least the dowry would stave off that shock for a bit.

"I assume you will take Miss Grafton with you?"

"For the time being, I suppose I should need to since I don't know Edmund's schedule or plans going forward." Suddenly, she didn't wish to talk about that any longer. The sun streaming in from one of the windows called to her. "If you can escort me to the window, I'll wait until it's time there. I want to stand in the sun for a bit." After he did what she asked, Anna sighed. "Thank you, Papa. For everything, but now I must move into my future on my own."

"Yes, I suppose you will." He patted her hand. "I'll just be seated across the room if you should need me."

She nodded and turned her face to the window and the sunshine. The prospect of leaving her father's home for the unknown left her discomfited. She'd need to learn a whole new floorplan, and for that matter, surely Edmund didn't plan to remain in his brother's house after they wed. That would be too awkward, but they hadn't discussed the possibility of renting a townhouse of their own.

Perhaps he had already taken care of those details.

As she stood there with hands clasped in front of her, other people came into the room, and already she could sense the tension between them.

"I can hardly believe you thought to marry before my own wedding. You knew how much planning I have already put into it," a woman said in a fierce whisper.

Anna recognized that voice as belonging to Edmund's sister.

"There was no other way around it," Edmund said with a surety in his tones that she appreciated. "It was imperative Miss Standish and I wed as soon as possible."

"But you'll go away on a wedding trip and thereby miss my own ceremony."

"It cannot be helped, Bea, but you'll be so busy you wouldn't even know if I was there."

"Were you c-c-caught in a compromising situation with this w-w-woman?" The gruff voice as well as the stutter betrayed the man speaking as Edmund's older brother, the Marquess of Grantley. "Or have you already impregnated her too?"

Dear heavens. Heat went through Anna's cheeks at the slight.

"Of course not. I have been nothing but a gentleman toward her."

The brother grunted. "Then why the haste? It is too soon to wed. You cannot possibly love her."

Anna strained to hear her husband-to-be's answer.

"I don't, of course. You already know this. She and I also are aware of that fact." A sound of annoyance left his throat. "This union is for convenience. You wanted me to clean up my life. This is how I'm starting. I assumed you wished for me to settle down as quickly as possible, which is why a special license was procured." He snorted, as if he couldn't stand the sight of his brother. "You can't have it both ways, Brother."

"God, you are i-i-impossible," the marquess hissed with anger in every word.

"So are you, which is why we are all here this morning." Anxiety and anger threaded through Edmund's words. "Once Anna and I return from Kent, I will make arrangements to rent a townhouse. Her dowry will go a long way into encouraging such a transaction. Then you will not have to see my face again. You can live out your perfect union in your perfect life and forget that you ever had a brother."

A tremble moved through her heart, for he was obviously hurt from wounds that went much deeper than differences between siblings. She wished she could help, for his family's dynamics were far too fascinating.

"Good." This from the marquess. "I t-t-truly hope this will encourage you to be a better man."

A soft sound came from Edmund's sister. "Can you two not get along for one moment? *I* might be temporarily annoyed with him, but Edmund *is* trying."

Both men grunted. Obviously, this rift between them wouldn't be bridged with a nuptial ceremony.

"Let us sit down." Lady Beatrice sighed. "There is the vicar. We shall talk later."

Anna stood frozen at the window, for to join any of them now would be the height of awkward. So she waited and wondered what sort of mess she'd fallen into. Not long afterward, the familiar scent of Edmund's shaving soap wafted to her nose, and her heartbeat accelerated. "I'm glad you are here. Doubts are starting to creep in."

"You wouldn't be human if they didn't. I am suffering from them as well." The moment he took both her hands in his, she relaxed by increments. "And, by the way, you are quite the vision this morning. That gown is pretty. The emerald color makes you seem so alive."

"Thank you." She hadn't truly given much thought to what she wore, but all the servants as well as her father had complimented her on it before they had left the house to come over.

Made of deep green silk, it had been shot through with golden thread. A sash of gold lamé went about her waist and the same fabric lined the hem and bodice. Puffed short sleeves reminded her of Christmas bells. There were even slippers to match, but they pinched her toes a bit. Her maid had spent copious time on Anna's hair to create an elaborate updo wherein she'd pulled curls out at strategic places. The heavy mass was held in place with glittering gold and tiny emerald-encrusted combs.

"As one of your wedding gifts from me, there is an emerald and gold parure waiting for you, and I cannot wait to see you wear it."

"Oh! I have always wanted lovely jewelry!" Heat went through her cheeks, even more so when he tugged her close.

He put his lips to the shell of her ear. "If we hadn't agreed on a marriage in name only, I swear I could eat you up." His tone quickened her pulse.

"Stop." But pleasure filled her chest. His scent threatened to drown her as she peered closely into his face. "You are quite handsome today."

"Well, being dressed in dark evening clothes including a tailcoat will do that for a man."

"No, it goes beyond that. I can see it in your eyes that you are ready for the changes this day will bring, and that you are a tad proud." She would like to hope it was because of her, but knowing him after what she'd overheard, he probably enjoyed inconveniencing his siblings more. Before he could answer, she rushed forward. "Are you certain you wish to do this? I will ask that you be faithful to me, even if our union is one of convenience."

"I…" Edmund took a step backward. He tugged at his cravat. "I will be for a time so there are no wagging tongues."

"Ah." Annoyance stabbed into her chest, but there was nothing she could do. He was still a stranger, and until she knew him better, until she could discover if they would suit in all the ways that mattered, there would need to be compromises. "Beyond everything, I despise being embarrassed. Please don't do that to me."

He brought one of her hands to his lips and then kissed the back. "I will not."

"Good." Tingles of anticipation played her spine and circled through her lower belly. Surely it was ridiculous to feel such things at her advanced age, but she enjoyed it just the same. "Thank you for the compliments. You give so many, I don't know what to do with such attention." Anna traced her gloved fingertips over his face. She swept her touch along his hair that had been manipulated into a popular style. "I know I shouldn't, but I feel quite fortunate to be doing this with you."

"I'll try to be the best husband that I can be for you."

She nodded. "What color is your waistcoat?"

He cupped her cheek, and the smooth kid of his glove molded to her skin. "Gold with silver and black embroidery."

"How wonderful." Nerves fluttered in her stomach but calmed somewhat when Edmund took her hand and threaded it through his crooked elbow.

"The vicar approaches, so it's no doubt time."

There was nothing in her line of vision except darker and lighter blobs that occasionally shifted if someone moved.

"Hullo. I am Mr. Gordon, and I will be officiating the ceremony."

"Welcome, Mr. Gordon." The emotion in Edmund's voice was true. "I'm glad your clerk has set up across the room."

"Yes, for you will need to sign the register to make everything official." The man cleared his throat. "If you would like to begin?"

"Absolutely."

Anna nodded. "Yes, please."

"Very good. I rather like this spot by the window. It will do nicely."

She smiled, for she did so adore the light and warmth. Behind them, fabric rustled as guests settled onto furniture.

Leather cracked. Had the vicar opened his *Book of Common Prayer*? "Dearly beloved, we are gathered together here in the sight of God, and in the face of this congregation, to join together this Man and this Woman in holy Matrimony; which is an honorable estate, instituted of God in the time of man's innocency, signifying unto us the mystical union that is betwixt Christ and his Church...."

Good heavens, this is truly happening! Anna clung to Edmund's arm. Never in her wildest dreams did she think she would ever be married, but here she stood beside a man of alleged scandalous reputation, a man who smelled so delicious, a man whose strength could be felt beneath her fingertips. It wasn't until he discreetly and softly cleared his throat that she ceased her woolgathering and attended to what the vicar said as he addressed the viscount.

"Wilt thou have this Woman to thy wedded Wife, to live together after God's ordinance in the holy estate of Matrimony? Wilt thou love her, comfort her, honor, and keep her in sickness and in health; and, forsaking all others, keep thee only unto her, so long as ye both shall live?"

Anna trembled. She held her breath held in anticipation. Did he truly understand the importance of those words?

In a clear voice, Edmund answered, "I will."

A snort originating from the marquess interrupted the sacredness of the moment. "Time will tell." Then he was scolded by a woman with an unfamiliar voice she assumed was his wife.

Her hands shook as the minister addressed her.

"Wilt thou have this Man to thy wedded Husband, to live together after God's ordinance in the holy estate of Matrimony?

Wilt thou obey him, and serve him, love, honor, and keep him in sickness and in health; and, forsaking all others, keep thee only unto him, so long as ye both shall live?"

She squeezed her fingers upon Edmund's arm. "I will." Her answer came out breathless and in a whisper, for tears crowded her throat. This was such a pinnacle moment. *I wish my mother were here to witness it.*

The viscount was instructed to take her right hand in his right hand, and hers shook so badly that he gently squeezed her fingers. He went so far as to put his lips to her ear and whispered, "It will be all right. I promise this is not a prison sentence. You'll have your freedom and the family you wanted."

"I know." Anna smiled lest he think she looked upon the ceremony with dread. This was the grandest thing she'd ever done in her life, and she did so hope she would make him proud that he wedded her. "I'm just so overwhelmed at the moment," she whispered back.

The vicar cleared his throat and continued. "Lord Evermore, repeat after me...." He intoned words Anna scarcely heard until Edmund said them to her.

"I, Edmund Richard Philip Ashdowne, Viscount Evermore, take thee Anna Marie Standish to my wedded Wife, to have and to hold from this day forward, for better for worse, for richer for poorer, in sickness and in health, to love and to cherish, 'till death us do part, according to God's holy ordinance; and thereto I plight thee my troth."

They were directed to release hands, and Anna was told to then hold Edmund's right hand with her right hand. "Ahem." The minister addressed her. "Miss Standish, repeat after me." He gave her the words, and she prayed she would say them in the proper order without bursting into tears.

"I, Anna Marie Standish, take thee Edmund Richard Philip Ashdowne, Viscount Evermore to my wedded Husband." She paused to swallow and squeeze his hand. "To have and to hold from this day forward, for better for worse, for richer for poorer, in sickness and in health, to love, cherish, and to obey, 'till death us do part, according to God's holy ordinance." She lowered her voice to a whisper. "And thereto I give thee my troth." How wonderful and slightly terrifying such a thing was.

Please show me this isn't a mistake.

They were instructed to again release their hands. Fabric rustled. Coins clinked. From her side, Edmund shifted. "What are you doing?"

"Giving the vicar a ring along with payment for his services."

"I thank you, my lord."

"Of course." The vicar must have returned the ring to him, for he then slipped it onto the fourth finger of her left hand. "Anna, the ring is a round emerald. Five carats, surrounded with tiny round diamonds. It is part of the parure I spoke to you about earlier."

"How lovely." She couldn't wait to put the ring close to her eyes in order to see it. "No one has ever assumed I might like to wear jewelry."

He grunted. "I rather think the people around you have been idiots."

"Repeat after me, Lord Evermore," the vicar said.

In his steady tenor, Edmund did so. "With this Ring I thee wed, with my Body I thee worship," his voice wavered on those words, for theirs was naught but a marriage in name only, "and with all my worldly Goods I thee endow. In the Name of the Father, and of the Son, and of the Holy Ghost. Amen."

Oh, goodness, we are truly wed. Anna kneeled when Edmund did, still clutching his hand while the vicar invited all in attendance to pray.

As the words of a prayer droned on, Anna closed her eyes and sent up a simpler prayer of her own, conveying gratitude and thankfulness and asking for strength to survive what would surely be a difficult adjustment to a brand-new life.

Suddenly, I will be a mother. She couldn't wait to meet his daughter.

When Edmund stood and brought her to her feet, the vicar intoned, "I now pronounce thee husband and wife."

And then it was over.

No longer was she unwanted or unmarried. She was now the Viscountess of Evermore. From the corner of her eye, she caught the green flash of the emerald that rested on her finger. Already, he'd been so generous when she hadn't required it, and though her father had bestowed upon her whatever she'd wanted, she'd never asked for much beyond a piano, but it was lovely being so pampered.

"Come," Edmund said into her ear. "We must sign the registry." They were ushered to a table away from the windows where they both signed the registry, which made the union official. When she struggled with finding the appropriate line, he was there, pointing out the place in the book. "That is that."

"I can hardly believe this is true." She kept a hand on his arm. His muscles were tight beneath her fingertips. "We are wed."

As fabric rustled, she assumed the various guests were filing out of the room to partake in the wedding breakfast. Anna's stomach growled, for she'd been so nervous, she hadn't eaten much dinner the night before.

"I wanted to be the first to congratulate you, Evermore."

Anna frowned, for she didn't recognize that voice, but Edmund stiffened beside her.

"That is much appreciated, Ettesmere. I hadn't known you were coming."

"I very nearly couldn't due to my schedule and with the baby being so fussy, but I managed it." He took one of Anna's hands, brought it to his lips, and kissed the back of it. "Good morning. I'm the Earl of Ettesmere, head of the Winterbourne connection. I'm sure you have heard the stories by now."

"Actually, I have not, for I wished to hear them in my husband's words and not have gossip color them."

"Clever girl." He released her hand. "Welcome to the Winterbourne family. You are one of us now, after a fashion, and Winterbournes stick together." Then he turned his attention to Edmund. "You've shown great character by choosing to keep the infant and to raise her, Evermore. I have much respect for you."

Her husband grunted. "I couldn't let her go to someone else for an unknown future."

"Agreed." Amusement and went through earl's voice. "Your brother told me you intended to spend your honeymoon period in Kent. If you want a change of pace, I have a property in Brighton that you are welcome to make use of. My mother is there currently, but I doubt she'll prove much trouble."

Excitement careened down Anna's spine. "Oh, I've never seen the sea." She chuckled. "Not that I will now, but I can feel it, breathe it in, put my feet in it." With slightly tightened fingers, she looked at Edmund. "Might we go?"

He patted her hand. "As if I could deny you anything."

"Wonderful!" The earl laughed again. "It's settled. Go there. I had it renamed to Quill House after my wife. She adores peeping at the stars from the shoreline. Refresh yourselves. And when you return to London, I hope you've found a few truths you needed that will carry you through and build a future upon. Now, I'm going into breakfast before leaving for home."

"Thank you for coming," Anna said as he departed. Then she was left alone with her husband. "My head is still spinning from everything."

"Mine too, but I promise you will have everything that life can offer."

"Does that include you eventually?" Though she'd agreed to a marriage of convenience, she couldn't imagine a union of perhaps twenty years or so stretching into the future where she would never enjoy intimacy from said husband.

Or never having his love.

"We shall see, but I won't discount anything." He cupped her cheek then pressed his lips to hers in a sweet kiss that left longing deep inside her. "Shall we greet our guests?"

"Yes." She wanted to trust him, wanted to have hope, but as fate had already taught her, there were no guarantees to a happily ever after. She would take it one day at a time.

CHAPTER SEVEN

December 13, 1820
Quill House
Regency Square
Brighton, England

THEY HAD BEEN married for over twenty-four hours, and in that time, Edmund had never been as exhausted or soul weary as he was right now.

Constant bickering with his family, the worries over hiring enough staff to help him take care of Poppy, and the trip to Brighton and knowing the dowager countess was in residence all chipped away at his will to be charming, but throughout the trip, Anna traded off with him in holding the infant, and seeing her with the babe had apparently tried to addle his brains, for he'd thought it was all too natural.

"I am glad the child has your looks," his wife said as the traveling coach made its way around the crescent toward the correct townhouse. She held the baby close to her face, like she'd done with him a few times in order to see her. "Such a lovely girl."

With his chest tight, Edmund frowned as he peered outside the window. "I fear I am not good enough to be her father."

"Do hush, Edmund. We are all learning. One doesn't become an expert in anything overnight. There must be practice."

"Perhaps." Yet he appreciated the insight. At least it wasn't raining. "I'd forgotten the earl's mother would be in residence even though he'd told us." He huffed out a breath. "Good thing ours is a marriage of convenience, for we certainly won't be alone." Her companion and the staff he'd recently hired were arriving in a second coach.

"There will always be something, but we *are* together, and this is our life." She cuddled the baby against her shoulder when the infant began to fuss. "We will soon find a rhythm."

"I hope so. The last thing I want is for my brother to think he's right about me." The long row of terraced townhouses featured white plaster stucco façades, long thin windowpanes, Greek columns, and balconies, all in a creamy ivory color. Not too far away was the sea; the surf pounding against the shore as the coach rolled to a stop drifted to his ears.

"Let the marquess have his opinions. You know the truth, and that's all that matters." She looked in his direction. "Promise me you'll try to relax while we are here. Regardless of what exactly our union is, you have made strides to give us all a future. That is nothing to sneeze at."

That lifted his spirits considerably. "Thank you. You are quite positive about this."

She shrugged. "Why shouldn't I be? This is a much better situation than the one I left. In the handful of days since I met you, I am married and at the seashore. For twenty-two years with my father, the only thing I'd done was practice piano and occasionally visit the shops."

When put in such terms, he supposed this *was* an adventure. "I appreciate you putting it into perspective for me." He laid a hand on her knee, and grinned when she gasped and blushed. While the driver put down the steps and then swung open the door, he stood. "Then I suppose there is nothing else to do except enjoy our honeymoon." Seconds later, he hopped out of the coach and then turned to assist Anna. "Hand me the baby before you climb out."

"Oh, but she's so snuggly I don't want to give her up."

For the first time in a couple of days, Edmund's grin was genuine. "Poppy does like to cuddle." And the fact she'd taken to Anna so quickly confirmed that he'd made a sound choice in marrying. "You will have plenty of time to be with her while we're in Brighton." Once the infant was back in his arms, he breathed a sigh of relief. Not realizing how worried he'd been, he held the girl against his shoulder. "Hullo, pet. Did you miss me?"

Poppy cooed and bumped her head into the side of his neck.

"Three steps, love." With his free hand, Edmund assisted his wife out of the coach just as the second one pulled up behind his. As soon as she cleared the steps and stood on the hardpacked street, he breathed another sigh of relief, for she was also one of his responsibilities. "The front door is after a short walkway past some shrubbery."

"I cannot wait to visit the shoreline. Already I can hear the surf and some birds."

He exchanged a grin with their driver. "Do you think you will wish to bathe in the sea? We can possibly rent one of those bathing contraptions that are driven into the water to give ladies privacy." The thought of seeing her bare legs and arms had the capacity to drive him insane.

"That largely depends on how I do when I dip my toes in," she said as he led her up the walkway. "If a creature should touch me, I am not certain how I would react."

How much did he adore her sense of humor or the way she found wonder in the world around her? "I will be there to defend against any sea serpents who might wish to be scandalous."

"So silly, Evermore."

Edmund bussed Poppy's chubby cheek. "Your mama thinks I'm silly." *Oh, God.* His chest hurt after he'd said those words, for they were true. Not only was Anna his wife, but she had immediately become the child's new mother. How was she doing knowing she held both of these new roles without experience in either?

Perhaps they would indeed learn together.

The front door opened, and he nodded to a butler who was probably in his early sixties. "Good afternoon, my good man. I am Lord Evermore, and this is my new bride. The Earl of Ettesmere has given us permission to stay at this house for the duration of our honeymoon."

"Welcome, my lord. The dowager is in residence and is currently occupying the drawing room, so that is where I'll take you." If he had thoughts about the baby, he didn't voice them aloud. "I'll have a few of the footmen help with the luggage."

"I appreciate it. We also travel with my wife's companion, my valet, a nursery maid, and a wet nurse as well as my wife's personal maid." The ride to Brighton wasn't a long trip, but doing so with the baby had made it more tiring than usual. With his free hand at the small of Anna's back, he guided her toward a staircase. "Stairs on your right. Take as much time as you need."

In short order they made their way to the second floor and were shown into a large, airy drawing room done in shades of peach and moss green. Paintings of seascapes hung on the walls in gilt frames, and sitting in curio cabinets or sitting on shelves were pieces of interesting driftwood or small glass bowls of seashells that gave the room a feel of the outdoors.

Then his gaze fell on an older woman with gray hair mixed in with her brown. Pursed lips, distrust lined her face, and she eyed them all with suspicion.

"Hensley, who are these people and why have they intruded on my solitude?" Her voice was short and shrill as she set a teacup on the small table at her elbow. A book lay open on her lap.

"I apologize, Your Ladyship. This is Lord and Lady Evermore." The butler cleared his throat. "Ettesmere gave them leave to stay here while they are on their honeymoon."

"Heaven save me from lovebirds," the dowager muttered beneath her breath. When she stood, her eyes lit when she saw the baby. "I expect they'll wish to freshen up, so please make certain the guest suite is ready."

"Of course, my lady." Then the butler quit the room.

"Newlyweds, eh?"

Anna nodded while Edmund transferred Poppy to his other shoulder. She was getting restless, which meant she needed to be fed, changed, and would have a nap before long. "We were married yesterday."

"Good heavens." The dowager huffed as if the marriage were a personal affront to her. "Another starry-eyed bride who assumes her husband will be faithful." She brushed an invisible piece of lint from the long sleeve of her brown dress. "Love lies, my dear, and there's no such thing as a man being true. Even when you love someone, and they profess the same, they'll betray you by also loving someone else."

"Oh my. Why would you say that, my lady?"

As Anna threw him a look of confusion, he bit back the urge to utter an oath. "I rather think that particular conversation can be postponed for a while." Yet it seemed his wife was in danger of being sucked into the sordid tale. Poppy fussed more loudly, and he tried without success to bounce her into a better mood.

"It is neither here nor there for the moment." The dowager's expression softened. "Whose babe is this?"

Heat went up the back of Edmund's neck. "Mine. She is six months old."

"Yet you only married your wife yesterday." As she peered between them, understanding dawned. "Ah, this is a by-blow from a mistress. I should hope you'll cease your womanizing ways now that you have become respectable." Bitterness wove through her voice.

"I should hope you would stay out of my business, my lady." Who was she to order him about or even view him with censure? Then he tamped down the urge to say more, for she was no doubt still hurting after the huge scandal that rocked both her family and his, and quite frankly, he was angry over the same thing. When Poppy continued to fuss, he tried gently patting her back. "Regardless of the baby's origins, she is mine and I'm raising her, but I don't know what I'm doing."

Anna wrapped her hand about his upper arm. "You are doing a wonderful job already."

The dowager snorted. "I'll withhold judgment, but don't be surprised if his attention wanes and you'll be stuck with a child not of your loins."

Anger lanced through his chest. "Enough, Lady Ettesmere. The babe is my responsibility and in that I won't fail. Period." He stared her down while she looked back with narrowed eyes. "Don't let your life's experiences color mine."

The dowager's lips twitched, but a grin didn't materialize. "At least you have a backbone, and you certainly have the Winterbourne looks." Her voice faltered slightly, but she shook her head. "I would be happy to watch the girl so you can concentrate on your new union."

"But I—" When she relieved him of the child, panic welled in his chest.

"You can still see your daughter every day, and I'm certain you have the proper nurses with you?" When he nodded, she continued. "There is nothing to worry about." The babe did quiet slightly in the dowager's hold.

"That is very kind of you, Lady Ettesmere," Anna murmured. "I would enjoy speaking with you later, for you seem an interesting person."

"Ha! I am only that because fate hasn't been kind." The dowager tsked her tongue. "Who else have you brought in your entourage? There were many footsteps on the stairs just now."

"Uh, my valet, my wife's maid, and her companion." Perhaps Miss Grafton would get along famously with the dowager, for they both shared a sourpuss disposition.

"Is there a need for a companion now that she has wed?"

He shrugged. "Anna is blind. She wants to have someone with her during this time of transition." Even if he wished to send her packing.

The older lady snorted. "Terrible idea. Best not let her come between you two. You need to concentrate on the marriage."

Her constant criticism didn't sit well with him. "I know what I'm doing."

"I rather doubt you do, Lord Evermore. Men are naught but idiots."

Anna's fingers tightened on his arm. Was she bothered by the constant barrage? "That might be your opinion and experience, but as for Edmund, he has been everything kind and solicitous toward me and the baby."

How much did he adore her for the defense? "Well, I…."

"It is an act, mark my words, Lady Evermore." She patted Poppy's back, but the baby continued to fuss.

Edmund glanced at his wife, who frowned. Clearly, she was confused about the scandal that had devastated the Winter-bournes and had caused the dowager to flee. Yes, she deserved an explanation, but that would have to wait. Exhaustion began to really set in. "If you can take Poppy to the nursery, Lady Ettesmere, I would appreciate it. I am going to have Anna and myself settled in and rested from travel. Will we see you at dinner?"

She nodded. "I haven't decided yet since my solitude has been interrupted by unexpected guests, and quite a lot of them."

"Fair enough." While he gritted his teeth to keep his thoughts to himself, he escorted his wife upstairs. Since they were apparently short of rooms, they would be sharing a suite instead of each having one due to the dowager's presence. He didn't know how he felt about that, for he was all too randy and knew he could be naughty and very convincing when he wanted.

Did he want to bedevil Anna so soon in the relationship?

The suite where they would be staying had been decorated in varying shades of blue, which immediately ushered in calm. A four-poster bed dominated the bedchamber, and seeing it only made his tiredness more acute.

"If the weather holds, we shall walk the shore before dinner if that would please you." Exercise would be most welcome, perhaps after a nap.

"That would be wonderful." Slowly, she turned in a circle in front of one of the windows while removing her gloves. Those she tossed to the top of a bureau. "My mind is whirling with the sudden freedom I have been afforded due to marrying you." Then she returned to his side and once more took hold of his arm. "I want to explore, yes, but I also want to talk with the dowager. And you." Concern clouded her emerald eyes. "The family I've married into is hurting and I would like to know why."

"It is a convoluted story, this is true, and has held us all captive for much of this year since we discovered a huge scandal around Valentine's Day."

"I understand that, but forever being at odds with your siblings won't make it any better." She laid a palm against his cheek, and the touch shuddered through him. "Your family needs to accept what has been and stop being angry."

"That's the rub. Graham and Bea have come to terms with it, but I have not. Where they have already met two of our Winterbourne siblings, I have refused, with the exception of the earl, but I don't know him well." He shook his head. "Though he and Graham have formed a tight bond."

Perhaps he was jealous of that.

"It's an excuse, Edmund." Anna held his head between both palms as she practically layered herself against him in order to peer into his eyes. "Do you think I asked to be mostly blind because of a fever? I could spend my life in bitterness, but that is a waste of time. I have more purpose than that."

Damn, no one could take him to task better than her. How interesting. "You are also a better person than I am. Than perhaps the dowager is." Having his life shaken by that large scandal and then having a baby deposited in his lap still stung. Would there ever come a time when things might even out, and he could try for respectability?

For his own little family?

She traced her fingertips along his eyebrows, his cheekbones, the slope of his nose, and every touch fired his imagination of how her hands would feel on various other parts of his anatomy. "It might prove an uphill battle, but I have faith everything will work out."

"Actually, so do I, and I have felt that since Poppy came into my life." Odd, that. "Since I met you the day of my accident." She made him feel a bit better, more hopeful, and he refused to question why that was.

"Good." Her smile was far too bewitching for a woman who'd agreed to a marriage of convenience. "If we are to be here for any length of time and especially to share Christmastide together, we should try to make the house festive."

"Ah." He'd never given thought to the holiday before, but he agreed. Anything to keep her happy in the moment, for he had rather asked her for much with the parameters of their marriage. "Of course. Whatever you want." As he cast another glance about the room, worry pulled knots once more in his belly. "If you don't feel comfortable sharing a bed, I will sleep on the floor or even on the sofa in the dressing room."

"Stop, Evermore." She squeezed her fingers on his arm, but her use of his title—his father's courtesy title as it were—was damned intoxicating. "We shall see, but first I wish to explore the house, if you don't mind? I would like to acquaint myself with the floorplan, so I am not fully dependent on others." Nothing except truth reflected in her eyes. "I can ask Meredith to come with me, but she will only lecture me, tell me it was unwise to marry you."

Annoyance for the companion's treatment of her lanced through his chest. "I would be honored, for I'd like to explore the place as well. The earl won't use it for a while until his child is a bit older, and if the dowager doesn't manage to drive me insane, our stay here might be extended."

She nodded. "He seems a lovely sort. I wish I could have spent more time with him before we had to leave."

Oh, she was a brick! Edmund snorted. "It's not as if the Winterbournes are going anywhere. They might be found family, but they seem to be quite intrusive."

"Pish posh." With a little nudge, she prodded him across the room with a sweet laugh on her lips. "Consider yourself lucky. You have people who care about you. I have just my father, and he thinks I'm a china doll to be packed away and looked at but not played with."

Oh, I would certainly enjoy playing with you. But he kept those thoughts to himself as his chest tightened. "You have me and Poppy now."

She turned to look in his direction even though she couldn't see him. "You have no idea how comforting that is to me."

Well damn. It seems I have much to learn from you.

How incredibly interesting, for his relationships with his mistresses had never piqued his curiosity outside of the bedroom before.

CHAPTER EIGHT

December 15, 1820

IT HAD BEEN two days since they'd arrived in Brighton, and everyone had more or less settled into a routine around each other. However, Anna hadn't truly had an opportunity to talk to Edmund about anything. Oh, there was conversation aplenty, but when it was just the two of them in their room at night, nothing of import was discussed.

Yet she found her new husband interesting. At night, after he'd fallen asleep—which was early, for he hadn't wished to relinquish full care of Poppy to the nurses he'd hired—she had taken to caressing his back and shoulders merely to feel what he looked like without clothing. The viscount slept in a pair of breeches, but when she'd questioned him, he'd admitted that before he'd been married, before he'd had a child, he was fully comfortable sleeping in the nude.

More's the pity he still didn't do that, for she would have let her fingers glide all over his body if that were the case. As far as she knew, he hadn't woken during her explorations, and if luck favored her, he wouldn't yet, for she liked that private time far too much.

If she were to admit the truth to herself, the man made her blood sing with his gentle teasing, his defense of her in front of the dowager, the way he took care of Poppy despite the very act being a scandal. The one fly in the ointment was the fact he hadn't shown interest in her as a woman. Ever since that chaste kiss he'd shared with her on their wedding morning, he had been everything gentlemanly and hadn't attempted to do anything of a physical nature with her. It bothered her, but she'd known that going in. A marriage of convenience was to be her lot in life, yet he was all too adorable with the baby as he learned how to interact with her. He was protective of her, as well he should be, and she hoped that would expand to her after a time.

Unless he wasn't proud of her or was embarrassed to have taken a blind woman to wife.

It was too difficult to say. Over the course of the last two days, the dowager had constantly picked and criticized various little things, and that had given Meredith leave to do the same, until Anna wanted to go out of her mind with the negativity. Too much more of that and she would explode. She was a viscountess, after all, and though the older woman held a higher rank, her companion certainly did not. Perhaps she would use that to her advantage, and soon.

Now, as Anna tried to court calm and a bit of relaxation for herself in the morning room following breakfast, Meredith swooped in with words of censure on her lips.

"I had difficulty locating you this morning. You should have given me a hint of what your schedule might look like today."

"I didn't know where I would be or at what time. All of this is new to me as well, and it's not as if I am in any danger here." In fact, she wouldn't have been surprised to learn that her father's worries regarding kidnapping and being used for ransom had been meant to keep her in fear so she would stay at home. *Well, no more. I want to see what I can do.* She turned her head in the direction Meredith's voice had come from. "Beyond playing the piano later today, I have nothing planned. Will you read me a couple of chapters? Lady Ettesmere told me the library has some lovely volumes of Gothic romance and angst. To say nothing of the salacious serials that she has accumulated during her tenure here. I am interested to hear them."

The companion snorted. "Why would you wish to immerse yourself in that filth when there are much more wholesome things to fill your head with?"

"What, like treatises on agriculture? Books on why the king—while he was Regent—made such a monstrosity for his seaside resort? I think not." Anna huffed out her displeasure. "It is not for you to judge my taste in literature. For that matter, I enjoy many different sorts of stories, but just now, I would like to discover those." It would take the longing out of her own less-than-ideal marriage.

"No need to fly into the boughs with me." Meredith tsked her tongue. "Perhaps I will read to you later. Just now, there are other things on my agenda that you and I need to attend."

"Such as?"

"Since you've married, I wanted to know if you'd given thought to changing your will, or even if that is something you'd wish to do." Meredith came close and sat in the chair near Anna's location. "Did you wish to make your husband a beneficiary of your mother's inheritance?"

"Oh, I hadn't thought about it, but yes, I suppose I should make the necessary changes." Because it was an inheritance, that coin wasn't immediately accessible to Edmund merely because he'd married her. "I'll ask Edmund if he would have his solicitor or man-of-affairs come out to Brighton with the appropriate paperwork."

"No need to bother anyone. No. I can take care of it for you."

"I would rather have someone with the knowledge look after my affairs." After all, being an heiress was nothing to sneeze at and far too many people wished to take advantage of her trusting nature.

"I understand that, but there is no sense worrying about it so soon after your nuptials. We shall take care of it soon enough." Meredith leaned over and patted Anna's hand.

She frowned. "Then why did you bring it up?"

"It was something on my mind since you married. I'm certain Lord Evermore has the same concerns now that he is responsible for you and his illegitimate daughter."

"That is true enough." It was something else they hadn't discussed between them.

"Did you have specific plans today, or will we do what we have always done before the arrival of the viscount when he apparently swept you off your feet." A tiny bit of bitterness threaded through Meredith's voice. Was she jealous that Anna had married where she had not?

"As I said, I intend to practice the piano. Lady Ettesmere told me there was one here but that it hadn't been played recently, so she scheduled a tuner to come in later today."

"How fortuitous," the other woman said with very little enthusiasm.

"I think so." Anna let it go, for there simply wasn't a reason to further feed Meredith's foul mood. "Beyond that, Edmund has promised to take me walking on the shore. It is rapidly becoming one of my favorite things here in Brighton." She adored how the ever-changing water felt against her ankles and calves, loved how the sand was a different texture than grass or dirt. "At some point, he promised to take me to a tea house. And we've decided to start decorating a few rooms for the upcoming Christmastide season." An unexpected laugh escaped her. "I have never been so busy, but I adore having things to finally fill my days."

"It *is* rather a large change from the life you had been living."

"Yes, it is, and I'm thankful for every moment." It was lovely having a husband, having someone to do things with beyond Meredith and her narrow-minded view of life in general, or rather Anna's life in particular.

"Let us hope it lasts and that his attention doesn't wane." Meredith sniffed, as if she didn't believe Edmund could be anything past the rumors. "He isn't exactly the type of man I would have chosen, but then, I wasn't desperate to get away."

The nerve! "You go too far, Meredith. It is no one's business but my own and my husband's why we married in haste." As hot annoyance bubbled through Anna's chest, she pleated a section of her skirting. "Besides, I enjoy spending time with him and Poppy. They have both brought light into my life, and yes, that life was a bit dark before."

Her companion snorted. "His bastard."

Anna huffed again. "The baby can't help what she is. It wasn't her fault how she was brought into the world; she is merely an innocent."

"Well, I think it's distasteful that he has kept her in an effort to flaunt the scandalous relationship he once had as if she is a trophy or a prize." Fabric rustled. Perhaps Meredith was shifting position in the chair. "He could have sent her away as any respectable gentleman of the *ton* would do."

"Ah, but you have said yourself he isn't respectable." It was lovely fun to needle the other woman, and for whatever reason, Anna had finally found her voice. "The viscount didn't do that because he wanted control over her care. Not that you need to know that. Quite frankly, I find it quite delightful. He's clumsy yet with her but once he grows more confident, he will make a fine father." Her womb longed for her to be a mother in her own right, but that wouldn't happen unless their marriage became something else entirely.

"Bah. He should reap the consequences of his actions, find out that he can't gallivant all over Town doing what he pleases and still live a decent life."

Perhaps he already is. Anna waved a hand. "If you will insist on being miserable, take yourself off. I am in no mood for animosity today."

"Then I suppose I will see you later this afternoon." Fabric rustled, indicating Meredith must have stood. "Enjoy your day."

Once she left, Anna released a held breath. Perhaps Meredith merely needed time to acclimate to all the changes.

"THANK YOU FOR agreeing to accompany me this afternoon," Edmund whispered into her ear after they were seated at a round table at a tea café in the shopping district of Brighton. "It has been a long time indeed since I have made the rounds in polite society."

"So far, it has been a lovely outing, and I adore being able to taste the salt in the air on my lips." Anna liked being in his company as well as his attentiveness, but she wished he'd try to kiss her. Obviously, he couldn't do so while out in public, but still. One would expect a former rogue to at least try and steal a kiss. After all, he'd done so twice before they said their vows.

Had that just been a ploy to win her over?

"Brighton isn't as bad as I assumed it would be." She heard rather than saw the grin in his voice. "I don't mind at all spending our honeymoon here."

"Describe what the interior of the café looks like."

"There are at least a dozen cozy tables like ours. Some seat two, some four. Marble tabletops. Table legs and chair legs are delicate and spindly. Lace edged curtains at the windows. Clientele is a mixture of men and women." The tenor of his voice lulled her into complacency. "Offerings on the silver trays of tea look delectable, or else I'm suffering from a powerful hunger from breathing in the sea air."

The clink of silverware against china echoed in her ears like the perfect melody punctuated by the tinkle of crystal and the low buzz of conversation.

"Tell me what you are wearing."

"Jacket of sapphire superfine. Waistcoat of brown brocade. Buff-colored breeches and my usual Hessians." Amusement lingered in his voice. "What else can I do for you?"

She was spared a reply, for a black-clad waiter arrived at their table with a loaded silver tray. As he was in the process of unloading its bounty to the table, the porcelain teapot teetered off the tray and tumbled into her lap. "Argh!" The top came off the pot. Scalding hot liquid seeped through her dress. Thankfully, she had added a second petticoat before going out due to the December chill in the air so she wasn't badly burned—she hoped—but it was still hot and caused a bit of discomfort. "Oh, goodness!" Acting on instinct, Anna jumped up with a squeal. Her chair toppled and crashed against the floor. Several gasps echoed in the air around their table. Finally, the porcelain teapot hit the floor and shattered.

"Dear God! Are you all right?" Edmund was immediately there with an arm about her waist, demanding answers from everyone around him. "Did anyone see what happened?"

"I am so terribly sorry, Lady Evermore." Horrified tones sounded in the waiter's voice. "Let me just go for some towels and a broom." Once he left, the proprietor of the tea café bustled over to their table.

"Lord and Lady Evermore, please accept my sincere apologies on behalf of my staff," the woman enthused while taking Anna's hand briefly in hers.

"This is highly irregular and most unacceptable," Edmund said. Concern shot through the words, and his muscles were tight beneath her fingers. "I sincerely hope my wife hasn't suffered serious injuries, else I *will* hold your staff accountable."

"Of course, of course." The woman fussed with Anna's tea-drenched gown. "Perhaps you should come into the back room with me so we can have a look?"

The heat of embarrassment went through her cheeks. This was the gown of fire incident all over again. "I would prefer returning home." Surely her maid as well as Edmund could assess the situation and let her know if she'd suffered burns.

"Yes, perhaps that is best," her husband said as he guided her away from the wreck of the teapot and her fallen chair. "Privacy is what is needed now." Then he ushered her from the café, grabbing their outerwear as he went. He said nothing else until they were in the confines of the closed carriage. "Are you in pain? Do your legs hurt?" Heavy concern threaded through his inquiries.

"It is difficult to say, for I'm quite embarrassed." She blew out a breath. "Perhaps I'm accident prone. This is the second one in a handful of days."

He snorted. "Have you always been?"

"Not that I have been aware of."

"Interesting. Perhaps it is nothing except misfortune." Apparently still not convinced she was all right, Edmund kneeled on the floorboards. "Allow me the liberty to see if you're hurt." As soon as she nodded, he shoved her skirting upward and then his hands were gliding along her stocking-covered legs.

A tremble of need moved down her spine. "It's not necessary. We can wait until we are home since it isn't a long drive." Though she still suffered from embarrassment, the gentle dance of his fingertips over her skin heightened her awareness of him and left her shivering for more of that intimacy.

"For my peace of mind, it is very necessary." Because they had both left so quickly, he hadn't donned his gloves, and the tactile feel of his skin against hers was amazing. "So soft." He explored her legs, the inside and outside of her thighs, anywhere he could easily access, and when his fingers glanced entirely too close to the curls at the apex of her thighs, she couldn't help a gasp.

"I'm fine." Oh, good heavens, his touch would soon drive her wild. "Do you see any redness? Burns or blisters?"

"Not immediately." He lowered his head and pressed his lips to the inside of one thigh and then gave the same treatment to the other one. "But then I would like to examine you properly in our rooms."

Once behind the privacy of closed doors, where would that exploration go from there? She gave into a host of shivers. "No need to inconvenience yourself. I'll have Meredith look me over when we are home."

"Absolutely not." When he glided his fingers around the tops of her garters, Anna bit down on her bottom lip to prevent crying out. "I'm taking care of you." Command and possession echoed in his voice.

"Very well." It was all too much, having him there and touching her, teasing her. "There is a certain loveliness in being protected," she said in a barely audible voice as she leaned toward him.

"Agreed." The viscount surged upward, caught her head between his hands, and then claimed her lips with his.

Oh, it was glorious and just what she needed in this moment! Through that medium, he introduced himself, questioned what she would enjoy, asked without words what she would like for him to do. As Anna thrilled from the tactile sensations, she drew her fingers along his shoulders while responding as best she could, for the only man she'd ever kissed was him. Awkward at first, she soon learned enough to make a decent showing and she mimicked his actions, so much so that he moaned.

Not able to stop a giggle, Anna pulled slightly away in order to peer into his eyes. Those cornflower blue depths had darkened with the same desire that coursed through her veins. She moved the same time as him, and once more they came together in a kiss, but there was more intensity in the embrace than there was before, and it left her head spinning and her heartbeat racing.

And she couldn't have enough of him.

Though he remained on his knees, he caressed her body, dragged his lips along the side of her neck, followed the edges of her bodice with little licks and feather weighted kisses, then after a slight pause, he blew out a ragged breath. "Do you wish for me to continue?"

Good heavens, he would give her more than a mere kiss? "Yes, please."

"God, but you're so prim and proper." Edmund encouraged her bodice down until her modest breasts popped free.

"Oh!" She gasped when the cool air hit her bared skin, gasped again when he put his hands on her, teasing that flesh, worried her nipples into stiff buds with the pads of his thumbs, nearly made her slide off the bench as pleasure swamped her. But he wasn't nearly done, for he took one of those sensitive peaks into the warm cavern of his mouth, and suddenly, her body came alive with wildly foreign feelings that were much like being lost in music. Anna clung to him, held a hand to his head and pressed him closer; this was the most amazing thing to have ever happened to her.

All too soon, they arrived at the crescent of townhouses and the carriage rocked to a stop. While it dipped as the driver climbed down, Edmund quickly returned to the bench next to her, waited until she set herself to rights before pressing a kiss to her temple.

"Thank you for that interlude," he said against the shell of her ear. "I promise I won't get out of hand again. This is supposed to be a marriage in name only."

Some of the joy he'd given her faded, and she frowned. Perhaps those rules could be relaxed. "Unless I ask you to change those parameters?"

A tiny growl escaped him. "Unless you ask, but even then, we would have to discuss what exactly we each want from the experience."

"Good." She sighed as the door swung open and the driver put down the steps. It would take some time to process how her husband had made her feel, but she wanted very much to experience that again.

CHAPTER NINE

December 16, 1820

EDMUND WOKE SHORTLY after dawn. The house was quiet; the rooms were quiet. The only discernable sounds were the ever-present crash of the waves against the shore as well as Anna's deep, even breathing from where she slept beside him.

As unobtrusively as he could, he turned over onto his side merely to watch her. That heated string of kisses in the carriage yesterday had haunted his dreams. Oh, he wanted more of that, but he alternately didn't. Why? She wasn't in his usual style. The dark arcs of her lashes resting upon her pale cheeks were like the most exquisite works of art. Her full, dark pink, almost red lips were slightly parted as if she were waiting for his kiss, and since she didn't braid her hair before retiring, the mass of her tresses was like a cloud of spilled ink all over the pillow.

What he wouldn't give to feel that waterfall sliding over his naked body.

If someone had asked him how he'd thought marriage would be a month ago, he wouldn't have known how to answer them. Perhaps naively he would have assumed a union would be full of bickering and sniping, especially one that had as little in common as his. Yet over the short course of their union, he'd been forced to interact with Anna differently than other women of his acquaintance. And he been forced to put forth more effort into trying to charm her. Oddly enough, he rather liked the challenge in that, and those times when she gave him a smile or giggled at something he said left him heated in a whole different way than that episode in the carriage. Yes, he'd married her knowing it was merely convenient, a way to remove them both from unwanted situations that no longer served either of them, but now? For the first time in his life, he had a purpose for existing other than making a nuisance of himself or finding scandal or spending coin he didn't have. And he rather enjoyed how she managed to boss him with a gentle hand.

The thought pulled a grin from him, and still he watched his wife sleep.

Her enthusiasm for kissing was delightful. She tackled it as she did everything else in her life, as if each new day were a miracle and she couldn't wait to discover what it held. Could she teach him how to do that? How to set aside his anger and resentment and guilt? How to summon enough gratitude for what he did have that life might feel familiar to him again?

That remained to be seen. They hadn't known each other very long, but she was years ahead of him in maturity. Not able to help himself, he tugged at a lock of her hair, twisted it around his finger so that it sprang away as a fully formed curl.

One thing he found fascinating about her was how she innocently explored him when she assumed he was sleeping. The first time it had happened, he'd been awakened by her tentative touches. The following times, his body had been ready for them. Those nights or mornings were precious to him, and he let her explore at will. If that was how it helped her to see him, then he would encourage it. Since they *were* married and apparently compatible, at least in a kissing capacity, perhaps he should encourage more of her explorations while he was awake, so she would have something to carry in her mind and imaginings.

God, it would be such hell to go through life beside someone and never truly know what they looked like. His respect for how she'd managed thus far without taking to her bed for months at a time rose.

Then he frowned. It was much too quiet, and he missed having Poppy in her cradle near his bed now that he had the proper staff to care for her. Deciding to let Anna sleep—she needed the rest after the whole teapot spilling debacle—he slipped from the bed. Once they'd returned home yesterday, she'd indeed been examined by him, and aside from some spots of redness that faded a few hours later, there was no permanent or immediate harm done. Perhaps he would spend some of the quiet time with his daughter when no one else was around.

It took next to no time to don a loose lawn shirt. Since he'd slept in breeches out of respect for Anna's sensibilities, it was easy to slip from the suite and make his way to the nursery. He softly greeted the nursery staff, and found out Poppy had already been fed. "Wonderful! Since the morning is so pretty, I'll take her on a walk outside."

As soon as he approached her cradle and peered in, the child lit when she saw him. His chest tightened. A wad of emotion stuck in his throat, and it took a few swallows to dislodge it. No one had ever been truly happy to see him come into a room before. Most everyone of his acquaintance gave him lectures or rebukes, or in the case of courtesans, frowns when he couldn't continue to provide them gifts, but this tiny girl liked him, maybe even loved him, for no other reason than he was her papa.

That hit him square in the breadbasket. *Oh God, I'm someone's papa.*

"I think she will enjoy an outing, my lord." The nursery maid outfitted the baby in proper clothes that would keep her warm and completed the toilette with a dear little lace trimmed bonnet.

"So do I." He nodded at the nurse. "It's been rewarding to show Poppy more of the world." It wasn't orthodox for a *ton* father to spend so much time with his offspring, but he didn't care. Clearly, he was enamored with his daughter. When he took her into his arms and she cooed at him, his heart trembled. "Let's go outside, pet." With a wave to the maid, he left the nursery suite.

Ethereal notes of a piano drifted to his ears from the floor below. Obviously, Anna had risen for the day and had chosen to practice her craft. There was no doubt to her talents, and easily he could see her on a stage performing in front of the world's most influential people.

They would need to discuss plans to make that happen.

A half an hour passed walking the shore as if in the blink of an eye. Edmund showed Poppy various things, chuckled when she touched the water, the sand, pebbles, and the like. Alternately, she would coo or squeal depending on how she found things. It was fascinating to watch her learn and discover the world around her. What sort of child would she grow up to be?

On his return walk toward the townhouse, he came upon the dowager, who sat on a blanket spread over the sand away from the shore. "Good morning, Lady Ettesmere. Would you mind some company?"

"Not at all." She gestured to the blanket. "Have you had a good walk?"

"I did. So did Poppy." He laid her on the blanket between them, and immediately, the baby flipped herself over onto her belly to look about her.

"The baby is doing quite well. Perhaps the air of Brighton agrees with her."

"That is good to hear. I'm afraid I'm out to sea when it comes to what is good or bad as a child grows." He glanced at his daughter and had to chuckle, for she rolled on the blanket between them, apparently finding joy in her fingers and how much she could drool.

"It's natural to worry, but don't. You are doing a fine job."

"Thank you." He nodded, tickled the baby's foot, and his world brightened when she laughed. "The wet nurse tells me she's working on getting in a tooth, which is the reason for the slobber and fussing." He felt so bad for her during those times, because nothing he did would comfort her.

"I remember those days. Give her something she can chew on to help the tooth erupt from the gumline. Once it does, she'll be in a good temper once more." As the dowager stared out to sea, she sighed. "I remember being so excited for each of my children's arrivals. In those days, it seemed everyone I knew was having babies. My neighbor too."

Dear God. How had they landed on this conversation so soon? A chill went down his spine. "My mother." Though he didn't wish to discuss the scandal that had rocked both his family and hers, if it wasn't for that scandal, he wouldn't be here today.

"Yes." The dowager nodded but kept her gaze on the water. "She had confided to me once that conceiving was difficult, that she didn't know if she and her husband would ever have children."

"As it turned out, she and her husband *didn't*." The words tripped out of his mouth before he could recall them. When he thought he'd gone too far, the dowager snorted in apparent humor.

"No, they didn't." She released a sigh of either annoyance or exasperation. "I suppose I should get out of this snit, but discovering that my husband, who'd pledged his life and love to *me* for so many years, had fathered children with another woman, simply because *her* husband couldn't conceive, and he wanted to help?" She shook her head. "It still confounds my mind. And if that wasn't enough, over the years he grew to love and adore her. It was too much to bear when the scandal broke, and I simply didn't know what to do."

For the first time he saw her as a woman who had been wronged and caught by surprise by her husband's unfaithfulness, and the fact that it was even more complicated than simply taking a mistress left him almost breathless with so many emotions. "I cannot imagine what you are feeling." He paused to gather his thoughts. "The only solace I can offer is that your husband *still* loved you, and perhaps he was so compassionate he couldn't bear to see a good friend suffer, but I rather doubt his feelings for you ever wavered."

"It will always remain a mystery and will haunt me until I can square with at least a portion of it." Then she looked at him with a scrutiny that made him a bit uncomfortable. "You bear resemblance to my husband. So do your siblings." A trace of a smile curved her lips. "You have a way of holding your mouth when you are displeased or even happy that reminds me of him."

"Ah." Shock plowed into him while heated embarrassment climbed into his neck. When Poppy started to fuss, he picked her up and held her against his chest. The little life was comforting next to his heart. Would he have betrayed his marriage vows to Anna for such a cause like the earl had? It was difficult to say, and that would have required hours of agonizing. Truly, he rather doubted the earl had nefarious intentions. He'd merely wanted to give a woman one of her most secret dreams… like *he* had by marrying Anna.

Damn. Perhaps that meant he was beginning to care about people beyond himself.

"I have shocked you." It wasn't a question.

"No, you actually haven't. I have spent months thinking over this very thing." Edmund pressed a kiss to Poppy's forehead, and when she grinned, he lost his heart all over again. "Regardless of what happened or how, I am glad you're still with us."

"Oh? Why is that?" Curiosity lit the dowager's eyes.

"I lost my parents—while they were arguing continuously for a divorce—and knowing you are here is… well… Suffice it to say, I'm glad. You give me back a bit of normalcy."

She snorted. "As if I could have that any longer." For the first time since he'd arrived in Brighton, she gave him a genuine smile. "But thank you. I feel much like my children did when they rebelled against rules and propriety."

That was a good analogy. "You had every right. Still do."

"Perhaps." She reached out and stroked the back of a finger over Poppy's chubby cheek. "Now, I think I have sulked enough, and it did no good besides. I might enjoy meeting your siblings and coming to know them. Perhaps in that way I might understand more of why my husband did what he did." Her voice faltered. "Life is far too precious to spend angry at the world. It only takes away the happiness in my own existence."

Another wave of shock came over him. "I have most recently had the same thoughts, only I don't know what to do about them."

"Well, you've married, so that's something."

"Out of spite to anger my brother, and she is an heiress, so it was a way to show him I didn't need to rely on his benevolence, except, now that I've been around Anna, I don't want her coin. I'll get through life on my own merits. Somehow."

"I can see that stubbornness about you."

They shared a laugh.

"But money *is* a powerful motivator and the two of you have a child to look after. You'll need somewhere to live, so let her help."

He nodded. "Her dowry will do that for a bit until I can figure something else out."

"At least you have gumption. That's more than some men."

For long moments they sat in companionable silence until he broke it. "It's not as bad as I feared, this being married. Being a father." Another wave of affection went over him as Poppy snuggled into the crook of his neck and shoulder. Clearly, her trip to the seaside had tired her out. "The addition of her was rather unexpected into my life."

"Since time began, there was always sex and unexpected children, Evermore. No matter how careful a man is, there is bound to be one by-blow."

"I suppose." He gently patted the baby's back. How was it that only last week he had no idea this child existed and now he couldn't imagine life without her?

"Will you come to love your wife?" Polite curiosity drove the question as the dowager looked once again out to sea. "Anna has such potential and is stronger than you think despite her affliction."

"She is… interesting. I am enjoying getting to know her, of course, and we married to the benefit of us both, but love? I'm not sure." At least it was honest.

"Life is short, Edmund. Love is precious. If you are fortunate enough to find it, hold tight to it." She flicked her gaze back to his face. All humor had faded, replaced by a somberness that made him pay attention. "If you will let yourself fall, you might be surprised at where your life goes from there."

He nodded. "I tried with this union to give her what she wanted most—freedom and a family."

"For all your worldliness, you are still naïve when it comes to women." Lady Ettesmere snorted with laughter. "Anna is good with the babe, I'll admit, but try to give her what she needs *now*. Affection from her husband. And make certain she goes outside more. Being blind doesn't mean being trapped endlessly inside a house. Show her the world around her. Show her how you enjoy it, and how you enjoy it more when she is there with you. Give her something of yourself so she can come to know you in a way *she* can understand."

That was good advice, and something he hadn't considered before. "We have shared a few kisses, but nothing more than that, so thank you for your insights." Did he want to move the marriage into a physical relationship? And what if it didn't stop there? He'd had his heart broken once before and wasn't keen on making himself that vulnerable again. "I… I'm frightened of what might happen if my marriage deepens." It was a difficult prospect to admit, but it felt right doing so now.

"Why?"

"The last woman I offered my heart to crushed it beneath her heel, threw me over for another man, one who had three children, a man she said could give her all that I could not." He shrugged. "I didn't understand what she meant at the time."

"Ah." For long moments, the dowager gazed at him. "Perhaps she was ready to settle down into everything domesticity meant, and you weren't. Women can sense that, and you *do* have a healthy addiction to bedding women."

Heat went up the back of his neck. "I did."

"Time will tell if you'll be faithful to Anna. However, in my jaded opinion, I can see there is something between the two of you." She offered another smile. "Give both of you a chance and the time to discover what is there organically before you fret your life away."

"Thank you." Her advice humbled him and gave him a modicum of hope.

She patted his arm. "We all have the capacity to be better people if we find our inner strength and stop listening to our insecurities."

"Ah." Edmund glanced at her with new respect. "Anna wishes to decorate the house for Christmastide. Apparently, the holiday is special to her, but she hasn't told me why. Is that something you would be interested in?"

"Now that is something I haven't done in a long time, so I'll help her." Remarkably, a chuckle emanated from her. "Don't worry, dear. I won't let my bitterness spoil her first holiday as a married woman."

Heat crept up the back of his neck. "Thank you. For everything."

"Of course you are welcome, and I think you have helped me as well. I needed someone to put me in my place. I admire how you are living your life regardless of the scandal that swirls around you." Surprisingly, she patted his cheek, and he reveled in the touch of a mother again. "You are a good man, Edmund, even if you don't think so. This year has marked a milestone for you, and I cannot wait to see what you'll do with yourself from here."

"I appreciate that." When she gathered her reticule and stood, he frowned. "Where are you going?"

"To write to Arthur and apologize for missing the birth of his child. He is quite enamored with his new wife, and I've been too soured to take part in that. So, it's time to repair a few relationships and forge new ones, don't you think?"

"I do." When he went to stand, she shook her head.

"Stay and enjoy the day. No doubt the rain will return soon enough. Do you want me to take Poppy back with me?"

"No. I want more bonding time with her." Already, the cherub was nearly asleep against his shoulder. He hated to disturb her.

Life was truly interesting, and he had much learning to do.

⊰⊱⊰⊱

WHEN HE BROUGHT Poppy to the house an hour later, everything was in chaos. Staff rushed through the corridors. The dowager was issuing orders, half of which were being countermanded by Miss Grafton.

"What the hell happened?" he asked of the butler whom he passed on the way to the front staircase.

"Apparently, Lady Evermore missed a step and tumbled down a half dozen treads. We are all trying to assess the state of her health now."

"Good lord!" Concern jumped to the forefront of his mind and pulled at knots in his gut as he ran through the corridor, trying not to jostle the baby too much. Anna sat on the bottom step looking disheveled with a blush in her cheeks while her companion and the dowager knelt on the floor before her. "Anna, are you well?

"Oh, Edmund!" Her head lifted and she held out a hand. "I'm so glad you're here."

He quickly pushed through the crowd of servants, handed the baby to the nursery maid, and then took Anna's hand. "Have you broken any bones?"

"We have already given her a cursory check," Miss Grafton said with a sharp tone. "No broken bones and it doesn't appear she is bleeding."

"I believe I asked the question of my wife." Ignoring the companion, he knelt on one knee before Anna. "How do you feel?"

"Disoriented and embarrassed. I can't believe I was so clumsy as to miss a step when I am usually extremely careful, especially in new environs."

The dowager touched his shoulder. "Take Lady Evermore upstairs. She should rest for the remainder of the day. I will manage things down here."

"Of course. Thank you." After standing, he helped Anna to her feet. "Can you walk?"

"I haven't tried yet."

"No need." Knowing the whole of the staff looked on, he scooped her up into his arms in a show that he could, indeed, care for his wife, he lost no time in carrying her up the two flights of stairs while Anna clung to his shoulders. To the butler who'd gone up with them, he said, "Please order tea for the viscountess. Perhaps that will soothe her jangled nerves."

"At once, my lord." Then the butler hurried downstairs with a pace that belied his age.

Once in their suite, Edmund carried her immediately to the bedchamber and then gently set her upon the bed. "Are you quite certain you are well?" This, on the heels of the dropped teapot incident, was quite alarming.

"I believe so, but oh, it is embarrassing!" In her upset, tears filled her eyes. "I was so frightened, but luckily, it wasn't the whole staircase." Slowly, she shook her head as some of her hair escaped its pins. "I thought there might have been pressure on my back or shoulder just before I fell, but I couldn't be certain. It was probably my imagination."

"Why do you say that?"

"I didn't sense the presence of another, but then I was distracted by thoughts of music... and you." The blush renewed itself in her cheeks.

"Me?" Gently, he sat on the edge of the bed and removed her half boots in order to massage her feet and calves. She trembled from his touch. "Why?"

"Why not?" Her giggle was tempered with a sigh. "The last kiss we shared was quite stimulating. I often keep remembering it."

"Ah." More heat went up the back of his neck while pleasure filled his chest. "If you'd like, I can kiss you again, so you'll have another memory." Damn, but he couldn't wait to do exactly that, only this time, he might not stop at just a kiss. Already, the warm softness of her skin beneath his fingers called to him like a siren's song. He wanted to explore her body, feel her skin, taste her, and she *was* his wife, after all.

"Oh." Another sigh escaped her. "I would like that. You make me feel like flying, which is how I feel when I play the piano." When she smiled at him, his world tilted for a moment. "However, I am starting to feel bruises form on my back and hip, so for now, sit with me. Tell me about your day. I like hearing the sound of your voice."

"Very well." Had he ever sat beside a woman in bed merely for talking? Not that he could recall. Then the dowager's words came back to him, and he nodded. "I would be happy to spend this time with you." Instead of sitting beside her, he arranged himself on his back so that his head rested in her lap while his lower legs hung off the bed. If she wished to touch his face or hair in an effort to see him, he wouldn't mind. "I walked the shore this morning with Poppy...."

CHAPTER TEN

December 17, 1820

ANNA WOKE, AND by the pressing darkness as well as the dead quiet, she suspected it was the middle of the night. A restlessness of sorts had come over her and left her both confused and slightly frightened, for the continuing random accidents were suspect. She wanted to be in her husband's company all the time now for protection.

As she turned over onto her side, various places on her body ached from the tumble down the stairs. After the rest in bed yesterday, Edmund had taken her to the shore, encouraged her to put her feet and legs in the surf. She'd clung to him each time the chilly waves lapped into her. She'd squealed with each new touch and feeling and experience, but he hadn't seemed to mind, for he remained at her side for the duration, constantly describing the scene to her, telling her of the variety of colors the sea possessed. The exercise had tired her, so she'd taken a nap before dinner, where the dowager surprised her by eating with them and telling her she would help with the Christmastide decorating. What was more, she'd put forth the idea of going shopping the next day together for baubles and decorations.

Now, as the longcase clock in the corridor beyond struck two, the need for something she couldn't quite explain continued to roll through her person.

Beside her, Edmund slept. On his back with an arm thrown over his head, he was never more relaxed than in slumber. As was typical with him, his chest was naked, but he wore a pair of breeches. When she'd questioned him, he said he wasn't one of those men to wear a nightshirt, that he usually slept nude but wouldn't here for her comfort. The warmth of his body, the gentle sound of his breathing called out to her. Anna's nerves felt strung too tight; she was highly aware of him, wanted his touch, but she couldn't resist exploring him through that same medium.

The faint scent of his shaving soap or cologne lingered on his skin as she pressed her lips to the column of his strong neck. The male form was so interesting, for he was hard with muscle yet soft in other places as she glanced her fingers over him. A sprinkling of coarse hair covered his chest with a thin ribbon of the same gathering on his mostly flat abdomen only to disappear beneath the waist of his breeches. Her hand stilled at that spot.

Oh, how she wanted to explore that part of her husband, but it would undoubtedly wake him. Unworried, Anna contented herself with caressing the rest of his body, learning through touch what he looked like so she could imagine him in her mind or dreams. He was so interesting and different from her, and he was charming in his attempts to be a good father to Poppy as well as a husband to her. That went a long way in raising her respect for him. She had remained adamant that she wouldn't listen to gossip or rumors regarding him in order to form her own opinions. Everyone deserved a second chance, and thus far, he had been everything lovely.

When she raised up on an elbow and pressed kisses to his chest, his body stiffened. Seconds later, he'd snaked an arm about her waist, rolled her over, and then covered her body with his.

Oh, dear. "Did I wake you?" The unaccustomed weight of him had her senses spinning. There was nothing to do but put her palms to his shoulders and wait.

"Yes, and quite deliciously too." His lips glanced over hers with each word. "Why are you awake at this hour?"

"Ah." Anna peered into his eyes. It was too dark to see him, but being pressed so tightly against him, feeling every angle of him fitting into the softer curves of her was heaven. "I'm feeling restless and don't know why."

"I am as well." Edmund shifted, put one knee between her legs while the evidence of his arousal rested at her hip. "Since we are both awake, I don't mind if you go exploring. It is your right."

Perhaps it was, but she also wanted his hands on her, longed to feel desired. She touched his face, his lips, glided her fingertips along his brow and temples. Truly, he was a gorgeous man. "Kiss me and we'll go from there." Where that daring had come from, she couldn't say, but nothing would change between them unless she made the first overture.

"Mmm, I like this side of you." He claimed her lips in a gentle kiss, made love to her mouth as if he had all the time in the world. When he pulled away, she felt his grin against the side of her neck. "Sleeping fitfully does have some advantages."

A giggle escaped her as he moved off her body to rest on his side facing her. "Rogue."

"That's the nicest of what I've been called recently." A hint of vulnerability rang in his whisper, and her heart squeezed.

"Hush." She reached for him, traced his face with her fingertips and then dared to explore even though he was awake. "Your form is quite lovely." Anna danced her touch along his bare chest, and except for a sharp inhalation of breath when she swept her fingers down his torso to his abdomen, he remained still. "Since the first time we met, I have had the urge to see what you truly look like so that I might carry that image with me always."

"How intriguing." When Edmund laid a palm on her belly, splaying his fingers, the heat of each digit burned through the thin silk of her frivolous night attire. "Have you dreamed of me since that day?" Slowly, he slid his hand upward, where he manipulated the satin ribbons that kept the placket of the night dress closed.

"Once." She forced a quick swallow to alleviate her dry

throat. "I always wanted more, though." Needing to tell him without words what she wanted, Anna continued to explore his body. He was strong and solidly muscled, and when she drew the fingers of one hand down his side to his hip, he blew out a breath. Perhaps he wanted her as much as she did him in this moment while shrouded in the dark.

"That is easily rectified… if you wish it." He pulled the filmy fabric apart, baring her breasts. The cooled air in the room tightened her nipples.

"I do wish it," she responded in a whisper while need trembled in her limbs.

"Good." Yet he didn't move to touch her further, perhaps waiting for further confirmation from her.

"Oh, Edmund." Anna lifted her upper half, slipped a hand to his nape, and she caught his mouth with hers. After all the teasing kisses they had already exchanged over the past week, everything would culminate in this one magical meeting as they consummated their union, moved it into new and confusing territory. How lovely was the press of his lips to hers!

Evermore plied her with kisses, each more intense than the last, and her head swam with sensation. In a thrice he'd encouraged the silky clothing off her body, tossing it away in a rustle of fabric. As she lay naked and exposed, he covered her body with his, and still he continued to kiss her. He plied her lips, the side of her neck, her shoulders with fleeting kisses, and the faint rasp of his nightly stubble added another exquisite layer to the pleasure he gave. While he roved his hands along her body, leaving not one inch of her unexplored or untouched, Anna did the same to him, couldn't have enough of him, for in this moment she felt he could truly be hers.

The sensation of falling assailed her, and a bit of panic set in, but Edmund must have anticipated her rapidly changing emotions, for he returned to her lips, telling her without words that all would be well. When he closed his lips on one pebbled nipple, her back arched and she moaned. This she remembered from the carriage ride, and oh my goodness, it was just as lovely as it had been then. He chuckled, and the sensation tickled through her chest, then the wicked man suckled that tip, and another soft moan escaped into the air.

As soon as he released it, he gave the other one the same attention. With each caress, every nip and nibble, Anna's heartbeat accelerated, and her blood turned to molten fire in her veins. She could barely breathe from the wonderful things he did to her, and her body clamored for more. Kisses and caresses soon wouldn't be enough to satisfy this new, unrelenting hunger chasing through her belly. As much as she wished to return the favor and explore him, such things were beyond her ken at the moment, for all she could do was squirm and sigh beneath him and revel in this new world of heady pleasure.

"Edmund, I need… something." The heat of embarrassment jumped into her cheeks, for she was far too inexperienced at this advanced age to not have an idea of what to ask for.

"Shh. I'll take care of you." When he slipped a hand between her thighs, furrowed his fingers through her feminine curls, she trembled, but as he glanced one of those digits over the hidden bud, the swelling center of her desire, she uttered a cry that had him laughing with masculine smugness. "I thought—" Ah, this was what she'd had a tiny hint of the other day in the carriage, but couldn't puzzle out why it had ignited her excitement.

"Enjoy. This is only the first of what I'll teach you." The viscount teased that nub of flesh as he kissed her lips, and once more she was lost.

"Mmm." Anna feared she would dissolve into a puddle of hot, liquid need, so great were the sensations he invoked within her. One didn't need sight for such intimacy, and knowing they were doing such an act hidden in the dark and their nuptial bed sent her need to the next level. Shivering from the streaks of pleasure that zipped through her body, she clutched at his shoulders, digging her fingernails into his skin. Horrible, amazing pressure deep inside her lower belly increased and stacked to bedevil her.

Dear God, how did she make it cease? "I need...." She panted. Words wouldn't come. Passion fogged her brain. Would he think her too stupid, that he'd made a mistake in marrying her?

"You need this." He circled that bud with his thumb and slid first one finger into her aching passage and then another, stretching her, testing her, making her ready, ensuring that she would be crazy with desire before too long.

"Oh!" Such wonderful sensations swirled around her. Not knowing what to do, Anna canted her hips in an effort to better receive him, and the bands of pressure inside her continued to build until she was certain she'd go insane from longing. Something glimmered just out of reach, but she couldn't quite grasp it. "Yes, more of that."

"Don't think too hard about going over the edge. Just let it happen naturally," he whispered against the shell of her ear.

As she tried to relax in the face of such splendid torture, he didn't relent on the pressure. Then, just as he said, the feelings inside her shifted, changed. Her body stiffened, then seconds later, she went pliant as the most wondrous sensations swamped her being. Heat rushed through her veins from the roots of her hair to the tips of her toes. No part of her was excluded. Between her thighs where he stroked his fingers in and out, her channel fluttered, contracting with the force of his attention, and she truly thought she was flying for a few brief moments.

All too soon it was over, and as she came back to herself, Anna collapsed against the pillows with a sigh. "That was like music. Floating on music, becoming the notes, living through the movements as I flew." Her mind still couldn't comprehend what had just happened.

"Lovely description of such an act, but we are not finished." Edmund left the bed, and when she uttered a weak protest, he chuckled. "I am only removing my breeches. I might be so damned hard for you that it hurts, but my shaft isn't powerful enough to tear through clothing."

An unexpected giggle left her throat. He was wickedly funny

when he wanted to be. "Hurry." Was it wanton of her to wish for a repeat of what just happened? While she stretched with a languid grace she'd not known before, the whisper of a garment hitting the floor broke the silence. "Now I know why women are so keen on being ruined."

"Oh, indeed. There is nothing that compares to a good bout of coupling." The mattress depressed, signaling his arrival upon the bed, and then he joined her once more, his body warm and strong over hers, his hips nestled in the cradle of hers, the hair on his chest both tickling and teasing her sensitive nipples.

"I'm glad we are here, that we met. It's much better than passing lonely nights." The simple joy of having his strong form in her arms and between her legs had the ability to steal anything else she might have wanted to say.

"As am I." He lightly nipped the side of her neck. "Where I thought I might detest everything that marriage would be, that fatherhood would entail, somehow I am rather enjoying myself… as much as I am able to do." Gently he spread her legs wider, and as he did so, the tip of his hardened member brushed her opening.

Her heartbeat accelerated as did her breathing. "You are doing admirably, and I am proud of you." Anna wriggled her hips, and when he didn't move, she held his head between her hands and kissed him. "Never think you are as bad as people have told you. Every day is a new chance to do better."

"God, I don't deserve you." As if he'd been given permission to go forward, Edmund captured her lips with his, and with a powerful flex of his hips, he slipped inside her, pushing through that slight resistance of flesh, and didn't stop until he was fully seated, and they were joined together as intimately as any two people could be.

"Oh, goodness." Anna gasped from the sharp prick of pain. She clutched at his shoulders, but as he began to move within her, the discomfort faded and, in its place, came sensations so pleasurable that she moaned from the sheer delight of the coupling.

"Damn, you are so tight, so wet." The whispered, suggestive words in the darkness worked to further suck her under into the world of heady bliss. He gathered her closer, gripped her hip with one hand and with the other encouraged her to wrap a leg around his waist while he increased the intensity of his thrusts. "I won't last, for I have been teased by wanting you for too many days, and it has been a bit since I had a woman in my bed." His breath caressed her cheek, ruffled the baby-fine curls on her forehead.

Not knowing what to do, she moved her hips in time to his and soon they fell into a pleasing rhythm that was as old as time. With each stroke, the pressure inside her built and grew, and once more she was pushed closer and closer to that shimmering edge of bliss. Harder and harder he pushed, scooting her deeper into the pillows. Faster his hips worked until all she felt was him, his hot, hard length inside her, his strong, solid body rubbing along hers, the crisp hair on his chest scraping over her nipples and adding another layer of awareness. This simple, physical act of solidifying their marriage quickly ushered her onto an entirely new path.

Then she broke. A cry of surprise left her throat as she shattered into a million pieces of light, fell into a world where there was no sound or sight, different than the one in which she usually lived. There was only feeling. Higher and higher she flew, her body drifting in clouds of sparkling white light. Edmund uttered his own shout of completion. He ground his hips into hers while his member jerked, but he withdrew from her body instead of spilling his seed inside her. On the heels of confusion, she floated back down. Her body tingled and shuddered as spent desire pulsed through every nerve ending.

"Dear heavens," she managed to whisper. "That was amazing."

"Indeed."

"I wouldn't mind indulging in that again." Did that make her sound too desperate?

His chuckle tickled through her chest. "I think we can manage that." The viscount collapsed against her then he pushed them both onto their sides. "I apologize for the mess, but will clean it as soon as I'm able."

As Anna returned to reality and her heart didn't pound quite so fast, she frowned. Why didn't he complete the act? If he didn't wish for her to get her with child, why didn't he first speak with her about it? Did he not want her to have a babe of her own? Or worse yet, did he not want that with her? Worries trotted through her mind, but as pleasant lethargy seeped through her limbs, she snuggled against his sweaty chest. While her eyes closed, she shoved the thoughts to the back of her mind. The concerns would keep for tomorrow, but there was no doubt she would need to talk with him.

Regardless of where their marriage rested after this night, there were decisions to make and at least an immediate future to contemplate.

CHAPTER ELEVEN

December 19, 1820

A
NNA'S FINGERS FLEW over the piano's keys as she lost herself in the music.

Even though she'd played the instrument nearly most of her life, it felt different now that she and Edmund had come together in physical intimacy. Just like he'd sent her flying that night, the music did the same, and now there was a richer quality to the experience, both playing it and immersing herself within it, and the enhancement there made the finished product even better.

"I don't know what has changed for you, dear, but you are playing beautifully," the dowager said from her spot on a low sofa where she'd told Anna she was embroidering the hem of a baby gown. "If I close my eyes, I could swear I'm at a concert hall listening to the most skilled pianist."

Heat infused her cheeks. "Thank you for the compliment, my lady." Finally, she was a proper bride, but since that exquisite night, they hadn't come together again. In fact, she hadn't seen much of her husband except at dinner, and then last night she'd retired before he had. By the time he'd joined her, she'd been asleep. To his credit, though, he had been spending time with Poppy and liked to take her to walk the shore or play with her on the nursery floor. He had also attended to correspondence; no doubt there were things he'd needed to take care of due to their marriage as well as Poppy, and he had mentioned seeking out the earl's friend, the man who would be hosting the Christmas night ball they were invited to due to Ettesmere's influence.

There was no cause for worry.

Was there?

Or now that he'd bedded her, did that remove his interest and he was ready to set his roving eye elsewhere? Cold dread twisted down her spine. Was he already contemplating betraying their vows?

A discordant series of notes intruded upon her thoughts, and with a start, Anna removed her hands from the keyboard. "Perhaps I am a bit fatigued and need to rest."

"Or you should get out of your own head," the dowager was quick to respond. The rustling of fabric indicated that the other woman had moved, and a dark blob in Anna's vision came closer to her. "Come. The footmen delivered two boxes of fripperies to this room yesterday, so let us begin the decorating. That will go a long way into lifting your spirits."

"I would appreciate that." When the older lady guided her up and around the piano, Anna smiled. "Christmas was always a special time for my family. It was the only time of year when my father would cease to work at his business. Mama would focus on my brother and me. If supplies were available, she would bake like a fiend, followed by cooking for seemingly an eternity, so there were always piles of edibles for a good two weeks."

"Ah, yes, you aren't part of the *beau monde*." The dowager's tone didn't suggest it was either a good thing or a bad thing. "In many ways, I envy your mother the freedom to cook in her own kitchens. I was never afforded that option, for Ettesmere wouldn't dream of having a countess who dirtied her hands in such a manner."

Anna patted the older woman's arm. "Mama enjoyed being domestic and looking after her family. She wanted that life for me as well."

"But you didn't share her feelings."

"No." Anna shook her head. "By the time I was eight years old, all I wanted to do was play the piano. At that point, I'd barely had a year of lessons, but I knew, felt it in my soul, that was where my passion lay."

"Did your parents encourage that talent?"

"Oh, yes. Papa was pleased. Thought it would be a way I could attract a titled gentleman and gain entry into the *ton*." She huffed and tossed her head. "I didn't care about any of that; I merely wanted to play."

The dowager put what felt like a tin bell into her hand. "If you don't mind me asking, what happened to your mother?"

"When I was ten, a fever swept through the village and sur-roundings where we lived. Since my father was in London, he was safe, but the rest of us fell victim to it. Mama and my brother didn't survive." Her voice broke, and she swallowed down the ball of tears in her throat. "The fever I struggled with had been so high, it destroyed my eyesight. I was left largely blind, but in an odd way, I felt that that event was when my life finally began."

"Until it didn't. I'll wager your father became overprotec-tive."

She couldn't help a grin as she shook the bell. The tinkle of it reminded her of Christmas. "He did, and after years that protectiveness was a prison, but through it all, I continued to play the piano. It was a refuge and gave me hope."

"I'm sorry for your history." The dowager then put a length of ribbon into her hand that felt like satin. "But you have come through those storms admirably, and you ended up marrying a titled gentleman anyway." Humor wove through her voice. "I suppose things happen just as fate intended all along."

"That's a lovely way to look at it." Again, she rang the bell. "I never had the hope of marrying until I unexpectedly met Edmund. He'd been involved in a carriage accident which occurred in front of my father's townhouse. I invited him in since he was slightly injured, gave him tea, and things went from there." Was it fate or sheer happenstance? "We needed the marriage for different reasons, and to be quite honest, I'm not convinced Evermore didn't marry me because I'm an heiress." Her father wouldn't live forever, obviously, and upon his death, she would come into quite a bit of his fortune since they had no other living family.

"That is always a concern." The sound of items being jumbled through a box met Anna's ears. No doubt the dowager was combing through the boxes of decorations. "And it's something women need to be aware of in this world, yet only you can decide if you trust the viscount, if he is a decent enough partner regardless of what happens with the coin."

Anna wandered about the area. When she reached the fireplace, she lifted a hand to touch the marble mantel, and felt the prickle of fir boughs. The pungent scent of pine wafted to her nose as she nestled the tin bells into the branches. "Oddly enough, I do trust him. Or perhaps he hasn't given me reason not to yet."

Would he do that in the future? Did his absence now allude to that?

The dowager tsked her tongue while joining Anna at the fireplace. The tinkle of bells sounded as she put them into the greenery. "My marriage to the earl was arranged. By our parents, when we were both children."

"Oh, no. Such high excitations for small children." She couldn't imagine.

"It was what noble families did in those days. I had barely heard of Ettesmere before I had to say vows to him, but over the course of our union, we managed to fall in love." A sigh escaped the older woman. "I bore him three children, and we mostly had a lovely life together." Sadness entered her voice.

Anna found one of her hands and held it. "I'm sorry."

The dowager huffed. "Of course, Ettesmere had also fallen in love with his best friend's wife." She sighed. "But I suppose I cannot blame him, for his compassion was also what had made my heart flutter for him. They had three children between them, so my advice of marriage or even love might not be the best to follow."

That struck her as funny. Anna chuckled, for the dowager was quite delightful. "While I'm sorry your life and marriage were surrounded by so much confusion and heartache, I can oddly understand why your husband might have done what he did." Her voice faltered. "Edmund is difficult at times to read; even more so because I cannot see his face, but if I make it a habit of falling back on wondering, on suspicion, I will never move forward."

"You have a difficult task ahead, but you are also a woman of strength. However, I don't envy you wading through those waters. Winterbournes are known to be both willful and stubborn, but then, so are the Ashdownes." The dowager tugged the ribbon from Anna's fingers. "I will do my best to help where I can."

"I appreciate that." For the first time, she felt an affinity for the older woman. "This is all very new to me, and there are many times that I feel as if I have no idea what I'm supposed to be doing, but I keep trying."

The other woman snorted. She temporarily moved away, and the tingle of bells indicated she'd returned to the boxes. "Everyone feels like that, but your situation is unique for the simple fact you are blind." When she returned, she gave Anna a glass ball. "Men can be difficult; even the best of them, and your husband is not the best."

The statement took her aback and she gasped. "Then the rumors are true?"

"Oh, they're most certainly true, but I have glimpsed changes within him since you both have arrived, so it's a good indication he wants to continue on that path even if he doesn't realize it yet." The bells tinkled again.

"Because of me?"

"You or his child, but it doesn't matter, for change is refreshing in this instance."

Anna nestled the ball into the evergreens. "How he cares for and interacts with Poppy is a good indication that he is truly invested in being a better person."

"Agreed. Edmund is a lovely man, and I've told him such, but he isn't the best."

Annoyance stabbed through Anna's chest. "Yet." She might not know exactly what her marriage entailed or what she and Edmund were to each other right now, but she was staunchly supportive.

"Ah." There was a smile in the dowager's voice. "Good girl. You must always be a team no matter what. Present a united front and let nothing come between you."

That advice was sound. Anna nodded. "Do you believe a blind woman can make a good mother?" It was one of her biggest fears, that Edmund would see her inability and continue to decide he didn't wish to impregnate her.

"I don't see why not, no pun intended." They shared a laugh. "You are quite nurturing, and placid. I have never seen a woman as unruffled as you."

Anna smiled. "Fate has handed me my fair share of challenges, this is true. There is no use in living in anger. That solves nothing."

"So I have learned." The dowager patted her shoulder. "Sometimes, though, venting your spleen is the only thing that keeps you sane." A sneeze escaped her. "Some bickering between a married couple gives spice to the union."

The words were perfect for the conversation. "I'll take your words under advisement."

"Don't worry about the sort of mother you are. There is no one type. In the grand scheme, it won't matter, for you will give Poppy—and any children you should have with the viscount—all the love you are capable of. After that, it is up to the children when they are grown to figure out what to do with those sacrifices you have made." She patted Anna's arm. "Don't think you are doing it wrong. There is no right way. You stepped in where others wouldn't. You stood by Edmund's side when the whole world branded him scandalous or a fool for taking on the baby, and believe in him even now. That shows integrity, and fate likes that."

It gave her a modicum of comfort. "I hope you're right."

"Time will tell, but if you want the romance, don't wait for it to fall into your lap. Men need to be prodded. Oh, and after Christmas, I am leaving the two of you alone so you can have a real honeymoon."

"Why?" Shock moved through her. "I have enjoyed having you about. You are quite interesting, and give me hope for my own situation."

"Ah, you flatter me, dear, but I have been away sulking long enough. I miss my family. So, I wrote to Arthur and told him I would return after Christmas. I want to meet his new babe, and I also wish to meet the three other Winterbournes and get to know them." Her voice broke, and it took a few minutes for her to regain her composure. "To tell them I wish them no ill will. The marquess' wife will have a baby of her own by next month's end. Babies are such a bridge to healing."

"Perhaps they are. Poppy has certainly started that with Edmund." She held the countess' hand and grew a bit misty eyed. "I wish you all the best and hope you can know that you have so much living and love left to enjoy."

The dowager squeezed her fingers. "As long as you realize the same."

"There is nothing more touching than coming into a room and seeing two beautiful women in the midst of decorating."

"Such flattery won't work on a woman my age, young man," the dowager said, but there was amusement in her voice.

The sound of *his* voice sent little tingles up and down Anna's spine. "Edmund! I assumed you were busy."

"I was, but now I'm not." Then he arrived at her side and bussed her cheek, put the baby into her arms. Immediately, she snuggled the girl against her chest. "Lady Ettesmere, do you mind too terribly much if I take Anna away for an hour? I'd like to walk the shore before tea, and my wife enjoys the exercise."

The other woman chuckled. "Go. Go. I will finish up here."

"Thank you." Then he wrapped a shawl about Anna's shoulders and escorted her from the room. The warmth of his arm about her waist sent awareness dancing over her skin, and the baby tugging on her shawl brought out a smile. "Did you enjoy your day with Lady Ettesmere?"

"It was quite lovely. She's soon going back to London."

"I got the feeling she is tired of being in Brighton and misses her family, but I don't blame her for wanting to be away." He put his lips to her ear. "Perhaps that will give us the opportunity to have a real honeymoon."

Her heart trembled. "There are things we need to discuss, though, and I don't want you to hide from me as you did the other night." She tried to keep her emotions under control, so the baby didn't pick up on her anxiety.

"I apologize."

"Do better, Edmund. I am your wife. We are a team, for good or for ill."

"Right." He took her hand, threaded their fingers together as they left the house through the rear door. Though there was a chill in the air, it wasn't too extreme. "I let confusion and other things get the better of me."

How interesting. "What are you confused about?" Had the coupling the other night temporarily knocked the sense from him like it had done her, and now he couldn't puzzle out what it meant?

A flush climbed his neck. "I don't wish to say until I can work it out in my mind, so it makes sense."

"Understandable, but talk to me next time." She whispered encouraging words to Poppy when she started to fuss, but then the girl put a hand to Anna's lips, she laughed, and the sound was quite cathartic.

"I will." He squeezed her fingers. "Poppy almost crawled today."

"Oh?" She bussed the girl's cheek. "What a brave child you are. Crawling is a big step for you. I'm very proud." She could just see the baby's blue eyes and the laughter there. "Never lose that determination, little one."

A sound suspiciously like a stifled sob came from Edmund. "You are lovely with her," he managed to gasp out.

"It's easy since she is such a loving little thing." She rejoiced when Poppy nuzzled into the crook of her shoulder. The barking of a dog in the distance went largely unnoticed as she cuddled the baby. "Such a sweetie," she murmured to the baby.

"Good God." Shock and horror threaded through Edmund's voice.

"What is it?" Alerted by his change of emotion, she held Poppy a bit tighter.

"A dog is running loose down the beach, and he seems to be coming this way. There is no other person in sight just now."

Barking grew more noticeable and louder.

"I'm going to take her back to the house." But there was no time. Before she knew what was happening, the dog was upon them, growling and snarling and snapping.

"Go!" Edmund gave her a bit of a shove. Then he threw himself bodily in front of her. He took the brunt of the dog's attack, but she couldn't leave him there alone. A grunt of pain came from the viscount, and he fell to the sand.

"Edmund!" The growling continued while Evermore grappled with the beast. She screamed, called for help while holding Poppy close to her chest. Eventually, someone responded to her calls. The man helped pull the dog from Edmund, but he apparently lost his grip on the canine, for he cursed and told them he'd try to wrangle him and at the very least find out to whom he belonged. "Thank you."

A groan from nearby gave her an indication of where Edmund was. With tears running down her face, she staggered to his location, and with the baby still clutched in her arms, she fell to her knees at his side.

"Is Poppy all right?" Concern threaded through his voice.

"Yes, yes. She's fine. I'm all right, but how are you?"

"A few scratches. A shallow bite that won't require a surgeon, but otherwise, I am well." Then his arms were around her, and she sobbed into his embrace with the baby between them. "What the hell is happening here in Brighton?"

"I don't know." In fact, she didn't want to contemplate it, but she'd been shaken to her core. "Let's go to the house and have you looked at by the dowager and perhaps the housekeeper."

An hour later, they'd both retired to their suite. Still ill-at-ease, Anna wanted Poppy with them. She held the baby while she slept but wanted Edmund next to her on the sofa in the private parlor. His wounds had been cleaned and patched up, but he didn't seem inclined to talk. Neither did she. Instead, he put his arms around her and the baby, then promptly fell asleep.

Anna sighed. She stroked the fingers of her free hand along the side of his face. In repose, he resembled a much younger man, and she lost a tiny piece of her heart to him in that moment.

I'm falling tip over tail for my husband. It was a marvelous feeling, and as she nodded off as well, she had the thought that with the sudden problem with accidents, she really needed to have her will changed. *Don't forget to ask Edmund about making use of his solicitor….*

CHAPTER TWELVE

December 20, 1820

EDMUND HUFFED AT the nursery window, for it was raining and had been for the bulk of the day. Boredom had set in, and since Poppy had just gone down for her afternoon nap, there wasn't a chance that he could use her as a distraction from the worries circling through his mind. Ever since he'd met Anna, strange accidents kept happening to her. Little in scope and most not menacing, and though they were random and seemingly unconnected, there were too many of them.

Who was behind them, if at all, or had she accumulated some honest misfortune? Or did someone in Brighton know she was an heiress? If they did, why not try to kidnap her instead of harm her? None of it made sense.

"My lord, the baby won't be awake for at least two or three hours." The sound of the nursery maid's voice broke into his musings. She gave him a sweet, tentative smile. "When Poppy has roused and has been fed, we will bring her to you. As we do every day."

The heat of embarrassment went up the back of his neck. "I apologize for my enthusiasm. I have never had a baby before."

"She is fortunate to have you."

"I think we're fortunate to have each other." He grinned at

her as he left the nursery suite. Perhaps he should seek out Anna. The last he'd seen her, she'd been in the drawing room practicing the piano.

Always practicing.

As he made his way to the second floor, he pondered how much his life had shifted in a short period of time. What would Graham or Beatrice think of him now? Would they applaud the fact he'd stayed true to his wedding vows this first week, that he was actually enjoying the responsibilities of fatherhood even if his child was a bastard, that he'd bonded with the dowager countess and come to understand the scandalous situation a bit better?

Or would they still look at him with censure and disapproval merely for being himself?

There was no way of knowing unless he went home to gauge their reception, and that wasn't something he was willing to do just now. Instead, he paused outside of the drawing room and simply listened to his wife play the piano. God, she was talented. He wished he had an ounce of her skill and passion. For something.

Anything.

Instead, he had wasted much of this life being a rake and a wastrel. There was nothing to show for his seven and thirty years. Well, there *was* Poppy. The thought had a grin curving his lips. Perhaps he might consider her his greatest achievement, and he didn't care she was a bastard or that her mother hadn't wanted her.

And then there was Anna.

He glanced inside the room, where she swayed to the music only she could see in her mind. Her eyes were closed, and her fingers flew over the ivory keys as she danced in a world that he couldn't see. The melodies she invoked were so intense, so powerful that he felt the music go straight through him, cleansing him, filling the cracks in his soul he'd accumulated over the years. The haunting song sent moisture to his eyes, swirled about his heart, and held him captive, frozen to the floor as he listened to his wife essentially give life to those notes.

Yes, life had certainly changed for all of them here, and they were discovering their own truths as they walked their paths. The most surprising of those changes was how much he appreciated Anna's companionship as well as the fact she trusted him enough to consummate their relationship.

Did he want their union to go further than that? Did he long for a lifetime with her as a real husband? Did he want children beyond Poppy? Uncertainty swooped in to fill his chest, taking away some of the joy brought by her playing. Put quite simply, he wasn't good enough for her, and he didn't know if he ever would be, for there would always be his past coming back to haunt him.

And still the notes emanating from the piano continued to swirl around him, taking his thoughts away and filling him with inexplicable hope, which he hadn't felt since his parents had died.

After the piece ended, the notes seemed to shimmer in the air before finally fading. Acting on impulse, Edmund applauded as he came into the room. "That was one of the most marvelous and memorable things I have ever witnessed."

"Oh! I didn't know I had an audience." A blush filled her cheeks. "Do you truly think it was good? I do so adore Beethoven."

"I'm quite certain you could give new life to any composer you choose to play." When he reached her position, he took one of her hands and tugged her off the bench. "There is certainly something special in how you play. The music connected with me, made me think." Which was a dangerous prospect because it made him want unattainable things.

"That makes me so happy, for I always hope I can reach people through my music." That emotion did, indeed, reflect in her gorgeous emerald eyes as she focused them on him, and even though she couldn't see him, he could pretend that she did. "It is what I adore doing."

"And it shows." This woman managed to humble and excite

him all at once. He held onto her hands as if she would suddenly vanish. "If you wish it, I can speak to the earl—or even my brother—and have them use their connections to perhaps put you on a stage in front of an audience. To gain you notice."

Surprise lined her face and her dark eyebrows rose. "You would do that for me?"

"I would, because you have done so much for me already." Already, her stamp on his life was invaluable.

"Perhaps." She nodded. "Let me think upon it. Such a potentially life-changing decision."

"Indeed." That was something he hadn't given thought to before. If she was an instant success, what would that mean for the future of their marriage? Needing a distraction else he would tumble into the turbulent emotions mixing through his chest, Edmund looked about the drawing room, at the holiday finery that had gone up, and the little touches his wife and the dowager had added to make the room festive, and he grinned. Suddenly he felt whimsical. "I am going to give you dancing lessons this week."

"Oh?" Excitement reflected in her eyes. "Truly?"

The fact he'd managed to make her happy had warmth cycling through his chest. "Of course." Beyond that, he would enjoy holding her in his arms again. "Since we're attending a Christmas ball thrown by one of the earl's contemporaries who lives nearby, I thought you might enjoy learning a few of the more popular sets."

"That would be ever so much fun." Such a simple thing made her so happy, that he was once again humbled. When he raised one of his hands to her lips, his heart squeezed.

"However, first, I thought we could sit quietly and do some talking. Lord knows we haven't done that enough yet." Wanting to be closer to her, Edmund led her over to a low sofa, settled onto it himself, then tugged her down beside him. "How do you manage to live with blindness? How do you not scream out in frustration for what is lost?" There was so much awe and respect he had for her, he couldn't manage to properly voice it aloud.

"At first, it took much acclimating, but because I was a child, I don't suppose I noticed it overly much, for I'd always had an active imagination." She glided her fingertips up and down his arm as she spoke, and with each pass, awareness of her tingled through his blood. "Then, when I grew older, being blind and moving through life was just what I had to do. There was no sense in feeling sorry for myself. It is merely something that happened." When she shrugged, her shoulder brushed his and caused another round of sensation through his groin. "I could be bitter about my circumstance, or I could meet my dreams. Everything has always been my choice." She trained her eyes on him. "We all have that choice."

Well, damn. Would she forever teach him little life lessons? "We do."

For long moments, she remained silent. "Has your anger tempered since we wed?"

"It has been days since I've thought about the things that caused me to be annoyed in the first place." He marveled at that. "Perhaps after talking to the dowager about the scandal, knowing that she had the strength to put such things aside gave me the freedom to do the same." With a frown, he gave the matter more thought. "Do I still wish to antagonize my brother? Most certainly, but that is merely because he's my older brother. Am I still annoyed at his highhanded treatment of me? Yes, but I can now understand why he was frustrated with my behavior and why my negligence had affected the family name."

"Then you are truly maturing." A slow smile curved her lips, and his attention dropped to her mouth. Damn, but he wanted a kiss. "Perhaps being distracted has been good for you."

"Make no mistake, this new life isn't a distraction. It is a conscious decision to do something completely different in the hope for better results." At the last second, he stifled the gasp that rose in his throat, for he hadn't wished to share such an intimate detail about himself.

"That is all to the good." She took his hand and threaded their fingers together. "There is nothing left in the past for you now."

"Agreed." For long moments, he remained silent. "Over the course of this week, I have come to know that. When I look into Poppy's eyes, or every time something I do—even the smallest things—that delight you, everything falls away and becomes unimportant."

"You are learning, Edmund, growing. I'm proud of you." So much happiness rang in her voice and was reflected in her eyes that his world tilted again.

"Those words mean so much." Emotion welled into his throat while tears stung his eyes. "No one has ever been proud of me since my mother died." God, what was this woman doing to him? He was becoming a bit of a wreck, but then he supposed people didn't know who they truly were until they broke. "Sometimes I fear I can only be who I am and will cock it all up." What if he did something like what had happened to his own father? There was no way he could stand to see the disappointment, the bewilderment, the incredulity in his wife's eyes due to him straying.

And damn if he didn't fall a little bit further.

"You poor thing." She bussed his cheek. "I have faith in you—in us."

Oh, God.

This was truly his life. He had a wife and a child. Neither of them was connected except through him, and together, they had the capacity to have a decent life indeed. All he needed to do was stop fighting it, stop trying to cling to the man he'd been and look forward to the man he could be, the man he was becoming.

Because of them.

"I don't deserve you, Anna." Damn, why did he say that? Too much longer and he'd be a blubbering mess. Before she could respond and make him even more confused, he struggled off the low sofa and then tugged her into a standing position. "Was it your idea or the dowager's to hang the mistletoe?" A few sprigs of the stuff had been bundled together and then pinned to the ceiling. It dangled near one of the windows from a red satin ribbon. Quickly, he told her where it was and what it looked like.

"It was Lady Ettesmere. I didn't know we had any." She frowned. Suspicion reflected in her eyes. "What are you about?"

"Well, you and she did a wonderful job decorating in here." It had been a long time indeed since he'd been excited to celebrate the holiday.

"Thank you." The blush in her cheeks was adorable. "She was quite helpful to me, telling me what each decoration looked like, letting me feel them so I could understand, then she would place everything within the greenery."

"I have learned much from the countess and will be sad to see her leave after Christmas."

"As will I. She has become a friend."

Edmund couldn't stand it any longer. He needed to touch her, kiss her, have her close. "Wouldn't it be a shame if we didn't make good use of it?" As she giggled with nervousness, he urged her over the floor and then under the sprigs of mistletoe. "Perhaps soon you will tell me why you like the Christmastide season so much."

"I will." She slipped a hand up his arm. "Though I'll be the first to admit it is taking some acclimation, but I like the path we are all on. It gives me hope."

Could she read minds? Not knowing what else to do, he said, "As do I." Then he took her into his arms, settled her into a comfortable embrace, and gently claimed her lips with his.

In that embrace, he introduced himself to her all over again, as if he were given a clean slate and wished to impress her, to tell her that she could trust him. Those petal-soft pieces of flesh cradled his in the perfect way, and when he needed more contact, Edmund held her head between his palms, furrowed his fingers into her hair, and then encouraged her to open to him.

As she'd done every time they shared kisses, Anna gave herself over into his care, matched his enthusiasm. She twined her arms about his shoulders and essentially layered herself against him in an effort to apparently kiss him as deeply as he did to her. It would be all too easy to let himself come undone in her presence, to give himself permission to complete the fall he'd begun with abandon and see where it led, but a part of him was terrified, for he might lose all that he'd gained.

And hadn't he had his heart broken once before? He absolutely did not want to go through that drama again, but Anna was so different than that other time in his life when he'd given out his heart. She wouldn't hurt him, yet was she only with him due to desperation? Was she starting to feel the same as he? It was too difficult to tell, and he hesitated to ask for fear that he would need to share all of his tumultuous emotions.

He would, of course, but not just yet. Instead, he kissed her, hoped that she might read between the lines, so to speak, and learn what he was too much a coward to say aloud.

"When we are like this, I feel I can truly see you as you are," she whispered against his lips. One of her arms was about his waist while the other rested on his shoulder with her fingers furrowing through the hair at his nape. "Like this, there is such a connection that it doesn't seem I am blind in your company. You are here and I can see you, right down to your soul."

"Is, it, uh, something you enjoy peering at?" Good lord, but he wanted her to see whatever she needed in him.

"Oh, yes." When she smiled up at him, he unexpectedly lost a piece of his heart to her. "You are beautiful, Edmund. Never think otherwise." Then she lifted onto her toes and kissed him, and he was once more lost.

Several moments later, to prevent himself from making love to her right there in the drawing room, he held her at arm's length. "Perhaps we should move into our first dancing lesson of the week, hmm? We will work on one of the more popular country reels. Obviously, during this dance you'll be partnered with many different men, but the gist of the steps is the same throughout."

For the next hour, he remained in her company, instructing her in how to move through the dance and what she would need to know about it if she might wish to participate, but somehow the thought of her in another man's arms—or even touching their hands—had jealously stabbing through him.

I think I'm in a spot of bother.

CHAPTER THIRTEEN

December 21, 1820

ANNA WOKE THAT morning before her husband. After the activities from yesterday, she figured he needed his rest, so after tracing her fingertips over his cheeks, his eyebrows, his lips, she quietly slipped from the bed. They had lingered in the drawing room with the dowager last night after dinner, and wonder of wonders, that lady had offered to read a couple of chapters aloud to her from one of the more exciting books the library had to offer. Once that had been completed, everyone retired.

Now, smiling as she did the necessary things one did upon rising, Anna left the bedchamber and quietly padded into the adjoining dressing room. Though she and her husband hadn't come together physically since that first time, he still initiated kissing quite frequently, and those times were quite lovely, but there was still that ever-present longing deep inside her that wanted a greater connection with him.

Would they ever have a real marriage full of everything it should entail? Was that what she wanted? It would certainly be a natural progression and help with becoming a true family, but until he could see that what lay ahead of him was every bit as exciting as his past had been, they wouldn't be able to move forward.

Once her maid had helped dress her for the day, Anna slowly drifted to the nursery suite. She softly greeted the maid there and asked if Poppy had been fed for the morning.

"Of course, my lady. She is quite active this morning if you would like to spend time with her." Nothing except bright greeting echoed in the young woman's voice.

"I would, indeed. If you don't mind, I'll take her to my room."

"She would like that. Wait here while I fetch her for you." It didn't take long before the nursery maid came close and put the baby into Anna's waiting arms. "She is still a tad fussy as that tooth is working its way through, but she is easily distracted with toys and attention."

"Thank you." Oh, was there any better smell than a freshly bathed baby? Anna cuddled the girl on her shoulder. "Come on, little one. Let's go wake your father."

Of course the girl didn't answer with words, but she did flail a little arm and try to pull at the braid Anna's hair was in.

With murmured goodbyes, Anna left the room. It was a gloomy day with intermittent rain, but none of that mattered, for the joy of holding a baby in her arms was an immediate mood lifter. She crooned happy words as well as ones that made no sense to the girl while entering the suite, and not hearing the sounds that would have meant Edmund had risen, she took Poppy into the sitting room portion of the adjoining room, set her on the floor, and then sat on the Aubusson carpeting near her.

A small ragdoll lay on the floor, so Anna gave the girl that toy as she talked to her, said nonsensical things in the hopes of making the baby laugh. And when that blessed sound echoed in the air, her heart squeezed. She couldn't help but smile. Would she ever bear a babe of her own? Not if her husband kept her at arm's length, but if she didn't, there was a certain level of contentment with Poppy.

It wouldn't do to become too greedy from fate.

When Poppy flipped over onto her back and cooed, Anna smiled.

"You are a strong, determined girl, aren't you?" She glided her fingertips over the baby's face, stroking them along the tiny eyebrows, the chubby cheeks, her chin, her nose. "And you have your papa's looks, which means you will grow up and be quite stunning." A pang of need went through her heart, for she truly wished to have a baby that resembled her even if she wouldn't be able to see it. "Already, you have your papa's heart."

Then the infant flipped onto her belly and kicked her legs, cooing the whole while as if she were excited to be in Anna's presence and hear her talk.

"Perhaps we should go shopping today, hmm?" When she tickled Poppy's foot, the girl uttered a delightful giggle that had Anna laughing. "I would like to buy your papa a Christmas present but have no idea what someone like him would want. He's of the *ton* and I am not, and I fear that anything I give him will seem too pedestrian."

The baby continued to coo and giggle, as if none of that mattered in the grand scheme.

"Your mama is a silly goose, I know." Again, she tickled the girl's foot to the same result, and it was quite hysterical. "What would you like, poppet? What would be fun to mark the holiday?" There was no answer except another giggle. "Perhaps we can convince your papa to procure an evergreen tree like is popular in the Bavarian region. I can only imagine how festive that might be."

"I shall do my level best to make my girls happy."

At the sound of Edmund's voice, Anna startled. "Oh, I'm sorry. Did we wake you?"

"Yes, but no one on this planet could ever be angry by coming awake to the sound of giggles and laughter from the two people he likes best in the world."

"What a lovely sentiment. Do you truly mean that?"

He settled on the floor next to her, and when she put a hand to his shoulder, tingles danced down her spine to find he was only clad in the pair of breeches he'd worn to bed. "Yes, I mean it." Then he took her hand, brought it to his lips, and kissed the back. "The longer we are here in Brighton, away from the world and London, the more I'm beginning to see that domestic life is quite satisfying."

Flutters went through her lower belly. A piece of her heart flew into his keeping. "Sometimes I can hardly believe this *is* our life. It is so different from what I knew before."

"Are you happy?" As he asked that, Edmund brushed the pad of his thumb over the sensitive inside of her wrist.

Sensation tumbled down her spine. How did that tiny little touch send so many tingles through her? "Yes, I am." How surprising to admit that aloud. "Before, the only thing I had to look forward to was playing the piano each day, and I still do, but now? There is you and Poppy, and you have both opened my world even wider and have given me such capacity for true joy that I don't know what to do with myself most of the time."

A strangled sort of sound came from him before he stole a fleeting kiss from her. "That is exactly how it feels." Emotion thickened his voice, then he chuckled. "Poppy has gotten onto her hands and knees. She is rocking back and forth."

Anna put out her hand to touch the baby, to see through her fingers what he was seeing through his eyes. "How thrilling! She will crawl soon."

"Then we will both be in trouble." Edmund put a finger beneath Anna's chin and drew her so close to his face that she might peer into his eyes. Happiness warred with confusion in those blue depths, but he said nothing about how he felt. "Please know that you are doing wonderfully with the circumstances, and I cannot think of a better mother for Poppy."

"Oh!" Tears crowded her eyes. His unexpected praise warmed her. "I appreciate that." Once they returned to London, would the contentment and ease they'd found here continue? Would his focus remain on his family and not of things beyond that?

When Poppy uttered a screech of enthusiasm, both Anna and Edmund laughed. They played with the baby for a bit, and Anna lost another piece of her heart to them both. Forever, they would be a family, and nothing could take that away from her. She and her husband must have had the same idea, for when Anna moved, Edmund was there. They each kissed one of the girl's cheeks and then laughed again. The baby rocked on her knees and cooed, for obviously she enjoyed the attention.

Truly, it was the best moment so far.

EXCITEMENT BUZZED AT the base of Anna's spine as she waited impatiently for her maid to finalize the preparations for her toilette. Edmund had asked her to accompany him on an outing for shopping and then perhaps tea since it appeared the weather was between rain showers. She couldn't wait, for she adored going anywhere that meant being on his arm and having him at her side. It might be a touch vain, but she quite enjoyed knowing such a handsome man was hers and could only imagine the looks they received from other ladies.

While her husband went downstairs to inform the dowager of their intentions and to ask if she needed any parcels retrieved, Anna tried to decide which bonnet to wear, for Edmund had been quite generous in allowing her to shop for fripperies.

"Oh, are you going out *again*?" Meredith asked as she came into the room. From the tone of her voice, one would assume that the whole of Anna's time was spent flitting hither and yon around Brighton.

"Yes. There are a few things I would like to attain before Christmas. Additionally, I'm to try on my ballgown one last time. It's for the Christmas Night ball Edmund is taking me to." Another set of flutters moved through her belly. The dancing lessons were going well enough that her confidence was building. It would be both terrifying and exhilarating to dance with him at a social event. "Once we return home, I'd like to walk the shore before rain comes again. I have grown to love the seashore since arriving here."

"I can't imagine why. It's so damp and dull compared to being in London."

Anna tamped on the urge to huff in frustration. "Not everywhere needs to be like London. Brighton is special in its own right."

"Well, mind yourself all the same. You have become all too prone to accidents of late. I hope that doesn't mean your health has been compromised since coming here."

"I hadn't thought of that before, but it's an interesting theory." Was it true, though? It might explain the accidents.

"Call for me when you return, and I'll assist in whatever needs doing."

Yet the woman hadn't offered to help with the decorating or anything else since arriving in Brighton. But Anna nodded. "I will. Do you need anything from the shops?"

"Not that I can think of. I have a friend who works in one who I can implore upon to get me whatever I need though."

"Ah." Over the course of their time together, Meredith hadn't really shared anything personal about her life, so Anna still didn't know after all these years who she truly was. "Enjoy the afternoon."

A couple of hours later, she and Edmund had completed their errands. They'd had tea at the café with no new incident this time. The last stop was the modiste. Edmund was all too congenial and charming to the staff there as she was ushered behind a privacy screen and helped with changing clothing. The deep tenor of his voice as he chatted with the modiste and a few of her seamstresses helped to keep Anna calm, but when the silken gown came over her head and cooled her skin, she shivered with anticipation.

"Oh, it feels lovely."

The seamstress tugged and fussed at the gown then urged her around the privacy screen.

"This gown is you personified, Lady Evermore." The modiste came near. "Shall I describe it to you?"

"Please do. The way it hangs, the way I feel while in it is amazing."

"There is raised embroidery all over the lavender silk gown. It took four seamstresses a few hours each day since you ordered the gown to complete the embroidery, but the result is quite lovely and one of my best pieces." Pleasure echoed in the older woman's voice. "We then added small fabric flowers to give movement and dimension to the gown. In the center of each small flower is a crystal jewel to catch the light. The sleeves and bodice are both plain, but the viscount said once you add the emerald jewelry, the look will be unparalleled."

"It's the most exquisite gown I have ever owned." She couldn't stop running her hands over the front and bodice to get an idea of what it looked like. "Edmund, is it what you have imagined?"

Then he was there, his scent swirling around her, and as held her hands, he brought each of them to his lips and kissed the backs. "It only enhances what you already look like, but yes, the gown is eye-catching." A tiny note of vulnerability sounded in his voice, probably not noticeable to anyone except her. "I fear you'll be charmed away from me on Christmas."

"Perish the thought." She put a hand to his face, traced his eyebrow, his cheek, his chin. "I made you a promise, and that will never be broken." When she thought he would have kissed her right there, the modiste put a hand on her arm.

"Let us get you out of the gown before your husband decides to devour you whole, hmm? I don't wish to see my creation ripped prematurely." Humor wove through her tones as she led Anna behind the privacy screen. "You are a fortunate woman, Lady Evermore, for your husband is quite enamored."

Heat seeped into Anna's cheeks and flowed through her veins. If someone else was able to see how Edmund reacted to her, then it must be true. "Thank you."

A few minutes later, she was helped out of the gown and then assisted back into her original gown of moss-green taffeta. As Anna went to follow the modiste out from behind the privacy screen, one of the seamstresses darted out from a back room and uttered a cry of warning.

But of course, Anna couldn't see whatever the danger was. Intense heat hit the back of her hand and wrist. Then there was a dull clatter and thud against the floor as something heavy tumbled down. Pain throbbed in her left hand, and suddenly, the shop erupted into cries, orders of command from Edmund, and tearful apologies from a seamstress who had apparently left a hot flatiron on a workbench near the aisle where Anna had passed.

"Good God, someone bring cold water and a towel or ice if you have it." Edmund was there, guiding her away from the scene of the accident then pushing her into a chair while he kneeled at her feet. His fingers on her burned skin were cool, and he shook from reaction. "Tell me how you feel," he asked, and emotion graveled his voice. "The skin hasn't blistered but it is red."

"It hurts, of course, but not overly much that it's uncomfortable." Before she could say more, a flurry of activity erupted around her. The modiste slathered on some sort of salve to Anna's skin, then Edmund wrapped a cool cloth around her hand and secured it with a knot. That helped to take some of the sting from the burn. "Will I be scarred?"

The modiste clicked her tongue. "I don't believe so. It's not a deep or severe burn. Just a quick glancing press against the iron, as if you touched a hot tea kettle." She patted Anna's arm. "You will be right as rain in a few days. Especially if your housekeeper has a salve for burns."

Edmund kept a hand on her knee. "I want to speak with the seamstress, to caution her against such inattention in the future."

Concern rumbled in his voice. "My wife could have been severely injured from such carelessness today."

"I understand, Lord Evermore." The modiste left their presence but returned quite soon. "I'm sorry, my lord, but the girl fled the shop after the accident. I don't know where she is, but once she returns, I will give her my own dressing down."

"Perhaps she was too mortified to face us," he said, and Anna could hear the frown in his voice. "I'm taking my wife home so she can rest."

"Again, I apologize for my employee. If there is anything I can do…."

Anna caught the woman's hand in her good one. "It wasn't your fault, or even the seamstress. Accidents happen."

"Yes, but for the life of me I cannot understand why she set the flat iron there when we have a specific worktable in the back for such tasks." The modiste patted Anna's hand. "Please know how sorry I am. I will not charge you for the next gown you order from me."

Edmund thanked her then he escorted her to the waiting closed carriage. Once their packages were stowed, the vehicle lurched into motion. "If I were a superstitious man, I would think these accidents you keep having are not accidents at all, but no matter how I rack my brain, I cannot think of how they are connected or even why."

"I'm beginning to feel the same way." She rested her hand in her lap. "It could have been so much worse today, though." A frown tugged at the corners of her mouth. "Which reminds me, will you please set up a meeting with your man of affairs whenever is convenient? I wish to change my will." It was time to admit a truth to him. "I, uh, would like the bulk of my mother's inheritance to go to Poppy, so she will never need to worry over her future."

"What?" He stilled on the bench beside her. "Are you certain?"

"Oh, yes. It is not her fault how she was born. I want her to know she is well loved and to have all the advantages I can give her."

"Dear God, you are amazing." He bundled her into his arms and merely held her, and it was everything she had ever craved from a man in this moment. Eventually, he stirred. "If you feel up to it, another dancing lesson tonight?"

"Of course." She patted his cheek. "I look forward to them."

Shortly after they returned to the townhouse, the dowager met them on the stairs. "I heard from one of the footmen about your accident with the iron." The older woman took Anna's hand in hers. "What do you need from me?"

"Nothing just yet. I'm a bit tired so wish to rest quietly before dinner though." She offered a smile to the dowager. "Edmund took care of me. He's quite protective."

"Oh, indeed. He is a good man, but I have news for you both." Excitement threaded through her voice.

"Is all well?" Immediately, Edmund went taut beside her.

"Yes, yes. Poppy began crawling this afternoon while you were out."

He gasped. "I missed the milestone. Already, I have failed as a father."

"Nonsense." Lady Ettesmere chuckled. "It's not as if she will suddenly stop crawling. There are plenty of other milestones for you to share with her." She patted his cheek. "I have a feeling you've fallen in love with that little girl, and it does my heart good to see that. It makes me remember when my children were young. Hectic times but really lovely too. Savor them, you two. They'll fly by."

"It's truly been a whole new world," Edmund said with emotion graveling his voice.

"Indeed. Now, go rest. I'm going out to walk the shore before the rain returns. We shall discuss our holiday plans at dinner."

Once Anna and Edmund had settled into their sitting room, she smiled. Somehow, the puzzling accidents didn't matter when such a beautiful life was waiting for her. As she rested her feet on an embroidered footstool, she sighed when Edmund rang for tea.

Her heart was full, and a lovely warmth came over her as contentment came over her. Was this what falling in love felt like? If so, she was all for it, but would he ever feel the same toward her?

Truly, they needed to find a few private moments where they could speak freely and from the heart if they wished to move forward into something neither of them had ever known before.

CHAPTER FOURTEEN

December 22, 1820

EDMUND PUT THE finishing lines to the letter he'd written to his solicitor when a knock on the half-closed door had his head yanking up and his heartbeat accelerating, for he thought it might be Anna. When he spied Miss Grafton standing there, he stifled a groan and then motioned her into the room.

"What might I do for you, Miss Grafton?" The last thing he wanted to do was have a conversation with this woman. He didn't care for her, and didn't trust her by half. There was something about her attitude and the way she pursed her mouth that made her off putting.

"I am here to rebuke you, Lord Evermore." She shoved the door open fully before storming into the study. "Since Anna has been in your care, you have not looked after your wife carefully enough. She never had accidents before, yet surprisingly, they have come fast and furious every day following the wedding."

"Just what are you accusing me of?" Slowly, he rose from his care and then crossed his arms at his chest. Did she truly believe *he* was at fault?

"Let me just say that nothing like this happened when I was her full-time companion." Accusation sat heavy in her voice. "Whether you want to acknowledge this or not, I am still Anna's companion, even if you try and block my access."

"Never once have I done that. The viscountess is free to utilize your services as she sees fit. Perhaps she merely enjoys spending her time in my company better now." Oddly enough, that pleased him, for he'd worked hard to charm the former Miss Standish. She was different from anyone he'd ever known, and he craved her attention.

Wanted her love.

"You have poisoned her mind against me, then," Miss Grafton continued, wrenching him from his thoughts. "She was utterly dependent upon me before you turned her head."

Edmund frowned. "I barely know you, so that accusation has no merit. As for you other one, don't you think it's possible—and quite logical—that she's now transferred that dependency to her husband?"

"You can't be all that she needs."

"While that is entirely possible, that is her decision alone, so don't come the crab with me because you don't like the fact that life is changing." Everyone acclimated differently to such things, and sometimes it wasn't pretty. He narrowed his eyes when she stood there and stewed. "Remember, Miss Grafton, I have the power of turning you out. If you wish to keep your position, then you will give me *and* her the respect of our stations. Lady Evermore is not a child. She knows her own mind and has for a long while. If she no longer has need of you, I expect that you will resign your position and wish her the best."

Miss Grafton frowned. Abject disgust roiled from her person. "She needs me because she is vulnerable."

He snorted. "We are all vulnerable, but you must let her see what she can do instead of coddling her." That he'd learned merely by being around her. One thing he admired about his wife was her strength and determination to live as normal a life as she possibly could. If she wanted help, she would ask for it. "She deserves the chance to try whatever she desires."

Miss Grafton huffed. "Obviously, you have a higher rank than me, and you are her husband, but if I discover you have only wed her to get at her money, I will come at you in a fury you have never experienced before." Before Edmund could respond, the companion stormed from the room.

God, she was a scare. Shaking his head, he returned to his chair, finished his letter, and then sealed it up for posting tomorrow.

Later, his spirits lifted when he met Anna for tea in the library. It always brightened his day whenever he had the opportunity to be in her company, and doing so in this room had been her special request today.

As he accepted a refresh of his cup from her, he grinned even though she couldn't see it. Somehow, she must have felt it, for a blush stained her cheeks. "How is your hand?" She no longer wore strips of linen wrapped around it.

"Well enough. No lasting damage and it doesn't hurt any longer."

"Excellent news. How would you enjoy spending the upcoming Christmas holiday? I don't know how one goes about that with an infant." Excitement buzzed at the base of his spine. No longer would he need to cater to what Graham and Beatrice wanted. He could make his own plans and traditions, and he would do that with his own little family.

Anna tilted her head slightly to one side. "I think merely spending time with Poppy, showing her she is loved, is the best foundation, but we can have candles and decorate the fir tree if one is procured. I bought her a silver rattle and a pretty, delicate baby gown yesterday."

"God, I would love to have an artist in sometime to have a family portrait done, especially if you would wear your new ballgown. The two of you would look lovely on a canvas."

Where had that thought come from? It shocked him, for when had he become so domestic? When had he ever wished to sit for a portrait? It had been an age since that had happened.

"What a lovely thought! Perhaps we can put that on the

schedule after Twelfth Night."

"I'll ask Lady Ettesmere if she can recommend a particular artist." It was so easy with Anna. In her company, he didn't feel the excessive need to rebel that he felt with his family. With her, he didn't have the pressure to be a rogue, to chase the scandal he'd always depended upon for attention. The only thing she wanted from him was his time and presence.

And he could gladly give that.

Once tea had finished, he drew Anna to her feet. "Come. Let us practice the waltz. You are quite fetching in that crimson gown; I cannot help myself." Yes, he wanted her, but he also wished to continue building up her trust so that they could have a marriage without complications.

She readily agreed. "I have been looking forward to this lesson, for the waltz sounds so romantic."

"It can be with the right partner." With a giddiness he hadn't felt in far too many years, Edmund swept her into his arms and in a soft voice instructed her on how to perform the steps.

As always, she was a fast learner. After a few questions and a few awkward steps and treading on his toes, she learned the basics. It took less than no time for them to move about the library furniture in a bid to pretend they were waltzing in a ballroom. Truly, she didn't need sight in order to dance, and he pulled her closer to his body, for it didn't matter if he wanted to be scandalous. They were married, after all.

The longer they twirled about the room, gliding around the groupings of furniture, the more he peered down into her gorgeous green eyes and understood the emotions flitting there, the more the sensation of falling assailed him. There was no point in denying that he was most likely tumbling tip over tail for his wife, but with every new thing he encouraged her to do, he was so proud of her. That meant she was gaining independence and confidence. Would she fly away from him and a marriage she hadn't truly wanted?

I cannot lose her!

"Why do your muscles tense? What are you worried about?" she asked in a soft voice as they drifted to a halt.

There was no point in lying. "That you will come to your senses and realize you can do much better than being wed to a viscount without full coffers, that you can attract a man with a sterling reputation, a man who hasn't tossed most of his life away on vices."

"Do hush." She laid her palms on either side of his head, brought it down to hers so she could stare into his eyes. "I chose you the same way that you picked me. We might have needed this marriage for different reasons, but now there is a new connection between us. Can you not feel it?"

Oh, how he wanted to believe her! But yes, he could feel it. "I do," he confirmed in a whisper as low hers. "Once you are a highly lauded and much sought after pianist of the stage, if you should happen to play for the king, your future will be set, and you will leave." This was the most vulnerable and open he'd ever been with anyone, but it somehow felt right to show that side of him to her.

"Do you truly think if I happen to meet such a dream that I would be willing to have it without you—my other dream? Do you believe I would leave you and Poppy behind?" The delicate tendons of her throat worked with a hard swallow. "You will always be a huge part of my life, Evermore, and never once think you aren't good enough. For anything."

A wad of emotion lodged in his throat as he stood there with his forehead pressed to hers. "It is difficult after being ignored by various people for years, after having no expectations from anyone...."

"Well, *I* expect you to be the best husband to me that you can." She glanced her fingertips along his lips, his cheeks, his temples, and it was the greatest form of heaven he had ever found. "Have you ever been in love, Edmund?"

"Yes. Years ago."

"Did it make you happy?"

"For a time. Until she decided I wasn't good enough, so she threw me over for an earl with three children."

"And tossed you further into the realm of the scandalous rogue."

"Perhaps." Quickly, he delved a hand into his waistcoat pocket and brought forth a silver locket with no chain. He took her hand so she could trace the trinket. "There is a lock of her hair in here to remind me that love is fickle and it means nothing most of the time."

"What you had before wasn't love if she walked out on you." Anna curled his fingers around the locket. "From the snippets of your past I've managed to glean, you have always been given skewed pictures of what love is, but you haven't truly experienced what that state is, what a person sacrifices for it, how it acts when it's true."

"It took me years to heal from that betrayal, and every liaison I had since then was a way to either put space between me and such an emotion as love or to show myself that chasing it wasn't worth it." He forced a hard swallow into his throat. "Now you know why I'm leery about giving away my heart again."

"I appreciate your honesty." She cupped his cheek. "But you have nothing to worry about. I will never stray, and once I complete the fall for you, I will never let a day go by where I won't show you in some way how loved you are. That is another dream of mine, to tell someone that I love them."

Oh, God. She is coming to love me?

When he didn't answer, she made a sound of annoyance in her throat, lifted onto her toes, and then pressed her lips to his.

"Are you hinting around for something in particular, Lady Evermore?" Edmund's pulse pounded loud in his ears and his shaft sprang to life. How was it in less than a handful of days she'd captivated him so perfectly?

"What do *you* think, Lord Evermore?"

What a minx she was! He crushed his lips to hers and spent the next few minutes acquainting himself with every inch of her mouth. When he probed the seam of her lips, she opened for him and he took full advantage, slipping his tongue inside and fencing with hers. The sweet taste of the sugar she added to her tea only enhanced his building need for her.

"Mmm, I adore how you follow hints." The soft moan that escaped her throat went straight to his stones. She pressed herself closer to him, all soft and warm and willing. He slid his hands to her back, moved them downward until he cupped the rounded curve of her buttocks.

"Ah, Anna, you are quite a marvel." Seconds later, he lifted her into his arms. *I've gone mad.* There was no other way to explain what had happened to him; he didn't give a jot to the fact anyone could come into the library at any moment. Three steps took him to a table that ran flush against the back of a sofa. He deposited her on it, regardless of the silver candlestick and a statuette that tumbled to the carpet with dull thuds, then drank from her lips again and again. She met each kiss, mimicked every thrust and parry of his tongue, mirrored each nip and nibble until his heartbeat raced and his breathing shallowed.

It simply wasn't enough. This woman who'd unexpectedly beguiled him from the moment he met her after the carriage accident continued to tease him merely by being herself. He wanted her, plain and simple, and here she was, more than willing, and what was more, she'd freely admitted she was falling for him.

His wife was coming to love him.

Nothing was more humbling than that, yet those same words refused to leave the tip of his tongue. Not ready to release the whole of his heart to her, he couldn't think past the haze of desire swirling through his brain. He left her lips in favor of nibbling a path along the soft column of her throat. Her apple blossom scent intoxicated him, and she clutched at his lapels in an effort to keep him near, keep them connected. The underside of her jaw beckoned, so he dragged a line of feather-light kisses there. The dip of her collarbones fascinated him, and he couldn't help but lick the area. Then the creamy swell of her breasts held his attention, so of course he explored that satiny skin. When he followed the scooped neckline of her gown with kisses, a shuddery moan left her throat.

"Ah, Edmund...."

"Hmm?" As she tugged on his cravat, he cupped her breasts. A soft smile curved her kiss-swollen, rosy lips, and a tiny piece of his heart flew into her keeping. "You are so damned beautiful, and every day I wake I cannot believe you are my wife."

"Sometimes fate manages to surprise us and give us what we need instead of want." When he didn't move, only kept his head close to hers so she could see him, she heaved a sigh. "By all means, continue to touch me, my lord." One of her eyebrows arched as if in challenge.

The impertinent "my lord" spurred him into action, just as she'd no doubt planned. He grinned. "Well, if you insist." As he brushed the pads of his thumbs over her nipples, those buds hardened, and he was lost. With a sound akin to a growl, Edmund hooked his fingers into the soft material of her bodice as well as the petticoat beneath and tugged the neckline down until her breasts popped free. "Never can I have enough of you," he whispered seconds before he dipped his head and took one of the rosy tips into his mouth.

"I adore this moment." She leaned back to give him greater access. As tiny sounds of encouragement left her throat, Anna moved a hand to his nape and held him to her.

Who wouldn't love this? Edmund fell into the heady world of showing his wife how much he delighted in her body. As he suckled one pebbled nipple, he rolled the other, and when her moans grew in volume, he claimed her lips with his, taking the sound into himself. It wouldn't do to alert someone to their presence. Desperation, perhaps adoration, guided his actions as did the pressure throbbing through his engorged shaft. The warm mounds of her breasts filled his hands, and gratefully he kneaded them, teased the hardened peaks with his thumbs while he continued his conquest of her mouth.

Why wouldn't he just let himself complete the fall and embrace everything this relationship was offering?

There were no answers, but he drank from her mouth as if she held the secrets to all his questions and the only way to get at them was to caress them from her tongue.

"Edmund, *please*." Her throaty utterance drove him wild and further tightened his member. When she pulled him closer, he settled between her naturally splayed knees. Her skirts bunched between them as she locked her heels at his arse, effectively trapping him. As if he would ever wish to leave. "Perhaps we should move upstairs."

"And ruin the moment?" He could bury himself in her wet heat now. "I think I'll take you right here," he murmured and slid a hand up her thigh beneath the rumpled fabric.

"Oh, goodness," she managed to whisper before she set out to explore his neck with her lips and fingers.

"Indeed." The silky glide of her thigh against his fingers urged him onward then he sucked in a breath and slipped his hand between her thighs. Unable to stop touching her, he planted a line of feather weighted kisses along the slender column of her throat as he glanced his fingers through the curls shrouding her sex.

"Keep going." She gave into a shudder even as she urged him closer.

He nipped the spot where her shoulder joined her neck. "Quite needy, are you?"

"Very." With a sound of impatience, she caressed a hand down his back and when she came to his rear, squeezed a cheek. "Make me fly, Edmund."

As if he hadn't thought about doing just that since he consummated their marriage. Heated desire shot through his shaft. He drew slightly back with his mouth hovering above one of her nipples. His pulse rushed hard and loud through his ears. "We aren't exactly in a private place."

"You are the one who ignored my invitation to move upstairs." She focused her gaze on him, and there was a specific invitation there he couldn't deny.

"Ah, Anna. You both confuse and inspire me." It wasn't a lie. Edmund stared down at her. With her flushed skin, her well-kissed lips, the ardent need in her emerald eyes, her skirts rucked up to her waist, and her white stockings and blue ribbons garters on display, she was every bit a woman in the throes of desire.

And he fell further down that slippery slope.

Again, he claimed her lips, bossed her tongue about with his as he slipped his fingers along her folds, and spread her open until that tiny pearl came out of hiding. The second he glided his touch over that bud, she nearly launched off the table. Her fingers dug into his shoulder in a subtle, quiet plea for him to continue.

Though his shaft throbbed with the need to bury itself into her honeyed heat, he ignored that urge the best he could, at least until he got her off. Again, he took a pebbled nipple into his mouth while he teased her nubbin with varying degrees of friction.

"Oh, oh, oh...." Anna squirmed on that shallow table. Her heel dug into his backside while the blush on her cheeks deepened. "Hurry."

He applied himself with more intensity, as if his only goal in this life was to bring his wife to completion. The soft inhalation of her breath gave away the first clue that she'd gone over the edge. As her body stiffened, he kissed her, silenced the cry of completion while she shuddered, shattered in his hold, and damn if that wasn't the most glorious sight. Surrounded by books, her splayed out on a table was the height of scandalous, but he grinned like a loon, for he'd put her into that state.

Then she slumped on the table, nearly slid from that piece of furniture, but he caught her before she fell. "I should be ashamed of how quickly I give into your ministrations," she whispered as she clung to his arm and tried to tug her bodice into place with her free hand.

Edmund snorted with laughter. "While I am quite smug at

that same fact."

She blew out a breath that ruffled a few strands of hair that had escaped its combs. "Come upstairs with me. We'll need to dress for dinner in a bit regardless, but before we do that, perhaps we can continue what we started here?"

Dear God, she would be the death of him. He nodded and grabbed her hand. "I believe that's a perfectly good way to pass the remainder of the afternoon." Miss Grafton and her complaints fell right out of his head as he tugged Anna from the room. Surely such happiness, such… completeness wouldn't last.

Would it?

CHAPTER FIFTEEN

December 23, 1820

"I AM GOING out to walk the shore," Anna said as she arranged a heavy shawl about her shoulders. The dress of a navy wool blend would keep her warm enough. "Do you want to come with me? I fear it will rain all too soon and remove any chance for exercise today if I wait."

"Of course I'll join you, but I'd like to bring Poppy down. Will you wait until I can get her changed and collected?" That winsome grin of his released a horde of butterflies in her belly.

"I am confident I can go down by myself." It was two hundred steps from the back door to the shoreline, and she didn't intend to go far out toward the surf. And what was more, she had taken to walking about in her bare feet. It didn't matter if it was considered scandalous. She would do what she pleased because she could.

"I admire your courage." He came close, wrapped his arms around her middle, and nuzzled her shoulder. "It's one of the many things I admire about you."

She giggled, for he was quite affectionate when he wanted to be. "Do hush. We slept in rather late this morning. Too much more time being closeted in here and we might actually have a real honeymoon."

What she had let him do to her yesterday in the library went beyond anything she could imagine, and then what she'd done to him after they'd gone up to their room still had the power to make her blush. She'd explored the whole of his body with her hands, and then when she timidly asked if he'd let her put her mouth on his shaft, he'd shown her how to go about it until they were both heated and quite primed. Afterward, they'd coupled and shared a deep connection during those stolen moments, and she'd lost yet another piece of her heart to him. Yes, she was falling tip over tail for her husband, though she worried he might not return those feelings. She'd even admitted as much to him, but he didn't reassure her with those same words.

Perhaps it was a learning process and she needed to be patient.

"I do like the sound of that," he whispered against the shell of her ear. "Staying in bed, having you all to myself…. Mmm. What man wouldn't reform if he knew there was such a woman waiting for him?"

She turned in his arms and bussed his cheek. "Perhaps once the dowager goes back to London, and we are left much to our own devices…."

"I'll hold you to that." Then he released her from his embrace. "Enjoy the shore. I'll join you as soon as I can."

"I look forward to seeing you with Poppy. It's one of my favorite parts of the day." Then she left the suite. On her way through the corridors of the lower level, one of the footmen came up to her.

"Excuse me, Lady Evermore?" He sounded uncertain of his reception. Perhaps he wasn't accustomed to talking to the people he served.

"Yes?" She waited until the man had joined her.

"This is from Cook." The man put a willow basket into her hands. "She'd heard of your plans to go to the shore and wanted to pack a late luncheon for you and the viscount."

"What a lovely surprise. Please convey my thanks to her."

Anna gave him a bright smile. It would be a perfect alfresco tea.

"I will. Enjoy your time at the shore."

She continued on her way, and by the time she went outside, she couldn't stop smiling. Life had become even greater than she had dreamed. On the shore, it was pleasant and breezy but only slightly chilly. The shawl kept her perfectly cozy. There was a certain smell to the air that signaled it would rain later, and she suspected the closer they came to the end of the year, the more that sort of precipitation would be likely. Would it snow this year? It was anyone's guess at this point, but the possibility of seeing Poppy's reaction to such a thing kept her in a constant state of excitement.

Counting steps, Anna reached a spot that she favored and then laid the basket on the scrubby grasses there. After she'd walked the shore and felt the surf on her feet, she would return and sit merely to listen to the sounds around her.

Occasionally, the murmured sounds of conversation reached her ears of people passing by or of children laughing and having the time of their lives while they dodged the ever-moving surf. Another round of counting ensued, and when she'd gotten to the end of her pre-calculated steps, Anna held her skirting up out of the water's way and went forward enough to put her feet into the surf. Oh, it was cold but not unbearably so. Truly, it was fantastic, and she couldn't have enough of the feel of the sand and water on her skin.

Never did she think when she was wasting away at her father's house, pampered and in prison, that she would ever have the freedom that she did now. One thing she adored about Edward was that he let her have her head on many things, let her explore as much as she was able, and he never hovered over her as her father and even Meredith did. If one wished to learn how to survive, one had to actually experience things for oneself.

With a sigh, Anna lifted her face to the weak December sun and breathed in the slightly salty sea air as the gulls passed overhead. So easily could she pass the hours of each day just lying on the sand and listening to everything around her. Or dreaming of what might happen. It would be difficult to leave Brighton when Edmund wished to go back.

Which was another topic of discussion she would need to have with him, for they couldn't linger here at the shore forever. It was almost as if he was using it as a crutch to avoid the life he led in London, or using her as an excuse to stave off interacting with his family. The reasons why would need sorting soon.

Eventually, Edmund joined her. "Poppy was a tad fussy and didn't wish to cooperate with the nursery maid who dressed her, but I think we've come to an understanding."

Anna drew her fingers over the baby's form. She was so sweet in an embroidered gown with a lace-edged bib, bare feet, and a delicate cap over her golden hair. "Poor little thing. That must be terrible pain for her." Drool dribbled down the child's chin.

"Indeed, so the dowager gifted her with a coral ring. It's tied about her neck on a satin ribbon, and she can chew on that to help ease the pain of teething. I hope it's working." His chuckle was a tad strained. "I don't know how much truth I hold in regard to the coral ring, but she seems to think the superstitions from when her own children were young still hold."

"I suppose whatever might help needs to be tried, and she did raise three children into adulthood." Anna touched the baby's face, felt the slobber, then put a fingertip into Poppy's mouth to feel along the lower gum line. "The tooth has almost broken through, though. Perhaps in another day or two it will, and she'll know some relief."

"I hope so. It's hell watching her suffer and knowing I cannot help. I'm going to put her feet in the water to see if she'll enjoy it today."

"One never knows with a baby."

The sounds of splashing reached Anna's ears, quickly followed by a squeal of delight from Poppy. Both she and Edmund laughed.

"I suppose she is in a better mood for the water today," Anna said with a smile. Babies were such a mystery, and she adored finding out more about them.

"Let us walk the shore while we still have the sun."

"Do you need to remove boots and socks?"

"Already done, love."

She stifled a tiny gasp. Had he meant the endearment, or was it merely something a man said during conversation with a woman? Not knowing, Anna contented herself with walking beside him while he bounced Poppy in his arms or alternately dipped her feet into the surf, which made her squeal. Feeling playful, Anna bent, scooped up a handful of water, and splashed Edmund, laughing when it took him by surprise.

"Naughty girl." The rumble of his chuckle tickled through her chest, but she squealed much like Poppy when he did the same to her.

For a few moments, they engaged in water fighting as if they were children before they bowed to decorum again and continued their walk. Poppy laughed and cooed in Edmund's arms. He told Anna how the girl wriggled and squirmed when he tried to keep her tucked against his shoulder so she could picture it in her mind. Obviously, the baby much preferred being held so she could see the people around her.

Tears sprang to Anna's eyes, for in that moment she could honestly believe they were a true, loving family. Because of that, she still had faith this would be forever.

Once hunger came upon them and Poppy began to fuss, they returned up the shore to the spot where Anna had left the basket. Then Edmund stopped abruptly. His entire body tensed at her side.

"Hold."

"What is it?"

"The picnic basket has tipped over." He put a hand on her shoulder and yanked her backward with so much force she nearly tripped on her hem. "Don't move. Don't get any closer."

Knots of worry pulled in her belly. Cold tingles went down

her spine. "Why? You are scaring me. What has happened?"

"There is an adder in the basket." Shock echoed in his voice. "The snake is beige in color with gray diamonds on its back. Why the hell is it in the basket among our tea things?"

Gooseflesh erupted over her skin. "Perhaps it crawled in when the basket tipped?" She forced a swallow into her suddenly dry throat.

"No, it was clearly curled amidst the edibles." Concern was heavy in his tones. "Protect the baby." He shoved Poppy into her arms. "I need to take the snake away so it won't bite anyone on the shore. From my knowledge, they shouldn't prowl around here, which is why I'm baffled."

"Oh, please be careful." She didn't know much about snakes in general or adders in particular, but such creatures weren't her favorite. While he was gone, she bounced the baby, talked to her in an effort to keep both of them calm. Her voice shook, but it was important to not frighten the child. Now she understood why mamas were protective of their children. Not even the cry of the gulls or the crash of the waves could soothe her while she waited for Edmund to return.

Then, unexpectedly, he was there, and his arms were around her and the baby. He held her tightly, as if she'd vanish into the ether if he let go. "God, if that thing had bitten you or Poppy, I would have been beside myself." Horror shook through his voice. He pressed his lips to her temple as his hands shook on her back. "It might not have enough venom to kill an adult, but an infant, certainly. I cannot imagine life without Poppy."

"Neither can I." She was humbled by his reaction and the emotion he exhibited, and she clung to him even though they were on a public beach. "The basket came from Cook. Surely, she didn't put the snake in there."

"I doubt it." He snorted, and by increments relaxed his grip on her. "Who told you there was a basket to take with you?"

"One of the footmen. He gave it to me."

"Do you know him?"

"No. He mentioned it as we were passing in the corridor. He said Cook wanted us to have a lovely time out here with a packed luncheon."

"Damn." Edmund hugged them both again. He kissed Poppy's cheek when she fussed. "I am no longer convinced all of these things are accidents. Something foul is at play."

Was that true? She frowned. "But why? Does someone hate you that much?" What had he done in his life in London before he'd met her?

"Not me, sweeting. You." Again, he pressed his lips to her temple. "All of these things have happened to *you*."

Anna couldn't even thrill to his use of another endearment, for fear twisted down her spine. "Me? I'm no one. I rarely left my house before you came along. I was never allowed to do anything." As her hands shook, she held the baby tighter but ended up laughing when the girl grabbed her nose and lips. "Why would anyone wish to harm me?"

"I don't know. Let me think upon the matter, but for the time being, we should return inside." He released her. "I'll gather the basket and its contents."

"No!" Anna shook her head. "If we do that, we will let whoever wishes to harm me win. I will not give into bullying or fear, but perhaps we won't indulge in tea just now."

"Damn, but I adore your spirit." He took her hand, led her a bit down the beach, and once he'd found a good spot, he sat down on the sand. "Hand me Poppy." Once she'd put the baby into his arms, he tugged Anna down beside him. "Per your request, we will sit here and enjoy the sunshine, because lord knows it'll be hidden behind rain clouds more sooner than later."

"I *am* quite content here." The sand was soft and sun-warmed, and having her husband and Poppy beside her was a lovely way to pass the time.

"I shall watch all the bathing wagons that line the shore. We can invent stories of who is within those contraptions, unless you want me to hire you a dipper."

Anna frowned. "What is a dipper?"

"It is usually a strong woman who comes with one of the wagons to 'dip' a woman of the upper class into the sea, so the current won't take the swimmer away."

"How very interesting and somewhat odd." She turned her head toward him. "If you must rent a wagon, I would rather go into the sea nude with you. If such a thing is allowed." Truly, she had no idea, but being in his company made her both brave and slightly naughty.

"I would imagine a patron can do whatever they please once inside a bathing wagon once they've rented it." Humor wove through his voice. "But that is definitely something I'll look forward to, for any excuse to have you naked and willing is a good day indeed."

Heat went through her cheeks. "Hush, you. Remember the baby."

"It is good for Poppy to be around us and know her parents get along." The viscount put the baby on the sand between them. "It will be comforting for her. My own parents were quite loving toward each other until the day my father became aware of my mother's betrayal." A trace of bitterness went through his voice. "I don't blame her, but I do understand why he felt the way he had. It was a difficult situation all around."

Obviously, that was one of the things that had prompted his push for rebellion. "Are you still angry about that scandal?"

"Not as much as I was before. Instead, I can understand what drove my mother and why my father was so upset about being lied to." He released a held breath. "However, my father always favored Graham over me even before the issue of paternity came to light. That made me feel slighted and less than, even somewhat unwanted."

"And now?"

"Now I don't feel I need to continually seek scandal in order to gain attention. Oddly enough, I am experiencing what true contentment feels like, and it surprises me each day." He slipped an arm about her waist. "Somehow, I either needed the catalyst of being a father or being a husband to force me to find the man I want to be."

"That makes me happy." Anna sighed. She smiled when Poppy patted her leg with a little fist. "I fear I'll have nightmares about that snake, so I'm glad I didn't see it. I don't like things that slither." A shiver moved down her spine. "Just thinking about how much damage it could have done…." Her voice broke. "And I wouldn't have been able to see it. Poppy could have been harmed because of me." Tears sprang to her eyes as emotion took hold. "She needs a better mother, Edmund. A mother who can see and keep danger at bay." How would that affect their lives as they moved forward?

"You cannot think that way." The low timbre of his voice promoted calm as it tickled through her chest. "Having a snake in a picnic basket could have happened to anyone. And Poppy has the exact mother she was destined to have. The way you care for her, nurture her, guide her is lovely." He pressed a kiss to her hair. "There is nothing wrong with you, Anna. You are exactly as you need to be, and neither of us have complaints."

Poppy chose that moment to squeal as she put her mouth to Anna's leg. Immediately, drool wet her skirting and slight pain followed as the girl teethed.

A few tears escaped to Anna's cheeks from his flattery and Poppy's attention. "Thank you. I truly needed to hear those words."

"I understand." Laying a hand to the side of her face, Edmund turned her head and then brushed his lips over hers. "I shall have to give you something more pleasant to dream about than that dratted snake."

There was so much promise in his voice, she shivered with anticipation. "Too much more of this and I'll follow you around like a star-struck puppy." Already, she was in love with the man. How much deeper would she go before he might match those emotions?

"I'd settle for a woman tip over tail, but I'll take what I can get." When Poppy bumped her head against Anna's leg, Edmund chuckled. "I think this outing has tired the poor thing."

"We'll go back soon. I want to soak up as much sunshine as I can." She lifted her face to the sky. "I will never forget this time at Brighton."

Yes, there was hope for her marriage, and despite the accidents that grew more dangerous with each passing day, she couldn't wait to discover what would happen next.

CHAPTER SIXTEEN

December 24, 1820

E
DMUND FROWNED INTO the cheval glass as he tried for a second time to tie the knot of his cravat while his valet stood off to the side, waiting patiently.

"Let me help you with that, my lord. It is why I am here."

He nodded at the other man. "Thank you, Andrews. I am having trouble concentrating today." It was Christmas Eve, and he'd promised to meet Anna at the shops around midday, for she'd wished to do some last-minute shopping. Apparently, there was a stuffed rabbit she simply needed to buy for Poppy. Since he'd had correspondence to attend to, he'd stayed behind. Then he'd spoken to the dowager about dinner tonight, for he'd wanted a special dish prepared, one that Anna had liked in her childhood, as a surprise—a delicately roasted quail stuffed with fig, onions, and chestnuts.

"So it would seem." The valet made short work of the cravat. "Is it the holiday that has distracted you or the fact you are in love with your wife?"

It had been twelve days since he'd wed Anna, and during that almost two-week period, his life had tilted, been upended, and was completely turned about so that he couldn't recognize it any longer. The between of the man he'd used to be and the man he was changing into now seemed as large and as deep as a canyon, and it constantly amazed him how different everything was.

"I couldn't say."

Andrews snorted. He scratched his fingers through his salt-and-pepper black hair and shot him a look of exasperation. "You can, but you are trying to deny the truth."

"Perhaps I am." Turning away from the cheval glass, he regarded the valet, who'd been a friend to him for many years. "I wasn't supposed to fall for her."

The other man laughed outright at that. "What did you think was going to happen once you wed her?"

"We had agreed on a marriage of convenience, a union in name only, to help us both, as well as to spite my brother." He shoved a hand through his hair, which upset the popular style Andrews had just made with the tresses, but he didn't care. "Yet every day that goes by, I find myself even more fascinated by her. It was supposed to be me charming her, but the opposite is happening, yet I cannot help but think what I'm feeling is only temporary."

"You are quite a nodcock, my friend." Andrews retrieved a silver-backed comb from a decorative wooden box atop the bureau. Then he began the task of restyling Edmund's hair. "It is a natural progression. There is no crime with falling in love. Especially with one's wife."

"Perhaps, but what if something happens?"

"Meaning?"

Quickly, he explained about the frequent accidents that were becoming more alarming as time went on. "What if she is attacked or even killed? How can I live with that on my conscience?" Knots of worry pulled in his gut. "How can I move forward knowing the best thing to ever enter my life is gone?"

"You do what countless men before you have done. Mourn their passing and then either let the death consume you or be willing to try once more."

"I am not strong enough for that, Andrews," he admitted in a soft voice. "Anna is coming to mean everything to me, and it's terrifying." For long moments he stared at the valet. "My parents loved each other with that sort of intensity, but my mother ended up straying. Her desperation to have children was worth more than remaining faithful to my father even if he was sterile." He shook his head. "If something were to come between Anna and I, make our union fracture after I've given in and let myself complete this fall, I would be devastated."

"That is understandable, of course, but might I remind you that you are not your parents? These are different times than when they met their struggles." Andrews finished with the hair. He replaced the comb into the box with the rest of the vanity set. "Perhaps your parents' fatal flaw was lack of communication. From what you have told me, neither of them was the best at sharing how they felt with anyone in the family. Yet you stand here with the chance to do better than they ever could because you can talk to Lady Evermore before trouble happens."

"This is true."

"Have you told your wife how you feel? After the incident with the adder, you were beside yourself and spent the remainder of the day at her side, as protection." One of the valet's eyebrows rose in challenge. "Last night the two of you were rather chummy as I found when I came by to see if you wished for assistance preparing for slumber."

Heat crept up the back of Edmund's neck, for he and Anna *had* been enthusiastically affectionate with each other last night, which had led to a heated coupling quite soon after they'd retired. "I have not, for in that, I've been a coward." It was that simple. Where she'd more or less told him of her feelings, he'd remained silent on his.

"Don't wait too long, my lord. Women with the viscountess' temperament and strength won't stand for such failures long. Women like her want to know they are loved, wish to be reminded that they are needed and wanted, even if you've already shown her in the protection of her, in the reassurance that she is a good mother for your child."

"What you say makes sense." And cheered him a bit. "How did you become so wise?"

"Perhaps I have learned from cataloguing your mistakes." They both shared a laugh. "Yet even a fool can see she is exactly the kind of wife you have needed all along. It is good to know you're a changed man because of her."

"It amazes me every damned day." He heaved out a sigh. "Right, then. I should go and meet her. She'll wonder what has become of me."

Andrews nodded. "Tell her, Edmund. Don't delay further, and for God's sake, don't cock this up."

He snickered. "I shall try my level best not to." But the chance that he would wasn't entirely gone.

ONCE HE'D REACHED the shops, he ran into one of his contemporaries, a man he hadn't seen for a few months.

"Evermore! Fancy seeing you here in all places."

Turning about, he greeted the man with surprise. "Crowley! Brighton is the last place I'd expect to see you." They clasped hands. "Are you here for the holiday season?"

"I am, but why are you here? I never thought I'd see the day when you voluntarily left London and all the entertainments there." The man had been an acquaintance for a bit, and they occasionally met each other at society functions or at their club, so he was well aware of Edmund's preferences.

"Well, I was recently married. Twelve days ago, in fact." There was some measure of pride that swelled his chest to tell one of his friends this information. "We came down for our honeymoon. I'm to meet her soon. She's been shopping."

Lord Crowley's eyes rounded with surprise. "You? Married? Now I know the world is ending, and soon, if you've gone into parson's mousetrap."

"Well, it happens to the best of us."

"Given up the life of gambling and mistresses, have you? I'll wager many of those fine fillies you used to frequent are in a temper. And to think you traded it all in for one woman."

"An heiress, too." As quickly as he could, Edmund divulged Anna's identity and who her father was. He frowned up at the skies as they began to spit rain.

"Ah, no wonder you married. But there's time enough to go back to your ways once you've got that heir, hmm?"

"Uh, sure." The heat of embarrassment went up his chest into his cheeks. He couldn't very well tell this man the truth of things, for he hardly knew him, but confusion ran riot inside him. Without thinking, he scrambled to pass the whole lot off as a joke. After all, the likelihood of seeing Crowley again soon was slim. "A man can suffer anything, even a blind wife, if there is enough coin to last a lifetime."

"I have an appointment that must be kept, but it was good seeing you." Crowley touched the brim of his beaver felt hat as he looked at someone over Edmund's shoulder. "Miss." Then he went on his way down the street, soon vanishing within the crowd of pedestrians.

A feminine gasp reached Edmund's ears. Of course he recognized the voice even if she hadn't said anything. Quickly, he whirled around. "Anna." How long had she been standing there? His heart dropped into his stomach. Dear God, had she overheard his exchange with Crowley?

"Did you mean that just now?" The shock on her face sent daggers of self-loathing into his heart.

"Uh, mean what?" Perhaps she hadn't heard what he thought.

"That you are merely suffering marriage to me to get at my money?" All color had leeched from her face. Disappointment and grief warred for dominance in her eyes.

His heart ripped asunder to know he'd put those emotions there. "I didn't mean that as truth. It was in jest." Though he hurried to her side, tried to take her free hand since the other carried a wrapped parcel, she yanked it away. "He is but an acquaintance. I didn't wish to tell him intimate details about our life." Which was also true.

She frowned, for obviously she didn't believe him. "Why would you say it at all, even as a joke?" Tears sounded in her voice. Moisture sprang to her eyes. Drops of rain dotted her maroon dress and pelisse. The delicate tendons of her throat worked with a hard swallow. "I thought we were getting along so well, that there was the hope of things to come, yet you said those horrible things...."

"Anna, you must believe me." He couldn't tell her why he'd made the joke without revealing his emotions, and when he did, he wanted them to be true. He wanted to be able to say to her, without the presence of doubts, that he was deeply in love with her. "I wasn't thinking... didn't want to be the butt of jokes about being married—"

"Yet you could do the same about me?"

"I didn't mean it that way."

When he once again would have taken her hand, she snatched it away. "Please leave me alone, Edmund. I don't wish to see you at the moment."

"But we were to spend the afternoon together and—"

"We were, but you destroyed that possibility." Anna shook her head. A few tears tumbled to her cheeks, and each one of those crystalline drops burned through his heart like acid. "I mean it. I'm quite cross at you and don't know what to think."

"I deserve that." His chest tightened, and he hated himself with every second that went by. People on the boardwalk stared as they passed. "At least let me escort you to the carriage. You can ride home, and I'll walk. You shouldn't need to be in the rain."

"Fine."

Not wishing to leave her vulnerable or have the crowds run into her, he slipped a hand about her upper arm, kept himself between her and the other people in front of the shops, and with every step he took, he couldn't find the courage to release the words that sat on the tip of his tongue. After two blocks, they reached the carriage, and he assisted her into it even as his heart was breaking. *I should have told her earlier. Hell, I should have told everyone.* "Please know those words do *not* reflect how I truly feel about you."

She frowned. Annoyance flashed in her eyes as she settled her parcel on the bench beside her. "Then how *do* you feel? You never answered me when I shared the contents of my heart. Perhaps you'll do so now."

"I... I..." Why the devil wouldn't the words come? He simply didn't have the courage to say what he ought, and because of that, he was in danger of losing everything. "I think, that is to say, I...." Fear kept a tight hold on him. Once he admitted to his feelings, there would be no going back to the man he'd been before.

"So I thought." She sniffled and scrubbed at the moisture on her cheeks. "What a fool I have been this whole time. Knowing you only married me to get at my fortune stings, but it's not unexpected, since that is what any man who shows an interest in me wants." Two spots of color blazed on her cheeks, but it was the disappointment, the shock in her emerald eyes, that completed Edmund's devastation. She rapped on the ceiling. "Driver, please take me home."

"Of course, Lady Evermore." The driver glanced at him for confirmation.

Edmund nodded as he gently closed the carriage door. As he hunched further into his greatcoat, he was left completely gutted on the side of the road. He'd behaved like a nodcock and had been entirely too careless. Fear shouldn't make a man act like that, yet he'd cocked things up exactly as he'd told his valet he would.

Damn, I'm an idiot. Would his marriage end not even two weeks into it?

By the time he reached the townhouse, he was almost completely drenched from the rain. He deserved to feel cold and wet and miserable. How would he make this misstep right? What could he do that would make Anna smile at him again? There were no easy answers, of course, but he needed to try. It was too important not to. And it was Christmas Eve to boot.

Not wanting to immediately seek her out, he ordered a bath instead. His very bones were too cold, and he needed time to think. Besides, according to the butler, his wife was closeted with the dowager with orders not to be disturbed.

On his way up, he shoved some coins into a footman's hand, told him to go to town and purchase a pretty floral bouquet for the viscountess, and to do so with haste.

An hour later, after he'd dressed and put himself to rights, he sighed, for Anna still hadn't entered their shared suite. His heart felt dead and heavy in his chest. How long would she punish him? When another hour passed and she still stayed away, Edmund went to the nursery. Poppy was having play time. Asking the nursery maid to give them a moment, he sat on the floor with the baby.

"I think I've cocked things up beyond repair with your mother," he admitted to her in a choked whisper.

Poppy trained her blue eyes on him and kicked her feet as she balanced on her belly.

"I was stupid and afraid." He stroked a knuckle along her chubby cheek, wiped at the bit of drool on her chin. "It is so easy with you. I can tell you how much I love you and I feel no fear, but with your mama, it's different. You are mine forever, but if I lose her...." Emotions crowded his throat and for a moment, he took refuge in letting them have at him. A trace of moisture on his cheeks surprised him, for when was the last time he'd cried? Perhaps it had been when his parents died—the people who first soured him on the idea there was such a thing as love at all. Perhaps he hadn't been angry over the years at that. Had the emotions he'd struggled with been grief all along? He allowed himself the freedom to cry for another few moments, then he gained control of himself. "Well, none of that matters. I have tried to do my best by you and her, and I'll keep on doing that."

Until I can find my courage.

Poppy cooed and laughed, and when he picked her up, covered her little face with kisses, she patted a hand to his cheek, and suddenly in that moment, he had the feeling all would be well. "I need to go find your mama." When he put her back on the blanket spread over the floor, the infant immediately pushed herself onto her knees and then half-scooted, half-crawled in his direction.

"I'll come back after dinner. Papa loves you." Merely saying those words caused his heart to squeeze, for he realized they were true. Never did he have such a capacity for love as he did for this little girl, and perhaps he'd needed to learn how to love her before he could be any good at loving someone else. In many ways, it was them against the world. They were both unwanted and misunderstood, but by themselves they were incomplete.

We need Anna.

His wife didn't make an appearance at dinner. The dowager told him she'd taken her meal on a tray.

Midway through the meal, Lady Ettesmere looked him in the eye. "If you don't make things right between you and your wife, young man, I will turn you over my knee. I don't care how old you are. That sweet woman didn't deserve your carelessness; she has done everything for you, had her trust bruised because of you."

"I know," he bit out, for he was well aware of the muddle he'd fallen into.

"Women are always more emotional during the holidays. Get up there and grovel, my boy. The two of you are good together. I'd hate for your marriage to crumble over something as stupid as what happened today."

"She told you?"

"Of course she did! I'm the closest thing she has to a mother. You broke her heart today, Edmund."

As if that made him feel any better. "I know."

"I'm telling you this just as your mother would." She pierced him with her gaze. "That woman loves you. Don't take her or those feelings for granted merely because you are too afraid to stand by your own."

The shock of those words slammed into him like a blow, but he deserved that too. "What if she doesn't forgive me?"

"Then she doesn't, but Anna is better than that. She won't toss you out over a few careless words. However, she's hurting and the longer you let this fester, the worse it will be."

He stood so quickly his chair toppled over. "I'm going up right now." Pausing long enough to right his chair, he then spent another few precious seconds in order to buss the dowager's cheek. "Thank you for the kick in the arse."

"You are welcome. My Gilbert was in a pickle with his wife not long ago. If he could manage to save his marriage, you can too." She waved him away. "I don't expect to see you before tomorrow morning."

If only he could be as confident.

As soon as he reached the suite he shared with his wife, he saw Anna on the bed, dressed in a lace-edged nightdress of green silk topped with a matching robe, propped up by a mound of pillows, her fingers constantly moving as if she played a piano in her head.

"Anna?" He approached the bed slowly. When she frowned at him, obviously still in a snit, he sighed. "I'll sleep in the nursery or the parlor tonight." It would be deuced uncomfortable, but perhaps he deserved that too.

"That might be best." Her voice wavered. "You hurt me, Edmund. It's a new experience, and I don't particularly care for it."

"I'm sorry." His chest ached so much he might die from it. "What else do you wish for me to say?" Why the hell was he such a coward and such a failure at merely talking? Because that had never been a part of his upbringing. Well, all of that ended now.

He wasn't his parents as his valet had said, and if he wanted different results, he had to live his whole life differently.

And that scared the spit out of him.

"I don't know." She moved her hands in a helpless gesture. "This has never happened to me before."

Though he wanted nothing more than to kiss her and cajole her into a better mood, he knew that would never work. Not with Anna. He could have bluffed his way with any of his mistresses in the past, but Anna was real. What they had between them was real and was worth repairing—keeping. And he was terrified he wouldn't get that back. In the end, his fear won. "I'll leave you to your contemplation. If you should have need of me though…." Caring for a woman as much as he did her was uncharted territory for him, and right now, he was thoroughly lost.

She nodded. "I'll call for you."

It was on the tip of his tongue to admit everything, but then his insecurities got the better of him and he realized he was nothing after all, good for nothing except scandal and hurt feelings and disappointment. That was all he would be. "Do you still attend the ball with me tomorrow?"

"Yes, of course." She gave him a tiny smile, but it was a watery affair. "I have looked forward to it, and perhaps I'll not be in a temper with you by then."

A modicum of relief swept through him. "You will be gorgeous, if that glimpse of you in your gown I had the other day is any indication." He hadn't anticipated spending Christmas awkwardly wondering about the state of his marriage.

"Thank you." For one second, he thought she might have thawed, for there was a softness about her expression and eyes, but it soon faded, and she waved him away. "Good night, Edmund. I hope you will come to realize what is most important in your life and where your heart and future truly lie."

Of course he already knew that, but how to tell her so it wouldn't seem as if he was only saying it to get back into her good graces? Then he drew inspiration from Lady Ettesmere. "I believe that occasionally, a couple needs to know a few bad times else the union will feel incomplete." Wasn't that what happened in the dowager's life, but then those things weren't discussed and pushed away, left to fester. "A life cannot be built on only good things and happiness, for how else will we come to appreciate those things when they come if there is no friction, no struggle?"

It was perhaps the most insightful thing he'd ever said to anyone.

For the space of a few heartbeats, there was absolute silence in the space, then a tiny sound emanated from her. "Oh, Edmund. I think you are right."

God, it was the sweetest benediction. He pressed a hand to his heart. "I *am* sorry, you know. Never would I have said those things ordinarily. Don't know why I did. I only knew what you and I share is too new, too special, and I'm too selfish. I didn't want to share any aspect of it." It wasn't an excuse, but it was honest.

"I do know." She held out a hand to him. Tears made her eyes luminous. "I don't want to fight with you, and we are still coming to know each other, but tell me the truth. Did you only marry me for my fortune?"

The time had come for at least a little truth. "I won't lie and say that an infusion of funds into my pockets wouldn't help the situation, but no, that wasn't the only reason." He joined her on the bed, sat beside her, dared to bring her hand to his lips and kiss the middle knuckle. "Quite frankly, the more time I spend with you, the more I am coming to wonder how I ever got along without you by my side." He cleared his throat. "And I also wonder what the devil I ever did good enough in my convoluted and scandalous life that allowed me to win you."

It wasn't quite the declaration he still needed to give her, but it was a start and would give him the time he needed to gather his courage, until he was quite certain he loved her without condition.

"Oh!" A sound much like a cross between a laugh and a cry escaped her. "You are such a dear." Then she pounced, caught him by surprise. The force of her attack propelled him onto his back, and they fell together in a tangle of limbs.

Edmund didn't mind, and he took full advantage of her forgiveness. After all, what better way was there to usher in Christmas than in bed with his wife?

CHAPTER SEVENTEEN

December 25, 1820

"OH, MY GOODNESS, I so wish I could see this gown on myself," she whispered to her maid. "It feels so luxurious."

"That is exactly how it looks, my lady." The maid tightened the laces at the back of the lavender gown. "With the emerald jewelry Lord Evermore insisted you wear, you will have all eyes on you tonight."

"If they are, I certainly won't know it." She shared a laugh with younger woman. "Do you think the gown fancy enough? The hue is not exactly a Christmas color."

"Think of it this way. Where other ladies will be wearing greens and reds and perhaps even whites, you will stand out in a color all your own. With your dark hair and eyes, no one will forget you." The maid fussed with how the gown lay on Anna's form. "Besides that, it shows enough of your décolletage that your husband will be pleased."

Anna snorted. "I don't want to be on display like that."

"It's quite tasteful, I assure you, and with your hair upswept like it is, you look like a queen." She patted Anna's shoulder. "I'm going to bring your jewelry over."

"All right." She put a hand to her temple, encouraged a thin curl to hang down then did the same on the other side. When the maid slipped jewelry about her neck, the coolness of the metal sent a shiver down her spine. It was every bit as elegant and exciting as she'd dreamed. "There is a possibility I'll play piano for the guests who will be at the ball tonight."

"Oh? That's exciting." After she fastened the necklace, she then fastened a bracelet around Anna's left wrist.

"It is. Evermore had either spoken with the host and told him about my talents or the Earl of Ettesmere did, but I was sent a note yesterday asking me if I would play a few Christmas carols for the assemblage. I'm both excited and nervous."

"You will be fine, and your father would be proud."

Tears welled in her eyes. "Thank you. I often wonder if he's given me thought since I married."

"If he hasn't, then he is a nodcock." The maid fussed with how the opera-length gloves lay on Anna's arms. "There is an emerald stick pin included in the parure. I'm going to thread that into your hair for added sparkle."

"Thank you. It's your artistry that makes me presentable. I cannot wait for the viscount to see me." Currently, Edmund was downstairs talking with the dowager and showing Poppy off to a few of her guests that she had in for an intimate dinner tonight.

With a smile, Anna traced the outline of her wedding ring beneath the glove. When he'd come upstairs last night, he'd been so sweet in his timidity and vulnerability. Though he'd apologized profusely, he still hadn't shared his feelings with her, but she was confident that would come with time. Various events from his past kept him reticent, and she understood that to a point. But they'd made up spectacularly and had spent the bulk of the night tangled in the sheets in various interesting positions.

No, it certainly didn't feel like their marriage was only one of convenience, and that pleased her beyond measure. Except for the fact he still withdrew before releasing his seed, everything was very nearly perfect. If he trusted her, if he were coming to love her after all that she'd shared with him, then why was he still letting fear control him instead of adding to their already little family?

"Your husband told me to inform you that the carriage would be ready and waiting in ten minutes," Meredith said as she sailed into the room.

The maid patted Anna's shoulder. "The pin in your hair is lovely." She sucked in a breath, but Anna couldn't fathom why. "Good luck tonight."

"Thank you." She waited until the maid exited the room before responding to Meredith. "I'm ready now."

"Ah, good." The faint clink of porcelain echoed in the space. "I brought tea. Thought it might steady your nerves, but Evermore will be pleased by your looks tonight. The lavender is a wonderful color for you."

"Thank you." Anna smiled. "The viscount really is trying, and because he is, he's quite endeared himself to me." The feeling of being in love was unparalleled. Was it difficult and hurtful at times? Of course, but then anything could be if it meant much to a person.

"How interesting. Do you love him?" There was nothing in Meredith's voice that revealed how she felt about it one way or another.

"I truly think I do. Before, I was only happy when playing my piano. Over the last few days, I have discovered I am happy when he is with me, and my piano playing is enhanced because of it. And the ability to be an immediate mother? Well, that has been life changing." The smile she flashed felt this side of loony. "It's a wonderful feeling. I hope you come to experience it sometime too."

"Ha." Meredith scoffed. "Being beholden to a man is not on my agenda."

"Oh, but it won't be like that with the right person." Despite the hiccups along the way, Edmund was so very different from other men. Now she knew why none of those men had asked for her hand; they were not for her.

"I shall bear that in mind." Porcelain clinked against porcelain. The tinkle of a spoon against a cup filled the air. "Regardless, I am glad for you. The viscount and I may never see eye to eye, and I still think it's beyond scandalous having his bastard as a prominent part of his household, but you seem content with this life." She put a warm teacup into Anna's hand.

"Thank you for the tea." She couldn't help a sigh. "Life is what you make of it, Meredith. You can either be miserable or be happy, but both take the same amount of effort. I learned that long ago when I lost my eyesight." When she sipped her tea, she wrinkled her nose. Despite the excessive amount of sugar in the cup, the drink tasted bitter. "Did this tea come from the kitchens?"

"Oh, it's a new blend I picked up in the shops. I thought it would be interesting to try. Do you like it?"

"It's…" Anna took another mouthful and shook her head. "It's horribly bitter. Why did you add so much sugar? I don't usually take my tea like that."

"I might have miscounted the lumps, but the tea should be good." An odd sort of excitement echoed in Meredith's voice. "It came highly recommended for my purposes."

"It is, ah…" An intense wave of exhaustion came over Anna. Why couldn't she keep her eyes open? The teacup drooped in her hand. "…doesn't taste good."

"Oh, I'm sorry to hear that." Meredith removed the cup from her lax fingers. Something thudded on the carpeting nearby. "Are you feeling quite the thing, Lady Evermore? You look as if you could fall out of your chair."

"I am…" What? She couldn't remember. There was a fog of some sort in her mind, dampening her thoughts and making everything else fuzzy. "…so tired. Need to lie down…." Before Edmund came up when the carriage arrived.

But where were they going? She couldn't remember.

"That's a good idea." Meredith half-pulled, half-pushed Anna to her feet. "Let me help you." Her words sounded as if they were whispered from a hundred miles away. "But I rather doubt Evermore will find you...."

Anna frowned, tried to fight off the companion's claw-like hold. "Why would you say that?" Surely Meredith didn't drug her.

No! But her limbs wouldn't obey her brain's slow commands to get away. As panic climbed her throat, she sank deeper and deeper into sucking darkness.

WHEN ANNA AWOKE, she couldn't move her arms or legs, and for the first few minutes, she didn't understand why. She certainly wasn't in her familiar bedchamber and there most definitely wasn't the pleasant warmth of blankets around her. The more she concentrated, the more she came to believe her ankles were tied, as were her wrists, and they were secured behind her back.

To say nothing of the fact that she was wet. That swept away some of the fatigue from her mind. It smelled like the sea around her, and she was quite chilled. So much so that her teeth were chattering. Then she became aware of the slap of water.

"I'm sitting in water!" It came up to her chest. Where the devil was she?

An odd but slightly familiar creaking sounded around her. As she tried to calm her racing heart and regulate her breathing, she thought about all the times she'd gone to the shore. Where along that stretch could she have been placed? Then the answer came to her, and it was more frightening than she could imagine.

"Dear God, why am I in the sea in a... bathing wagon?" Panic welled in her chest in a hot wave. She tried without success to tug free of her bonds, but the knots held too well.

"It's about time you woke. I began to fear I'd given you too much laudanum." Annoyance wove through Meredith's voice. "Not that I would have minded your demise in that way, but there is a part of me that wishes you to suffer."

"Why?" The hatred coming from the other woman slammed into her chest like a blow. "Please help me. I'm freezing." Then she gasped. "My gown is ruined!" And where was Edmund? The panic grew and expanded upon itself. "Where is my husband?"

"If luck is with me, he's already gone to the ball." Meredith came close enough to dig the fingernails of one hand into Anna's shoulder. "For years I have catered to whatever *you* wanted to do, which was nothing."

"I don't understand." Truly, she didn't. She shook her head and tried to ignore her discomfort. "My father hired you as a companion. Did you not understand what the position entailed?"

"Don't you dare think to mock me." Meredith moved quickly even through the water. She splashed about until she was in front of Anna. Then there was a swift, hard slice of pain through her cheek when Meredith slapped her. "Do you know how dull you are? We could have gone to the opera, museums, taken carriage rides through Rotten Row, mingled with titled men at society events, flirted our way into gifts and other fripperies, but you dislike society."

"None of that is real! It's all a big game of cat and mouse. I didn't want that. I wanted love. That was all."

"Your head has been stuffed full of fairytales and stories that will never come true." There was no mirth in Meredith's laugh. "All you wanted to do was play the damned piano."

"That is where my passion lies! Besides, my father never allowed me to do anything outside of the house. You knew that too." She shook her head. "If you didn't enjoy that the life you had with me, why didn't you give notice? My father would have found someone else." None of this made sense. And she was so cold. Shivering became uncontrollable.

"Because as dull as you are, getting my living through you was too good to relinquish." Bitterness sat heavy on the other woman's words. "Just when I thought I had you relying exclusive-ly on me, that damned carriage accident happened, and you met

Lord Evermore." She spat as if the very utterance of his name was foul to her. "The two of you came up with a ridiculous plan. Then you married the king of scandals after knowing him all of two days."

"What difference does it make to you? If you despise me so much you should be glad I'm not your responsibility any longer." She was done with being pushed around by this woman.

"Are you that dense?" Meredith grabbed her chin and yanked her head upward. She stuck her face close to Anna's, but the bobbing illumination from a lantern hanging near the far end of the wagon didn't allow for much recognition. "I don't like you. I have never been fond of you. The only thing you were to me was a way to make a living and enjoy the luxurious life while I could."

Tears stung Anna's eyes. "You used me, just like everyone else always wanted to." It was demoralizing to know she couldn't see what this woman had truly been. "I thought we were friends."

"How could I be friends with the likes of you?" Such disgust threaded through the inquiry, it smacked into Anna's chest. "So now, I'm taking my revenge and your money." She snorted. "Didn't you ever wonder how so many accidents could happen to one woman?"

Anna gasped. A frown pulled at her lips as all of those things flitted through her mind. Could one woman have been able to accomplish each one of those things by herself? Perhaps, but that answer rankled. "You were behind them all?" At least she had a reason, and it wasn't because she was suddenly unlucky.

"Of course."

"How could you have procured a snake by yourself?" It didn't make sense, and neither could Meredith have been in two places at once since the companion wasn't even at the scene of some of the accidents. "You had help."

"A pity you're so clever. It won't help you to escape, but yes. There were others who I paid to make certain things happen to you." A certain smugness lingered in the other woman's voice.

"I don't understand." Anna shook her head, for she was still quite groggy from the drug. The effort to puzzle everything through was nearly beyond her. "Why would you do this?"

"Marriage, and letting that womanizer fuck your brains out, has taken the remainder of your intelligence." More annoyance threaded through Meredith's voice as she released Anna's chin and gave her a shove.

"There is no need to be vulgar." Once more Anna pulled at her bonds, but the other woman—and whomever had helped her—had done her work too well.

"*Why* did I do this?" Meredith laughed, and it was a horrible sound that Anna didn't recognize. "Because of your will. You never managed to change it. I got a look at it when we both had to sign it, remember? *I'm* your sole beneficiary, because *I* was your only friend until *he* came along with his baby and turned your head." She splashed around until she once more stood at Anna's back. "Well, I want the life that was promised to me with that money."

"And the only way you can have it is to kill me." A gasp escaped Anna. "*How* did you manage the accidents?" The need to know wouldn't leave her.

"Finally, your head is out of the laudanum clouds, and you can see." Her laugh was nearly a cackle. "I wanted to hasten your death instead of waiting years for you to die naturally. I want to actually live where you have let your father coddle you into being fearful, and I'll do so from your inheritance."

"That is completely mad." Anna's teeth chattered loudly together. "If you wanted more money over and above your salary, why didn't you just ask?"

"Because you have been handed everything you've ever wanted, yet you don't want anything!" The lantern light swung wildly, no doubt bandied about in the breeze. "You're blind and people can't help but like you. I'm me, but no man ever turns an eye to me when you're in the room."

This line of thinking was ridiculous. "Jealousy doesn't become anyone." Anna scoffed and shook her head. "Also, I don't recall any offers. Once men realize I'm blind, they stopped coming 'round."

"You are such a fool. Do you think Lord Evermore was the exception?" Incredulity rang in the question. "That he saw something in you none of the others had? You assumed no other man could accept your blindness?" Meredith's laughter made her even colder than she already was. "*I* warned potential suitors away. Told them you had the pox, for how else were you blinded?"

"Dear God, you are a horrible person." Hot anger stabbed through Anna's chest. How could someone close to her want to sabotage her life so badly? And how had she not known about it? But then, Meredith had always been slightly negative. Apparently, it wasn't merely an off-putting personality.

"Perhaps, but that all depends on the perspective." Her chuckle made Anna want to cast up her accounts. "I have always been good at making friends, manipulating people, really, to suit my purposes. In my experience, people don't wish to think too deeply on their own, so if someone with the talent for managing comes along, they'll follow right behind. It was quite easy to do with a few members of the staff, or the tea café. The list goes on. When it comes down to brass tacks, many people are motivated either by physical gratification or coin. It matters not to me as long as we all have our needs met."

The more she discovered about the woman, the more appalled she grew. "Why did you become a companion, then?" It was bizarre to carry out a conversation while she was tied and sitting in the sea, facing certain death at the hands of a mad woman.

"Variety? Boredom? Does it matter?" Meredith snorted. "I saw you as a mark, so wanted to make certain you remained alone, lonely, unwanted, with no one except me, your *adoring* companion, your only friend."

Anna gagged, and when a bit of bitter bile made its way into her mouth, she spat it out then swallowed a few times to prevent that from happening again. "I wrote you into my will, and I *trusted* you." What did that say about her? She gasped. *"That's why you didn't want me to change it immediately."*

"Oh, *now* you have a brain in your head?" Meredith laughed, and in the damp darkness, it was an oily sound. "Upon your death, I'm a very wealthy woman."

As panic continued to climb Anna's throat, she tried to remain as calm as she could. "You'll truly let me drown after being with me for so many years? After I thought we were friends?"

"You truly are pathetic. I was never your friend." For a few seconds, she remained quiet. "And yes, I have no qualms in letting you drown. I plan to tell your lovesick husband you decided to go ahead of him and that you'll meet him at the ball."

The implications of that chilled Anna's blood, but the other words gave her pause and an odd uplift in spirit. "He loves me?"

"You're even stupider than I realized, even if you are blind." Meredith dug the toe of her half boot into Anna's side, laughed when she cried out. "Of course he loves you. He follows you around the house with puppy dog eyes, hangs on your every word, but he's got it into his head he's not good enough, that he's too tainted by scandal to truly let himself tell you of his feelings. Perhaps, after all, you *are* well-matched. Too bad you'll be dead."

"But—"

"Enough." Meredith grabbed a handful of Anna's hair and yanked her head backward. "By the time he realizes something is wrong, the tide will have come in and you'll meet Davy Jones personally." Again, she laughed, and Anna's stomach muscles convulsed. "Once I receive my money, I'm going on a tour of the world with one of the footmen in your father's employ. We have been seeing each other for years, and hatched this scheme between us so we can finally know how the other half lives. Let someone else cater to *us* for a change."

A wad of tears lodged in Anna's throat as the reality of the situation pressed in. "You're insane."

"Perhaps, but at least I have lived, and don't we all need to be slightly insane to survive this life where the divides are so wide?"

When she tried to protest, Meredith was quick to wrap a dirty fabric gag over her mouth.

"Sweet dreams, Anna. So foolish you are, and it will serve your husband right. Perhaps his reckoning has come, and while he grieves, I shall enjoy myself thanks to your benevolence." After another laugh, the dratted woman said, "Happy Christmas, Lady Evermore." The light bobbed. Splashing reached Anna's ears. The sound of a wooden door banging into place echoed, then Anna was alone with the ever-moving tide.

Never had she felt as low or as hopeless as she did now. To be completely betrayed by a person she'd trusted left her stunned, yet in a way, she wasn't surprised. Her sheltered upbringing and the vulnerability of her blindness—perhaps even her longing for acceptance and love—had opened her up unsavory types. The water was nearing her chin, and that caused her to panic even more. She wouldn't be able to tell Edmund goodbye or how grateful she was that he'd been in her life for that brief time. Her only regret was that they hadn't met sooner, to have more time together. Or that she wouldn't live long enough to see him grow into the man she knew he could be.

Tears sprang to her eyes and made hot tracks onto her cheeks. Would Poppy miss her? She wouldn't know what happened to her surrogate mother, and poor Edmund would be lost too deeply in mourning, he would probably never marry again. In one fell swoop, Meredith would destroy three lives.

What was this world coming to when women preyed upon other women, all out of a love for money? Despite trying to rally, to rise above her circumstances, a sob of hopelessness escaped.

I am so sorry, Edmund. I never wanted anything like this. For any of us.

CHAPTER EIGHTEEN

December 25, 1820
Night of Christmas Ball

D AMNATION.

The long case clock in the corridor struck the ten o'clock hour as Edmund left the nursery suite. He was running horribly behind schedule after proudly showing Poppy to the dowager's dinner guests as well as engaging in conversation with them. Since he and his wife were expected across town at a ball most imminently, they needed to hurry.

"Anna? We must go. We are already grossly late," he called as he strode along the corridor, tugging on his kid gloves as he went.

Oddly enough, there was no answer from their suite. When he'd left her earlier as she'd begun the task of dressing, she had been excited about the evening's entertainment.

"Anna?"

"You won't find her there, my lord."

He frowned as Miss Grafton came up the stairs toward him. "Why not?"

"Lady Evermore decided to go ahead to the ball. She wished to warm up on the piano, but she asked me to tell you that she can't wait for you to arrive."

Interesting. "Thank you." Yet muscles pulled in his gut.

Something wasn't right. "How does she have the address? I didn't mention a name or anything else that would direct her to the correct townhouse."

Slight panic jumped into the woman's expression. "Uh, she must have gotten it from the butler or dowager."

"Ah." Except he hadn't told anyone that information. There wasn't a need, for he had intended to escort Anna to and from the ball himself. The dowager had declined to go due to other plans. The only other person who had need of the direction was the driver, and he was currently waiting at the curb. "I suppose that makes sense." He frowned when the woman relaxed. "Oh, and Miss Grafton. You had best change clothes."

"Oh, why?"

"It seems you have been walking the shore. There's a salt rim on your hem that has crept up quite a way into your skirting." Again, another oddity, for it was far too late at night for anyone to be prowling the shore, especially since high tide was upon them. Unless one had a lantern, it was pitch dark outside, especially with the clouds rolling in.

"Ah, yes. Well, walking the shore is good exercise and with rain expected tonight, I wanted to do it ahead of the weather. I suppose I'd forgotten that the tide is almost at its highest point just now." She didn't drop her dark gaze, and he continued to hold it as he contemplated her answers. "Well, enjoy your evening, Lord Evermore. I'm quite certain it will be a night you'll not soon forget."

"Indeed." He narrowed his eyes. "Happy Christmas, Miss Grafton." Then he continued down the stairs to the ground floor. Something wasn't right, and that unsettled feeling wouldn't leave his gut. Anna wouldn't have gone ahead without knowing where the ball was being held, and quite frankly, she wouldn't have wished to go without him. That was out of character for her. And after how close they had become in recent days, how affectionate they'd been toward each other, after knowing Lady Ettesmere wished to show Poppy off to her guests, his wife would have certainly wished to do all of that with him. To say nothing of the fact that she'd wanted to make sure he and she entered the ballroom together with her on his arm.

It was a matter of pride with her and she'd been quite giddy about it, for she wasn't of the *ton*, and this was to be more or less her debut as Lady Evermore.

With a soft curse, Edmund turned around and ran back up the stairs. There was a decent chill in the air tonight, so he wished to wear a jaunty red muffler Anna had bought him from one of the shops. As he opened the door to his suite, he startled Andrews, who was tidying the adjoining dressing room.

"My apologies, old chap," he murmured with a slight grin. "I came back for a muffler."

"No need for apologies. I had intended to seek you out, in any event, before you left for the night." As the man came toward him, shadows pooled in his eyes. Lines were more prominent on his face as worry shaped his visage. "I witnessed something quite ominous earlier that has left me at sixes and sevens."

"Oh? What was it?"

"That damned Miss Grafton." The valet shook his head. "I have never cared for her. She puts on airs in the servants' hall as if she's better than her position."

"I can just imagine." So it wasn't just him who'd gotten a specific feeling about her.

"Well, I'd happened to glance out the window earlier tonight to see if it had started raining yet. It was rather dark, but she was down on the shore, holding a lantern and dragging a rather large bundle being assisted by a man I didn't recognize."

Edmund frowned. "What was the bundle?"

"I couldn't tell. Seemed to be wrapped in a cloak. I don't know. It was too dark."

"Where did they take the bundle?" If it was rubbish, surely they wouldn't have disposed of it in the sea.

"They left my line of vision, so I couldn't say, but later, one of the maids commented on the fact someone had left the kitchen door open and it was too cold for that nonsense."

"So then Meredith and whomever was with her left through the kitchens." Edmund's frown deepened. "Did the cloak come from this house?"

"It could have. Would you like me to go through the clothes press here first?"

"Absolutely. It should be a rather easy search, for I don't own such a garment, but I believe the viscountess does." Cold foreboding twisted down his spine as he followed the valet on his rounds. "Please tell me everything is in order."

Andrews was quite meticulous as he went through every piece of clothing in the clothes press, bureau, and everywhere else garments could be stored. "My lady has two cloaks. One in black and one in navy. The navy one is missing." When Edmund would have reacted, he held up a hand. "It might be with the butler, for she might have planned to wear it tonight."

"Oh, God. Miss Grafton told me Anna decided to go ahead to the ball and wanted me to meet her there."

"I highly doubt that, my lord." The valet closed the doors of the clothes press. "She was quite excited to attend with you. As her maid said, the lady was aflutter."

Though he grinned, it was tight. "What the devil is going on here?" He moved into the bedchamber. Nothing seemed out of place. "Take a quick tour of the dressing room and search for clues."

"Of course." It took less than a minute before Andrews called out for him with a trace of panic in his voice. "Look there," he said when Edmund joined him. In front of Anna's vanity, a teacup lay on the plush carpeting, with a dark stain of liquid beneath it as if it had been dropped unexpectedly or completely forgotten. "The lady is usually quite meticulous."

"So she is." Damn it all. This didn't bode well. Kneeling, Edmund pressed a finger to the stain then brought it to his nose, and sniffed. "There isn't really a strange scent." When he experimentally licked at the tea, he immediately spit. "It's bitter.

And overly sweet. Perhaps to cover—"

"Laudanum," they said together.

"Shit." Edmund sprang to his feet. "Where the devil is my wife?" Hot panic welled in his chest. His heart squeezed to the point of pain. "I don't believe she went ahead without me."

"Neither do I, my lord, but I haven't seen her since she came upstairs to dress."

"Damn, damn, damn." He strode across the room and yanked at the velvet bell pull. "I'm beginning to have a bad feeling, Andrews."

"As am I, my lord." One of his hands curled into a fist. "If I discover that horrid Miss Grafton had anything to do with my lady's disappearance…." He slammed the fist into his opposite palm.

"I appreciate your support, my friend." As he waited for Anna's maid to arrive, he paced the space between the door and the window. "Could someone have snatched her because she's an heiress?" When they'd first met, she had mentioned that as being one reason her father was overly protective. "Will I receive a ransom note shortly?" God, what a coil. His coffers weren't that full, and that meant he'd need to apply to Graham, who would lecture him and tell him, once again, that he was a disappointment.

"At this point, anything is possible," Andrews said with a fierce frown. Obviously, Anna had made quite an impression on the staff here in Brighton.

Finally, the maid came into the room. Her eyes widened when she saw him and Andrews, and to her credit, no doubt, they looked quite menacing.

"Is something amiss, my lord?"

"That is what I'm trying to determine." He crossed his arms at his chest as he stared at her. "Where is Lady Evermore?"

"I couldn't say, my lord. I finished with her toilette at least two hours ago."

"Did she say what her plans were?"

"Only that she was waiting for you to come up and escort her downstairs to the carriage that would be along any moment."

Damn it. He exchanged a speaking glance with Andrews before resting his gaze back on the maid. "So she had every intention of going to the ball with me tonight?"

"Of course, my lord." Confusion crossed the young woman's face. "Why would she go without you? She was all aflutter and couldn't wait to dance with you."

"Why indeed." He heaved out a sigh of frustration. "Did anything untoward occur while you'd last seen her?"

"Not that I can remember." She frowned as she darted a glance between him and the valet. "I left when Miss Grafton came in with a tea tray. She glared at me as if I'd done something wrong, so I hastened my retreat."

It seemed that none of the staff had a fond word to say about the companion. "Thank you for your help. You're free to return to your room."

She bobbed a curtesy. "Is all well with Lady Evermore? She is a lovely woman, and it would break my heart if she is ill."

"Let us hope she isn't ill, but she *is* missing. If you would go to the kitchens and servants' hall and ask about?"

"Of course, my lord." The maid fairly flew from the room.

He threw a look of inquiry to the valet. "What now?"

"It sounds more and more likely that Miss Grafton knows something regarding your wife's disappearance. Where is she?"

The urge to cast up his accounts grew strong. After he swallowed to stave off retching, Edmund said, "I passed her on the stairs not twenty minutes ago. That's when she told me Anna had gone ahead to the ball."

"I'll search the house for her."

"Good man. If you find her, secure her to her room until I return. Tie her to a piece of furniture if you have to."

Once the valet left, Edmund immediately went to the nursery suite. His pulse rushed hard through his veins, but he took a peek at Poppy, who'd been dressed for bed and currently was lost to dreamland, asleep in her cradle. The nursery maid startled in the chair nearby. She glanced up from the handiwork in her lap. "Is all well, my lord?"

"Lady Evermore is missing. Please do not leave the baby alone until we have located the viscountess and have brought her home." The last thing he needed was an attack on the baby.

"I will lock the doors behind you," the maid said as she rose to her feet.

"Thank you." Once in the corridor, the telltale click of the locking mechanism sliding into place reached his ears, and he nodded. Andrews came bounding up the stairs with his expression mirroring a thundercloud. "Tell me."

"Miss Grafton is gone, and there is evidence a bag was packed rather hastily."

"Damn it." He shoved a hand through his hair. "I'm going to the shore. Miss Grafton had just come back from there, for the bottom three or four inches of her dress were damp and had a salt rim."

"I'm coming with you."

"While I appreciate that, I need you to look for the damned companion. Under no circumstances will she be allowed to leave Brighton this night. Stop every damned vehicle on the street if you have to. I want her found and to be held accountable if Anna is...." He couldn't finish the thought as emotion rose in his throat. "Well, just find her. I will engage Bow Street if need be to bring that woman back here."

Andrews put a hand to Edmund's shoulder. "Keep the faith."

"I am trying." They both ran down the two flights of stairs at a reckless pace then separated once on the ground floor. He bellowed for the butler, and when that man appeared from a small work room, looking slightly frazzled, Edmund grunted. "My greatcoat, if you please. Lady Evermore is missing. I'm going out to try and locate her."

"Missing, my lord?"

He followed the butler to the coat closet in the entryway.

"Apparently so. Her companion told me she went ahead to the ball and for me to meet her there. Did she?"

"No, my lord. I didn't let either of them out of the house, and the carriage driver said no one ever came to the vehicle, so when it began to rain, he returned to the mews."

Damnation. I should have paid more attention.

"I feared as much." After yanking the outerwear from the other man's fingers, he shoved his arms into the sleeves. "Andrews is out searching for Miss Grafton. We believe she is behind Lady Evermore's disappearance. Render him assistance if you need to. Meanwhile, put the housekeeper and everyone else on alert. Both women are gone, and if something dire is at play, we might need to summon a doctor for the viscountess."

"Of course, my lord." The butler laid a staying hand on Edmund's arm while a look of concern crossed his face. "I wish you good fortune on your quest. She is quite vulnerable and—"

"I am well aware of that, but I won't come back without her." He could do no less, for that woman held his heart in her more than capable hands.

Then he was off like a shot, running through the corridors despite the dowager's guests gawking at him from the floor above. A footman waited at the rear door with a lantern in hand, the candle's flame dancing merrily behind the glass.

"I appreciate the foresight. Thank you." After that, he jogged down the short stretch of lawn and when he finally arrived on the shore, he lifted the lantern.

As Christmas went, it was a miserable night. The darkness was complete. Rain drummed down upon his bare head, quickly saturating his hair. With his free hand, he turned up the collar of his coat to keep the worst of the moisture away from his body. The pounding surf echoed the frantic thud of his heartbeat. There were no obvious clues as to Anna's disappearance nearby, so he walked a bit down the shore, before stopping once more.

There! In the sand, nearly obliterated by the rain were what appeared to be drag marks, as if someone had brought something heavy through the area and perhaps rested it here before heading onward. Two distinct sets of footprints marred the smoothness of the sand, not yet taken away by the creeping tide.

Quickly, with his heart in his throat, Edmund followed the tracks, but when Anna didn't turn up—alive or dead—the worry knotting his insides grew. Where the hell was she? Surely the damned companion didn't bury his wife....

Then, the hulking shadow of a bathing wagon came slowly into view. He hadn't seen it before due to the dark and the rain, and by all accounts, it shouldn't have been out on the shore at this time of night. The contraption had been pushed a bit from the shore; the high tide was halfway up its side.

Oh, hell. Instinctively, he knew.

"Anna!" As fast as his feet would go, Edmund ran over the sand, fighting to stay upright as the wet sand shifted beneath his shoes. "Anna!" There was no answer. Only the quiet of the night and the unrelenting surf.

His thoughts were a mess. He couldn't lose her now. Not when he loved her beyond all doubt. There was no more fear as courage swept in to obliterate everything else. Why hadn't he told her how he felt when he had the chance? If she had died thinking he didn't care....

Running into the surf, Edmund was forced to battle through the strong waves. He tried his best to keep the lantern out of the water. Finally, after being pushed back more times than he could count, he reached the wagon. The damned rear door was locked, and no amount of tugging would gain him access. Using the wagon itself for stability, he carefully made his way around to the front part of the vehicle that dipped downward into sea. Once more battered by the waves, he kept his footing by a miracle. A flap of canvas acted as the door on this side, and it fluttered like mad in the wind and rain. Somehow, he went through and clambered over the wagon's frame.

"Anna?"

A muffled shout mixed with a gagging sound met his ears.

"Anna!" *Oh, God.* He held up the lantern, for his wife sat on the sand while the waves kept crashing over her head. Why didn't she get up? After hanging the wire loop of the lantern on a nearby hook in the wooden frame, Edmund maneuvered to her feet and knelt onto the sand. The waves nearly knocked him over, but he planted his knees as she put his hands beneath the surf to explore. "Damnation. Your ankles are bound." When she nodded and made a noise again, he leaned over her and wrenched the rag off.

"Edmund, you came!" Anna whimpered, and the sound went straight to his heart. "It was Meredith. She's crazed. Trying to kill me for my money."

"We eventually figured she was behind your disappearance but didn't know why." When a wave slammed into his back, he faltered. "Over my dead body will she accomplish her plans." Quickly, even though his fingers and toes were freezing, he worked at the knots in the rope that bound her ankles. "Where is she?"

"I… I don't know." Her teeth chattered together so much she could barely form words. "Said she planned to r-r-return to London, t-t-tour the world with a footman in my father's household."

"Living a lavish lifestyle on your inheritance." Anger filled his voice. He moved behind her, discovered her wrists were tied in the same fashion, then worked on those knots. "She's a real piece of work. I'll send a Bow Street man after her, make her come back and answer to her crimes."

"How could I n-n-not sense what she truly was?"

"You trust easily, assume people have the same heart as you." Finally, the knots were undone, and the rope fell away from her wrists.

The cry of relief mixed with pain tightened his chest, but he stood and pulled her up with him. "We have to get you out of here. You must be freezing." Now that he had a good look at her in the weak lantern light, there was a slight blue tinge to her lips. Her hands in his were far too cold for his liking. "How you managed to survive so long with the tide breaking over your head.... If I had waited just a half hour more, you could have been...."

He'd almost lost her.

"I tried my best to free myself." She held up her wrists. Evidence of scratches and claw marks marred the skin. "But it did no good, so I prayed and I hoped, but I knew you would come in time," she whispered as she clung to him when the waves almost swept her off her feet. "I am sorry we've missed the ball. I so w-w-wanted to dance with you after all our lessons."

That's what worried her? "Silly goose." He pressed a kiss to her wet temple as he guided her toward the flap of canvas. "There will be plenty of parties during the social season here in Brighton."

Once he climbed over the wooden frame, he turned back to assist her over. Anna stumbled. She cried out, just beyond his reach.

"My skirts are caught on something below the water." Panic threaded through the statement, and he couldn't imagine what she'd already endured while alone.

The tide went ever higher as they lingered. "Shit." Edmund came back over the frame. When he reached her location, he took her skirting in hand and then wrenched with all of his strength. The sound of wet fabric tearing echoed dully. "I promise to buy you three new gowns to replace this one. Just come out of here with me! You are far more valuable than a damned frock."

She clung to his hands, pushed through the waves as he guided her over the wooden frame. With the partial blockage of the bathing machine not there to temper the waves, the sea tried its best to suck them into its mass. "Don't let go." Her words were tremulous and full of fear.

"Never." Then the ever-mischievous sea made an instant liar of him. On the next wave, she was torn from his grip, and her scream echoed in his ears. "Anna!" His wife was in the sea, but there was enough of the anemic light from the lantern for him to catch a glimpse of her lavender gown. With his heart in his throat, he threw himself in that direction, paddled about until he was able to close his hand around the fabric then he quickly reeled her into his arms. "Dear God, don't do that to me again."

"I'll try not to." She coughed and sputtered as she wrapped her arms about his shoulders. "I don't know that I'm q-q-quite as fond of the sea as I was before."

The fact she had the wherewithal to joke at a time like this made him grin. "I don't blame you." Edmund picked her up while the waves battered them, and then half-carried half-pulled her around the bathing wagon and finally, after seemingly a lifetime, they reached the shore. Already winded, he didn't stop until they were a bit away from the crashing surf. "Anna, I—"

The unexpected arrival of Miss Grafton interrupted his words. "Why couldn't you just stay away long enough for the sea to claim her?" With a cry of pure rage, she came at him with her hands extended, her fingers curled like claws, and she attacked him with enough force that he was ripped from Anna's hold and sent flying onto his back.

Though the wind was knocked out of him, he wheezed out a few words while struggling to his knees. "At least now I can save myself the expense of having someone track you down and England the coin in prosecuting you, for you won't leave this beach alive."

Above all, protecting Anna was his first priority.

CHAPTER NINETEEN

ANNA SCREAMED WHEN Edmund was wrenched away from her. She didn't know where he'd gone. All around her the rain fell and the surf pounded. They both muffled sound, and she was so cold that she shivered uncontrollably, but her husband was in danger from her companion, who'd apparently gone mad.

I have to do something.

The sounds of fighting drifted to her ears. Would Meredith kill him? She seemed incredibly angry when she flew at him. As Anna ventured away from the area to find something—anything—to use as a weapon, the strong band of a man's arm went around her middle and he lifted her off her feet.

"Put me down!" She kicked out with her feet but couldn't quite catch her captor.

"I will, once you're in the damned sea where you belong." His voice was familiar to her, and she gasped as he carried her toward the pounding surf. He was a footman in the townhouse from London, and he'd no doubt fallen beneath Meredith's oddly hypnotic spell. "I won't be cheated out of my new life."

"Neither of you actually worked for it or earned it." As she renewed her efforts to free herself from his hold, he continued over the sand. Then there was the feeling of being weightless for a few seconds before she hit the cool water of the constantly churning sea. Her scream was swallowed when she went beneath the waves.

Immediately, the fight to survive was renewed. Anna was forced to summon strength from a deep reserve she never knew existed. Kicking her feet and scooping the water with her hands, she fought her way to the surface. When her head broke the surface, she immediately sucked in lungful of air before another wave crashed over her.

The overriding thought that kept her moving and striving toward shore was helping Edmund get away from Meredith. Was the footman waiting for her on the shore? Oh, if he was, she would fight him tooth and nail because on the other side of this horrible night was everything she'd ever dreamed of having in her life.

After what seemed like an eternity, Anna let the power of the waves spit her out onto the shore where she then crawled the rest of the way up until the waves barely brushed her stocking-clad toes. Somehow during her stints in the sea, she'd lost her slippers but was too exhausted to care.

Bang!

The report of a pistol echoed through her ears and sent a stab of worry through her chest. Had the footman shot Edmund? Had her husband somehow got hold of a pistol and shot Meredith? Worry twisted her insides into knots as she staggered toward the sound, but the closer she came, the more dull thuds and grunts indicated the fight hadn't yet ended.

"You fool woman! Instead of shooting me, you killed your partner in crime!"

Oh, dear God, thank you! The sound of Edmund's voice at least reassured her he still lived and that there wasn't an obstacle to her path.

"That *is* unfortunate, but he wasn't that important, really. There are other men." Meredith's words were quite winded; perhaps she was tiring. "Now my money will go that much further."

Anna's skirting caught on a piece of driftwood, and as she

wrenched the fabric from the branch, she uttered a tired sigh. Would this horrible night never end? Then an idea came to her mind. She bent, explored the driftwood with her fingers. It was the perfect length to be able to hold. Perhaps she could wield it as a weapon and in that way help Edmund fight off Meredith, for she was just so sick of being cold and wet.

Above all, she was sick of being told by everyone what she should or shouldn't be doing with her own life.

Wrapping the fingers of one hand around the driftwood as if it were a cane, Anna staggered once more to her feet. She held the makeshift weapon in front of her like a sword, and with every step she took, she strained her ears for clues of how the fight was progressing.

"Give up, Lord Evermore." Meredith panted between words. "I have rage and desperation on my side, and I will not quit until you are both dead."

"Ah, so you've graduated from killing just my wife. If one is good, two bodies must be better?" Edmund grunted. "Why not use your devious mind to actually work toward a decent goal?"

"I have wasted half my life on poor, blind Anna." The sarcasm in her tone was obvious and heavy. "Now I will live for myself."

"Funded by my wife!"

"I deserve it! She owes me for what I've sacrificed." She uttered a cry, and Anna could only imagine that she'd charged at the viscount again.

The dull thud of a body hitting the wet sand drifted to her ears, and it was close, so very close. Hoping the rain and the pounding surf would cover any warning of her approach, Anna crept onward. She tripped over a boot, presumably from the man who'd recently been shot. After righting herself, she took a chance and hoping against hope her instincts were right, she swung out with the piece of driftwood. The jarring *thwack* that resonated in her ears was just as satisfying as feeling the thud of the makeshift weapon as it found purchase somewhere on

Meredith's body. As soon as her former companion crumpled to the sand, Edmund's tired whoop of victory echoed in the night.

"Good show, Anna! You got her."

The next thing she knew, he was on his feet and standing next to her, relieving her of the piece of driftwood. "Is she dead?" In an abstract portion of her brain, Anna didn't care any longer. All she knew was that the woman had tried to kill her, attempted to do the same to Edmund, and there was no other option except to defend herself and her family. "Is it truly over so easily?"

"The sea can come and claim her, for all I care." A soft thump sounded, and she assumed he'd dropped the driftwood. "Yes. It's over."

She put out a hand and clutched his wet sleeve. "For me, please check. I don't know if I can live with myself knowing I took a life, but I need to know."

"Very well." Seconds later, he returned to her position. "Miss Grafton has quite the gash on the side of her head. She is breathing, but shallowly. If you wish it, I will drag her sorry arse back to the townhouse. Otherwise, I am going to leave her here and let the sea have at her as poetic justice for what she would have done to you." His voice broke, and even through the rain there was no mistaking the emotion crowding his throat. "She would have killed you, Anna, with no remorse, for she only wanted your money."

"I know, and she would have killed you as well, just like she'd killed her lover." She could hardly force the words from her own tight throat. "Leave her, then. Meredith has already reaped her fate." She sucked in lungful of breath. "I suppose if she survives, we should see her put into prison. It's what she deserves."

"Agreed."

A sound that was a cross between a snort and a sob escaped her. "This isn't how I'd planned to spend Christmas night. I had a gift to give you and Poppy."

Edmund's tired laughter blended with hers. "On the other hand, knowing that you and I are still alive after the events of this night is a most welcome gift. Wouldn't you say?"

"Yes." Though the whole mess saddened her in a way she would never forget, knowing the nightmare was over brought relief pouring over her. A large shiver racked her body. "Can we please go inside now? It will take hours to warm, for even my bones are frozen."

"Of course." Immediately, he whipped off his mostly wet greatcoat and bundled it about her shoulders. Apparently not content with that, he slipped his arms around her and claimed her lips with his as if he hadn't seen her for years. Over and over, he moved against her mouth, perhaps in an attempt to warm her before he pulled away. "Once everything has quieted down, there are things I wish to say to you that will not be put off any longer."

"I cannot wait to hear." Another shiver shook her frame. It would be so lovely to be in the dry warmth again. "Except, just now, I would rather sink into an overly hot bath, reassure myself that Poppy is safe and blissfully unaware of the night's horrors, and try to forget about what happened tonight." She sighed when he put an arm about her waist. "My slippers were lost in the sea." Thinking upon that now, it was absurdly funny, but all she wanted to do was cry. The night had been so terrible, and those feelings of terror and betrayal wouldn't soon be forgotten. Would the memories forever mar Christmas?

"Then allow me one last chance to play hero," he said against the shell of her ear. Then he scooped her up into his arms and with slow, steady strides, carried her over the sand and toward the townhouse.

EDMUND WAS BESIDE himself with so many emotions as he brought Anna into the house that he could barely think. The beating he'd taken from the insane companion had put cuts and bruises all over his body, but those minor inconveniences were quickly forgotten in the face of knowing his wife still lived and she was finally safe. There would be no more accidents.

Barely had he brought her to the staircase at the front of the house when most of the staff as well as the dowager and her guests greeted them.

Everyone exclaimed at once. They swarmed around them, talking and exclaiming when bits and pieces of the story emerged. Anna drooped with exhaustion, but Lady Ettesmere took command of the situation. She ordered the butler to carry Anna upstairs while telling the housekeeper to immediately have a strong, hot bath drawn. A bevy of maids was dispatched to provide Anna with tea, fresh soap, cold compresses, fluffy towels, and anything else a woman who was nearly murdered could need.

Andrews came over to him, exclaimed over his battered state, and then they compared stories. "I will dispatch a messenger to the Standish home in London telling your wife's father of the traitor within his midst."

"Thank you, but don't bother. She killed him. His body is on the beach. Please also send a messenger to the hosts of the ball we were to attend. Give them our regrets with a brief story of what happened. Perhaps we can come to celebrate the New Year with them instead."

"Of course, my lord." Andrews lifted an eyebrow. "What of the companion?"

He rubbed at his eyes. "She was left unconscious on the sand with a large gash on her head from where Lady Evermore thumped her with some driftwood." His lips twitched. "Bring her sorry arse back to the house. I want her thrown into prison for her crimes."

"I'll take a few footmen with me, my lord."

"Thank you." All Edmund wanted to do was drop onto the nearest horizontal surface and sleep for a thousand years, but there was something much more important to attend to still. After heaving a shuddering sigh, he looked about at the remainder of the people crowded about. "I thank you all for your caring and concern for Lady Evermore. That means more than you can ever know, and once she's feeling more the thing, I'm sure she will thank you herself."

Lady Ettesmere bustled forward. She pushed him toward the stairs. "You are about to drop, my boy. Go upstairs. Set yourself to rights. You can regale us with tales on the morrow after we attend Boxing Day activities."

He shot her a grateful grin. "Thank you. Truly, this has been the most memorable Christmas, and knowing my family is safe is the best gift." Slowly, painfully, he climbed the stairs, but before he retired into his suite, he stopped off into the nursery. He couldn't help it. After the horrific events he'd been through, he needed to reassure himself that his daughter was safe.

When he peered into the cradle, glided a knuckle along her satiny cheek, moisture sprang into his eyes. Everything became clear as he watched Poppy sleep. Nothing was as important as his family, as the people in his life who cared about him and whom he cared about in return. In that moment, all he wanted was to make amends with his siblings. It was ridiculous to spend time holding onto stupid disagreements or holding grudges not of his making when life was so precious.

Once his honeymoon had concluded—not until well after Twelfth Night or beyond, he hoped—he would take Anna to London where they would begin their married life, and his family would be a definite part of it. Beyond that, he wanted to spend time with his Winterbourne half-siblings, come to know them, because they were found family, and that was all that mattered.

On the heels of a yawn, he left the nursery with a nod to the maid, but when he entered his suite through the dressing room door, Anna was no longer in the bath. The water had cooled to lukewarm, and he would make good use of it soon, but first, he moved into the bedroom, and his heart squeezed.

She'd been tucked into bed already, clad in a shift with the covers pulled up to her chin and her black hair damp and curling on the pillows. A cheerful fire crackled behind the decorative metal grate, and the added warmth was much appreciated. The poor dear was already asleep, the dark arcs of her lashes a stark contrast against the paleness of her cheeks. With a tired grin, Edmund returned to the adjoining dressing room.

After pouring out a cup of tea, he gulped down the tepid brew and then had another cup. It took mere moments to strip out of his wet and ruined evening clothing, and his groan was overly loud as he slipped into the bath water faintly scented with lavender. Immediately, some of the aches went out of his muscles. Closing his eyes, he gave himself up to rest and relaxation for a time before emotion overwhelmed him. Then he quietly cried in the tub with his thumbs pressed to his closed eyelids, and what was more, he wasn't ashamed of meeting those feelings. He gave into the emotions racking his insides, let go of the things that no longer mattered, grieved for the things he'd put aside for far too long, gave thanks for everything he did have that helped to make his life complete.

Eventually, once the water went cold and he'd scrubbed off the salt and the grime, Edmund dried off by the fire, then joined his wife beneath the bedclothes. He stayed close to her, for he refused to leave her alone in the night.

IN THE HUSH just before dawn broke, he was awakened by gentle kisses that whispered along his cheeks, beneath his jawline, against the column of his neck, over his pectoral muscles. When he opened his eyes, Anna kneeled beside him in the gloomy darkness, very much like a specter in her lawn shift with her dark hair flowing over her shoulders.

Truly, it was one of the most erotic things to ever happen to him, and his shaft took a hearty interest in her proximity. "Good morning." His voice sounded rough from sleep and being out in the elements earlier that night.

"Good morning." Once more, she leaned over him, and the cloud of her fragrant hair skimmed over his face leaving the scent of apple blossoms behind. "I am glad you're awake."

"How could I not be when you have made certain I am so deliciously back in the here and now?" When he reached for her, she tsked her tongue and batted at his hand. Perhaps it was just as well, for he didn't need to be distracted just now. "We need to talk."

"I imagine we do." Her eyes were dark and glittery in the inky shadows. "When someone you love nearly dies, that usually makes a person think." Concern twisted through her words. She laid a palm on his chest, and he swore her fingertips seared into his skin. "I need to touch you, to remind myself that I am truly awake and that I survived."

"You are and you did. And I am all the gladder for it." That was one way to introduce the subject that loomed between them, but the uncertainty in her expression tugged at his heart. "However, there are words I'd like to say to you."

"I'm waiting, Evermore. In fact, I woke from a dead sleep worrying about those exact things, for they will either further bind us together or pull us apart."

"Oh, sweeting." A wave of love poured over him. Even in sleep she agonized over the state of their union. It was the dearest thing. He cleared his throat. "I want you." Did she still not believe that his feelings were real? "When I thought that damned companion of yours had truly drowned you...." He had to pause to battle back the emotions that were rather too close to the surface again.

"I already know how you physically feel." The clever girl drew her hand slowly down his naked body, danced her fingers over his torso, skimmed them along his abdomen and the clenching muscles there to hover her palm at the pinnacle of his erect member. "Your body reacted almost instantly to my teasing."

He sucked in a quick breath in anticipation. "Anna, I...." How to start this much needed and long overdue conversation? "I am not good at words when they matter. Yes, I can charm any woman I choose when the words are empty and meaningless, but speaking from the heart? I'm rubbish at it."

"Try. For me. Because we both need to hear them." Slowly, she took his length into her hand and wrapped her fingers around its girth. "Else I'm afraid playtime will be postponed."

When had she become such a tease? But he quickly sobered. "All my life, I have felt ignored, pushed away in favor of others, or have been told I'm a dismal failure. I've run away from anything personal or emotional because I believed deep in my soul I wasn't worthy of anything, that I couldn't live up to the Ashdowne or even the Winterbourne legacies." Forcing moisture into his dry throat with a swallow, he continued. "When I met you, I didn't feel any of those things, and as time went on, you made me feel like I'm a damned hero."

"Do you assume you are not?" When she just as slowly pumped her hand along his shaft, Edmund nearly vaulted off the bed.

"For many years, I did all that I could *not* to be that type of man." He laid his hand atop hers, stilling her movement lest he come prematurely. "I didn't want to be noble or to care about anyone. I thought chasing scandal and sin a better use of my time than charity or domestication, but then came you."

"I did nothing."

He snorted. "You did everything! You quietly bossed me, moved me in the ways I needed to go, showed me a better way to behave and why." His voice broke. "When I couldn't find you, in that moment I realized how much I did indeed love you, and I feared I wouldn't have the opportunity to tell you...." The words felt pulled from him, even though he'd thought of nothing else even while he'd slept. "I'd never been in love before, not a love like this. Since you cannot see the masks I've lived behind, you looked deeper and saw the real me, the man I've hidden all these years out of fear, or spite, or anger, and you married me anyway. *That* was the moment I started my fall for you."

Her eyes welled with tears. "That makes me happy to hear."

Suddenly, he needed to hear the same words from her, for much the same reason. "And you?" His voice sounded raw from all the emotions clogging his throat. "Did you only tell me you loved me days ago as an effort to try and charm me?"

"Of course not." A couple of tears fell to her cheeks and broke his resolve. "I meant what I said. I love you, now and always, no matter what is in your past or what waits for you in the future. You will always be the man who holds my heart. You are everything I want from a husband, and when I thought one or the other of us wouldn't survive the night...." Her bottom lip quivered as she stared at him with moisture clinging to her lashes. "I… I need you, Edmund. Not merely as a way of survival, not in a marriage of name only, but because you make life worth living." A tiny hiccupping laugh escaped her. "You make me smile, help me to see the world. I wish to be in it because with you, things aren't quite as frightening."

"Ah, sweeting." He couldn't take it any longer; he had to touch her. Before she could protest, he put his hands on either side of her waist and dragged her over his body so that she straddled his waist. "You have no idea how humbled I am you chose me." Because he'd already waited what seemed like an eternity for this moment, he claimed her lips in a series of long, drugging, demanding kisses that left him panting for breath and her staring down at him with stars in her eyes and love illuminating her expression. "I hope I will always deserve your praise and pride. I hope I will prove worthy of remaining by your side as your husband."

"You haven't failed thus far." With a little squeal, she slid down his body until she lay sprawled on top of him. The friction of her form against his nearly had his eyes crossing. "Have you finished your speech, or is there more?"

"As I said, I am not good with words, but for you, I will spend the rest of my life practicing, just as you do with the piano, until I get it right." Again, he kissed her, and his length pressed painfully against her belly. When he allowed them both to catch their breath, he said, "I love you, Anna. Your infinite patience with me, your nurturing joy with Poppy, they are merely two of the things I hold most dear in my heart."

"And you claim you aren't romantic." She rested her forehead against his while peering into his eyes. Though he would give anything to know what she saw in him, he quietly rejoiced that she'd found something she adored. "I love you too. Perhaps simple is best in matters of the heart."

His world shifted, came back into clarity upon hearing those words. "I don't deserve you. I have nothing to recommend me, and will no doubt need to find gainful employment in order to make a decent life for us."

"Hush, my love. You deserve every good thing in your life. Everything will work out like it is supposed to. Don't lose hope."

"Finding you is enough to ensure that I won't." Edmund found her lips again, and he took his time, seduced her, made love to her mouth, reacquainted himself with the wonder that was his wife. "I want you, sweeting." He cupped her breasts, teased the nipples with the pads of his thumbs, and when she moaned, he smiled. "We are still on our honeymoon, but I will wait if you wish to regain your strength. After all, you were nearly murdered earlier tonight."

The sound she uttered was quite like the purr of a contented cat. "I have rested enough for a while. I'd rather not lose any more time with you."

Was there any wonder why he loved her to distraction? He didn't answer with words. Instead, he framed her face in his hands and plied her with kisses, drinking from her as if he'd never have enough. Once more, the sensation of falling assailed him as he nibbled a path beneath her jaw. Running a hand down the length of her back, at the hem of her shift, he gathered the fabric in his fist and tugged. She took the hint and helped him divest her of the garment. It fell to the floor with nary a whisper, then he covered her exposed skin with kisses, teased and tormented her with his tongue and lips, all in the hopes she would believe actions over words.

Anna's breathing was decidedly labored. "I need you."

"Surely I must do as my lady commands," he whispered, and as his body tensed, he flipped them both over in the bed. The sheets twisted around them. "I didn't fall in love with you, sweeting, I arrived kicking and screaming against being domesticated until I realized this is exactly where I was meant to be all along."

She trembled in his hold. "Perhaps fate was right after all."

"I am not convinced that fate was at play." He plunged a hand between their bodies, slipped his fingers through her feminine curls and found the swollen center of her pleasure. "But every day that goes by, I will walk this path with you because I believe we are both better together than we are apart." He rubbed his fingers over that button and didn't relent until she was near to breaking. "You truly are my catalyst for change, and every day I will count myself grateful that carriage accident landed me on your doorstep."

"Oh, Edmund!" His wife shattered in his arms, coming undone with a gentle sigh and the luxurious arching of her back. She looked at him with eyes luminous with tears. "I rather thought there would be... more tonight after words of love were exchanged."

He grinned, couldn't help it. "It just means I need another chance to do better." Again, he claimed her mouth in a kiss, drugging and deep, showed her with his tongue exactly what he intended to do to her body in mere seconds. When he fit his tip to her wet opening and then stroked inside her welcoming, honeyed heat and tight passage, he uttered a sigh mixed with a moan. "I would fight for you over and over, because you are mine, and I love you, so, so much."

And still he fell, down, down, down into the green pools of

her eyes and the radiant depths of her soul, until all the broken pieces of her filled all the jagged holes of him.

"Ah!" She panted as her body closed around his. "I knew you were a true hero." Anna moved with him, matched his thrusts with encouragement and the enthusiasm to which he'd become accustomed. Her knees framed his hips as she held him impossibly close. "You and I are building a solid foundation." But she looked into his eyes, and for one moment, his world tilted wildly again. "I want everything that entails with you. *Everything*, come what may. Understand?"

Ah, she referred to his penchant for withdrawing just before he came during intercourse. Heat crept up the back of his neck as he stroked into her lush body, made love to his wife, his movements growing ever more forceful, the act all the sweeter for the emotions behind it now. "I do understand, because I want that too, now I know there is nothing to fear from being in love or letting myself be the man I was always destined to be."

Too soon, frantic desire took control, and Edmund renewed his efforts to make her come undone. Pleasure and need streaked through his length and into his stones. Sweat trickled down his back, and with each stroke he went deeper into her, and she met him just as determined as he to tumble over that edge. Their movements together went quicker, faster, more intense. It was almost as if they were dancing, only he had a feeling she was playing him with the same mastery that she brought to her piano keys. Her fingernails bit into his skin and soon her body tensed. As she convulsed around his member, he was sucked into a release so strong his knees nearly gave out. Instantly, he was lost in that swirling nirvana, barely heard her cry of release while flying through his own, and for the first time in his life, he knew exactly what love felt like.

For long moments, as the residual tremors left his body and Anna went pliant in his arms, he held her close. Then, when she sighed and blinked open her eyes, he smiled and gently kissed her lips. This was the beginning of a whole new life together. Now he felt as if he could finally breathe and be the man he was always supposed to be without censure.

Truly, it was a bright new path, and he couldn't wait to travel it.

EPILOGUE

December 24, 1823
Melody Place
Manchester Square
London, England

EDMUND WAS, BY turns, exhausted and elated, for a miracle had truly visited his house this Christmastide season. Their little family of three had had another member added to it not four hours past.

Truly, his life was much different than it was three years ago, when he'd been sullen and angry at the world, bound and determined to play the part of a rebel and to annoy his siblings with his penchant for scandal.

Never in his wildest dreams would he have thought he'd grow into the part of a doting father and a loving husband, a man who didn't wish to be anything other than that. It still managed to catch him by surprise even now. As he held onto his daughter's hand while leading her up the stairs, he thought about how much life had changed since that horrible Christmas when he'd nearly lost Anna to the machinations of a madwoman.

After returning to London following his honeymoon, he'd rented this townhouse. Anna had promptly come up with the name due to her musical background, and they'd chosen the neighborhood because it was a quiet area within Mayfair where they might raise Poppy away from the haughtier sections of Town.

Soon after, the Earl of Ettesmere—Edmund's oldest Winterbourne half-brother—had used his connections to have Anna perform on stage in front of the king and some of his advisors, his court, and close friends. That was all she needed, for her career as a professional stage pianist became a whirlwind after that. She traveled all over England, playing for some of the country's most important and influential people. Then she was given the opportunity to travel to France, Spain, and various places on the Continent. Seemingly overnight, she'd become a sensation, and everyone had rushed to extend her invitations.

Edmund couldn't have been prouder of her, and true to his promise, he followed her everywhere with their daughter in tow. It wasn't a bad life, and hearing the music Anna made with her piano was always an otherworldly experience. No longer was he jealous of the attention she received over him; she deserved every one of those accolades, and her talent only grew.

Eventually, the coin she earned from each performance more than paid for their townhouse. They bought a carriage, were able to hire more staff, especially a governess that traveled with them for Poppy as she grew. And when they were in England, he made inroads into forging strong bonds with his siblings—all of them.

As for his sister, Beatrice was thriving and quite happily content with her major and their active grown children.

Graham had a one-year-old daughter to add to his already three-year-old son, as well as a beagle named Wellesley.

And the dowager was in her element with taking all the children of the family under her wing and lending advice—or giving her support, especially if it ran at cross-purposes with those children's parents.

It seemed the families had been liberally sprinkled with forgiveness along with their willfulness. They had even taken a few holidays to Brighton together, which was a small miracle unto itself, but through it all, Edmund never failed to remember to remain grateful for everything that he had.

Last summer, though, Anna put a temporary end to their travels abroad, for she'd announced the news that she was increasing with the babe due to be born in December. He'd been wildly shocked but outlandishly pleased, for conceiving children had managed to elude them, and now the day had come when he was a father all over again.

"Papa, why is Mama in bed in the daytime?"

The sound of Poppy's voice yanked him from his musings. He waited patiently as she climbed each step slowly beside him. "Because your baby brother arrived early this morning and she needs to rest."

I have my heir. A son. The child of us both.

Not that it meant he loved Poppy any less, for he couldn't imagine his life without her.

At the second landing, the little girl paused. She had a stuffed rag rabbit tucked beneath one arm. "Why is he a brother?"

Edmund couldn't help but chuckle. "That's what we were given, and that is what you call him since he's a boy." He tousled her golden ringlets. "Do you want to meet him?"

"Will I like him?"

"I hope so, because your mama and I love him."

Confusion clouded her blue eyes. "You love me too."

"Oh, yes, indeed. That will never change." If anyone within the *ton* remembered the scandal of her birth, he didn't care. To him and Anna, she was simply their daughter. Despite what anyone said, Poppy would be launched into society whether it was allowed or not, and if anyone took exception to that, then they could tell that to his face, and he would set them straight. "But our hearts have room for much love."

"All right." She nodded as if the explanation made sense.

It was incredible to watch the little girl grow and come into her own understanding. The governess and the nursery maid as well as Anna coordinated with each other regarding Poppy's education, and she was such an intelligent creature that she took to each new subject with alacrity.

Slowly, carefully, they ascended to the next floor of the townhouse and Poppy clung tightly to his hand. When he came to the room where Anna had birthed their son, he paused at the door. "Are you ready?"

Poppy peered up at him with a serious expression. "Yes." She nodded. "Will Baby Brother like me?" she asked in a hushed whisper.

Ah, so *that* was what bothered her. "I am quite certain he will adore you, poppet, just as we all do." After he depressed the latch, he pushed open the door and ushered his daughter inside. "Anna? Are you ready for visitors?"

"Of course!" She gestured them toward the bed where she sat propped against a mound of pillows. In her arms was the tiny infant swaddled in soft blankets. "Come here, Poppy. I want you to meet your brother, Charles."

Edmund's heart squeezed, for they'd named the child after the man who had actually sired him and his two siblings, which had been the former Earl of Ettesmere. In a way, he felt that his life and the Winterbournes had come full circle because of that. While Poppy clutched his hand, they approached the bed. He lifted Poppy up and set her beside Anna while he occupied the chair next to her. Across the room, his niece Eliza helped the midwife with cleaning up. The young woman was studying to be a nurse, and she couldn't have been more pleased to assist in delivering his son.

"Poppy, this is your brother." Anna proudly held up the tiny infant for the girl to see. "Isn't he lovely?"

It had taken her almost a full day of laboring until she was delivered of the babe. It had been one of the most difficult days of Edmund's life, but damn if he wasn't proud of all of them.

"Why are his eyes closed?" she wanted to know.

Anna chuckled. "He is very tired from his fight to come into the world."

"Oh." Poppy peered into the tiny face. "Hullo, Baby. Do you want to play?" Then she shoved the rag rabbit against his head.

Gently, Edmund encouraged her hand and rabbit away. "Perhaps later when he's stronger. He's still very fragile yet."

For long moments, Poppy looked at Charles. Then she huffed and wriggled off the bed. "He is dull. May I find Miss Reed?"

With a quick grin, Edmund nodded. "Of course." Once she left the room to seek out her governess, he put a palm to the side of Anna's face. "Do you think he's dull?"

"No, I think he's wonderful, and so will she when the baby is a bit older." She took his hand, pressed a kiss to his palm, and then traced her fingertips over the boy's face. "He has your looks."

It never ceased to amaze him how she could see through touch instead of sight. He peered into the babe's face. "Well, he does have fuzzy golden hair." Then the infant's eyes opened, and they were most certainly of the Winterbourne blue hue. "Other than that, I feel he favors you." Every other feature Charles had, right down to the fingers and toes, was clearly his wife. "He is perfect."

"He is." Anna bussed the top of his head. She trained her eyes on Edmund, and there was so much joy in those emerald depths, it stole his breath. "Thank you."

"For what?" Truly, he didn't understand.

"For making me a mother, for giving me everything I have ever dreamed of having in my life." Tears filled her eyes. "For supporting me in all that I have set out to do."

"It is my honor." Emotion thickened his voice. "I am truly in awe of you."

She squeezed his hand. "Hush, you."

"It's true. Without you, this life we both have wouldn't be possible," he said in a whisper. Then he put his lips to the shell of her ear. "Thank you for believing in me. In us together. That is the best gift I could ever be given." He brushed his lips over hers. "Oh, but there is one more thing." He delved a hand into the pocket of his waistcoat and brought forth the locket that had once contained a scrap of hair from the woman he'd first loved and had his heart broken by. Quickly, he pressed it into her hand and curled her fingers around it. "I want to give this locket to you, perhaps put a miniature painting of you and the children in it for you to have close, either on a ribbon or made into a pin. It only just occurred to me that I still had it tucked away."

"Oh!" A tear slipped down her cheek. "It's perfect, especially now."

He nodded even though she couldn't see the gesture. "Happy Christmas, Anna. I love you so much I sometimes cannot comprehend that this is my life."

"Happy Christmas, Edmund. I love you too." With a smile, she bent over the babe and pressed a kiss to his forehead. "I cannot wait to see what we will all do next."

"Neither can I." And God willing he would always be amazed, for life was entirely too precious to grow bored.

The End

About the Author

Sandra Sookoo is a *USA Today* bestselling author who firmly believes every person deserves acceptance and a happy ending. Most days you can find her creating scandal and mischief in the Regency-era, serendipity and happenstance in Victorian America or snarky, sweet humor in the contemporary world. Most recently she's moved into infusing her books with mystery and intrigue. Reading is a lot like eating fine chocolates—you can't just have one. Good thing books don't have calories!

When she's not wearing out computer keyboards, Sandra spends time with her real-life Prince Charming in central Indiana where she's been known to goof off and make moments count because the key to life is laughter. A Disney fan since the age of ten, when her soul gets bogged down and her imagination flags, a trip to Walt Disney World is in order. Nothing fuels her dreams more than the land of eternal happy endings, hope and love stories.

Stay in Touch

Sign up for Sandra's bi-monthly newsletter and you'll be given exclusive excerpts, cover reveals before the general public as well as opportunities to enter contests you won't find anywhere else.

Just send an email to sandrasookoo@yahoo.com with SUBSCRIBE in the subject line.

Or follow/friend her on social media:
Facebook: facebook.com/sandra.sookoo
Facebook Author Page: facebook.com/sandrasookooauthor
Pinterest: pinterest.com/sandrasookoo
Instagram: instagram.com/sandrasookoo
BookBub Page: bookbub.com/authors/sandra-sookoo